Community Board

ALSO BY TARA CONKLIN

The Last Romantics
The House Girl

Community Board

Tara Conklin

MARINER BOOKS
New York   Boston

FIRST EDITION

Designed by Emily Snyder

Library of Congress Cataloging-in-Publication Data
Names: Conklin, Tara, author.
Title: Community board / Tara Conklin.
Description: First Edition. | New York : Mariner Books, [2023]
Identifiers: LCCN 2022031325 (print) | LCCN 2022031326 (ebook) | ISBN 9780062959379 (hardcover) | ISBN 9780062959386 (trade paperback) | ISBN 9780063297098 | ISBN 9780062959393 (ebook)
Subjects: LCGFT: Novels.
Classification: LCC PS3603.O5346 C66 2023 (print) | LCC PS3603.O5346 (ebook) | DDC 813/.6--dc23/eng/20220708
LC record available at https://lccn.loc.gov/2022031325
LC ebook record available at https://lccn.loc.gov/2022031326

ISBN 978-0-06-295937-9

23 24 25 26 27 LBC 5 4 3 2 1

For my parents

Then you begin to give up the very idea of belonging. Suddenly this thing, this belonging, it seems like some long, dirty lie . . . and I begin to believe that birthplaces are accidents, that everything is an accident. But if you believe that, where do you go? What do you do? What does anything matter?

—Zadie Smith, *White Teeth*

Wherever you come near the human race, there's layers and layers of nonsense.

—Thornton Wilder, *Our Town*

Community Board

Winter

HOW DO YOU KNOW WHEN one time is the last time? Occasionally there's a ceremony, a notice, a threat. Like the big red clock in a basketball game or the drive from Providence to Boston. If you're paying attention, you'll see the sign for the last exit. You'll notice the numbers counting down. But more often the end comes, kaput, without fanfare or signal. You're whistling along in your usual way, driving home from work, swiping snow off the mailbox, fixing two mugs of that sweet and spicy tea you both like, and then, with the turn of a doorknob, the beat of a heart, everything changes. Everything stops.

In the second week of the year 2019, this happened to me. My husband's name was Skip. Or rather, his name remains Skip but, from that day forward, he was no longer my husband. Or rather, he was still technically my husband but we would no longer live as husband and wife. His intention to be my husband, forever and ever, amen, had changed.

The turn of a doorknob, the beat of a heart.

Darcy, Skip said. His boots shed little mounds of snow onto the tiled floor. He cleared his phlegmy throat. I met someone, her name is Bianca. And . . . I think we're done here.

Our mugs of tea waited on the kitchen counter. The clock clicked to 6:04 p.m.

Done? I asked. It sounded like something you'd say to a waitress who hovered over the table, wondering if she should clear the plates. One summer I'd worked as a waitress at a pasta place in my hometown of Murbridge, Massachusetts, but that had been thirteen years ago. I was twenty-nine years old now, a legitimate adult woman with a legitimate adult job to which I wore blazers and high-heeled shoes. Skip and I met on our first day at South Boston Junior College, waiting in line for beer at a new-student happy hour. We slept together later that week, said the word *love* later that month, got engaged the following year and had been married for eight years, two months and nine days.

I didn't know it then, but there would be no tenth day. This was the last.

Us, Skip said, pointing a finger first at me, then at himself. We're done. And, listen, I'm sorry. I am. I just. Well. My lawyer is really nice, she'll email you. Skip re-zipped his coat, returned his hat to his head and left. On the table, steam rose from the tea. On the floor, a trail of dirty slush marked his exit.

LET ME TELL you about Bianca. She's an interesting woman. Skip met her at a team-building event organized by his employer, Re-Gro Diagrams Inc., a company that sells Re-Gro diagramming software to small- and medium-sized businesses. Bianca is a professional skydiver and it was her job at this particular event to shepherd one lucky Re-Gro employee—that would be Skip—through a ramped-up five hours of skydiving education and training, and then, tethered by an unbreakable bungee cord to her charge, leap from a Cessna T240 flying over Boston Common. Who knew that the team built that day would be a small one, consisting of exactly two members? All the other Re-Gro employees jumped but none, as far as I know, moved in with their skydive instructor just three months later.

The day after his abrupt departure, Skip returned to pack up his things. In the driveway, a silver Prius waited, Bianca herself in the driver's seat. I peeked through the curtains: long dark hair, thick eyelashes, a middling kind of nose. She wore a light purple sweatshirt and her nails, I noted from the hand that gripped the steering wheel, were painted lavender to match.

Skip noisily gathered up his shirts, his Xbox, his hair products, his mountain bike and artisanal salt and loaded them into Bianca's trunk. I followed him out the door and stood, shivering without a coat, sniffling without a tissue, on the front steps of our condo. Skip shut the trunk, looked at me and shrugged. He opened the passenger door, disappeared inside and then, muffled but distinct, I heard a *whoo-hoo!*, the cry Skip made whenever he scored a basket in his Saturday afternoon basketball league.

As I watched the departing rear of Bianca's car, with its COEXIST bumper sticker and vanity license plate, FLYERGRL, I began to weep. I wept with rage and true sadness. My life, it seemed to me then, was located inside that car. My life, speeding away from me, leaving me alone and unloved, bereft and abandoned. How to explain this tragic turn of events? How to tell my friends and colleagues?

How to tell my parents?

My parents adored Skip. After just five months of our dating, Mom had presented him with a Christmas stocking she'd sewn from felt and glittery trim. Along the top she embroidered *Skip* in festive red thread, the shade matching exactly the color of *Darcy* sewn onto my own stocking, the one I'd hung every year of my life from the wooden mantel in my childhood home. Every Christmas since our wedding, Mom would hang those two matching stockings side by side and fill them with candy and knickknacks and oddly shaped pottery castoffs from her weekly ceramics class.

What would become of that *Skip* stocking now? And our monogrammed his-and-her robes? And our couples membership at the

Y? What would become of our Saturday night couples bingo? Every week, we played with our friends Saba and Saul, Aleeyah and Felix, Min and Jed. Every week we'd make nachos and margaritas. One couple would host, another would bring the tequila. The idea of playing bingo alone, just me, Darcy, was ludicrous. It was sad and pathetic. Ditto for Tuesday movie night. Ditto for Wednesday waltz lessons and Sunday morning crosswords and Monday evening cupcake bake. Skip and I did everything together. My friends were his friends. My activities were his activities.

After Skip left, I wept all day and all night. I wept all Saturday and half of Sunday. When my vision wasn't completely obscured by weeping, I wrote Dear Skip emails that cataloged my pain and confusion, my remorse and undying love. I typed, deleted, typed, deleted and typed some more, but I never pressed send.

Then, on Sunday night, the phone rang.

It was our friend Min. She'd heard the news from her husband, Jed, who'd met Skip for a beer near Fenway.

Oh Darcy, I'm so sorry! said Min. I just can't believe it. I told Jed, I just cannot believe Skip would do such a thing.

I had stopped crying to answer the phone but now I began again. I—I—I, I hiccuped.

Maybe this is just a phase, Min continued. Maybe he just needs some excitement. Darcy, I'd say this is an early midlife crisis. I bet he'll come crawling back with his tail between his legs.

I calmed my hiccups. Is that what Jed said? I asked.

Pause. Min coughed. Well, no, he said Skip seems happy as a clam. *Dodged a bullet,* I think were Skip's words. But he's clearly just under some kind of sexual spell. It'll wear off. It always does. Min snorted. I mean, look at me and Jed. We could hardly keep our hands off each other but *now.* Well. I think if you just wait it out, if you let Skip have his fun, he'll realize all the security and stability he's missing, and he'll come back. Mark my words, you just wait.

But how long? I'm almost—almost—I stopped. I couldn't say it.

Oh, that's right, Darcy, you're almost *thirty*. Wow, I forgot about that. Min whistled. Listen, I don't know how long it will take. Maybe six months? A year? Two? Just wait it out. I mean, Darcy, what else have you got to do? Min started laughing. She laughed and laughed and the sound took on a vaguely hysterical tone.

Min? I asked. Are you okay?

Oh my goodness, I am fine. Just fine. A pause. Maybe you should treat this like a vacation. Jesus, what I wouldn't give for Jed to leave *me* for six months. I could watch all the TV shows I wanted to watch and eat all the food I wanted to eat. She paused again. I really hate bingo night. Hate it.

Should we meet for coffee or something, Min?

Oh, that's sweet, Darcy, but I can't. Jed doesn't want me to see you for a while. He thinks divorce is contagious or something. I think it's best if we keep our distance. Nothing personal.

The next night, it was Saba who called.

Honey, pull yourself up and get moving, she said. If he wants to shack up with some slut of a skydiver, let him. Tell him you'll lawyer up and take every last penny he's got. Don't his parents have money? What about stock options? You could be set for life. Seriously. You'll never have to work again. He's guilty of adultery, the bastard. He'll be paying you for years. Divorce can be very lucrative for women. It's almost like winning the lottery.

But I don't want to win the lottery, I said. I just want Skip. Min said he'll come back with his tail between his legs.

Ha! Don't be ridiculous, said Saba. Now, honey, stop sniffling and start planning. I've got some names and numbers for you. The best divorce lawyers in the state. I keep tabs on these guys, just in case. I love Saul, I do, but it never hurts to be prepared. Half of all marriages, Darcy, *half* end in divorce, and the way this world is structured, it's the wives who suffer. It's the wives and mothers who end up holding the short end of the stick. Unless you know how to play the game. I'll send you some YouTube links. There's a lot you need to learn. You better get started.

Three nights later, I heard from Aleeyah. Of all our friends, she was the one who knew Skip and me best. We met her the second week of junior college in an Intro to Econ class. We formed a study group of three. I helped her pack when she transferred to BU. She helped me pick out curtains for the condo.

I always wondered what you saw in him, Aleeyah said. Her voice faded and I heard a loud rustling sound.

Am I on speakerphone?

I'm packing, Darcy. Sorry. Anyhow, I always thought Skip was a little bit, oh, I don't know, wannabe frat boy.

Frat boy?

Yeah. Like trying too hard to be manly. Beating his chest kind of thing. Maybe a little.

I mean, perfectly nice. Don't get me wrong. Skip is great, wouldn't hurt a fly.

I sniffed.

You know what I mean, Darcy. Aleeyah's voice faded again, then returned. He's just not a very *inspiring* individual. I'm honestly surprised he had the get-up-and-go to have an affair. That takes real motivation.

You almost sound impressed.

Listen, you can do better than Skip Larson. I know it sucks right now but trust me, you're twenty-nine years old, your life is not over.

It feels like it's over.

You've got at least another year or two before your collagen levels start to drop. Your skin is at prime elasticity right now.

I smiled for the first time in six days. Aleeyah, I miss you, I said. Can we grab drinks?

Oh Darcy, I'm so busy right now. I have a week in Denver for a conference, then another in Miami, then microblading on March first, a big presentation mid-April and Felix decided we need to go to St. Barts for our two-year anniversary. Can you believe him? Crazy, I know. And then when we get back I'm sure I'll be slammed. Maybe early summer? Like, June?

I guess five months isn't that far away.

It will just fly. Okay, I need to meditate now. It was great to chat. Hang in there.

I hung up the phone and sat on the couch, staring at the gas fireplace, the feature that Skip and I loved most about the condo, the feature that had prompted us to say—yes, we will slap down our life savings for this pile of brick and plaster and here we will build our life together, right here. I hadn't lit the fire since Skip's departure, preferring instead the metaphor of its cold, dark emptiness.

I sat, cold and empty myself, and considered my recent conversations with Min, Saba and Aleeyah. Their words played on repeat as I sipped some tea. And then without warning, my throat seized up. I couldn't swallow. A strange, bitter sensation came bubbling up from somewhere deep within, I'm guessing from the organ that processes bile and waste. The sensation moved up my torso, tickled my nose in an unpleasant way and settled in the back of my throat. I burped.

The sensation became a feeling that can best be described as intense dislike. An aversion, in fact, to my friends. All of them. Their lives continued, untouched and unbothered. They still signed up for vegan cooking classes; they still wondered about waist cinchers; they still searched Expedia for a dream vacation package. Life per usual. Future planning. Forward motion. Predictability and routines. A daily momentum you don't even notice until, *whammo,* it's gone and you screech to a halt. My life was halted, the screech still ringing in my ears, but my friends continued merrily along the path.

And did they glance over a shoulder to check my position? No. Did they reach out a hand to pull me along? No, they did not.

My friends lacked the capacity to understand my current emergency. No, I decided then, my friends lacked the *desire* to understand my current emergency. If my friends didn't make me feel better, if they failed to comfort me in my moment (my first real moment!) of desperate need, then what good were they? Why keep friends who make you feel crappier than you already feel alone?

Draft email files

Dear Skip,

It's been three days since you left. I can't stop crying, Skip. What did I do wrong? Was it my new bangs? Bangs typically grow out in four to six weeks but my hair grows extra-fast so we're looking at three to five, tops. And in the meantime, I can wear a hat or a wig that looks just like my old hair. Or maybe a wig that's kind of sexy, like long pink waves or a Joan Jett black mullet. Would you like that, Skip? Just tell me what I did wrong, please. Is this a joke, like that time you showed up with a fake tattoo of Justin Timberlake on your neck? If this is a joke, ha ha ha! Really funny! So fucking funny, Skip, you sure got me! Now please come home. Please. Please, Skip. I sound desperate, I know, but desperate is exactly how I feel. Just come home and I promise I'll never

WITH MY SOCIAL LIFE AND marriage no longer requiring attention, I became free to focus fully on my career. I worked as a junior actuary at Castro Insurance Agency Inc., based in Roslindale, Massachusetts, a cute Boston suburb with a Dunkin' Donuts on every corner and plenty of Thai takeout. True, the hour-long commute from Back

Bay was a pain, but, before Skip's departure, I would use that time to listen to podcasts about actuarial science or celebrity romance.

After Skip's departure, I used my commute time to weep. Despite my best efforts, the weeping followed me from the Castro Insurance parking lot into the reception area, down the hall, past the kitchenette and into my own cubicle. Once inside my semi-private zone, I tried to stem the flow but everywhere I looked, Skip Larson gazed back at me. Photos of me and Skip on our honeymoon cruise. The *My Wife Is Hotter Than My Coffee* mug Skip gave me on my first day of work. The dried rose I'd saved from Valentine's Day. Thus surrounded by Skip memorabilia, I found it difficult to write my daily reports and compile my weekly spreadsheets. I found it difficult to speak coherently on the phone or remain upright in meetings.

After three weeks of this, my employer, Mr. David Castro, suggested I take a sabbatical. Mr. Castro was too young to be my father, and I wouldn't replace Daddy for the world, but our relationship had always held that vibe. He built the agency from the ground up and maintained a spectacularly trim physique. I looked to him for guidance, both with reference to spreadsheets and, I realized then, life.

Darcy, Mr. Castro said after yet another tear-filled staff meeting. You must take care of yourself. Look at you.

I looked down; sure enough, I'd misbuttoned my button-down.

You are a bright shining star, he said. Your mind is a beacon, your heart is a gem, but you need to take some time. To put the pieces back together. To recover the spring in your step. Here is what I can do. A six-month sabbatical, with my blessing. Your job waiting for you on your return, guaranteed.

Mr. Castro was a prince among men. After three seconds of reflection, perhaps four, I accepted his offer.

Thank you, David, I said. I'll be back on my feet in no time.

Be kind to yourself, he said, and placed a hand on my shoulder. Darcy, I don't often tell this story, but my heart too was broken and the pieces stomped upon by a very cunning woman. Simone. It was many years ago, but I remember the feeling well. Hopeless and filled with an unspeakable rage. But listen—here he smiled brightly—I got over it! I moved forward. Never does her wanton image darken my mind. Never.

I felt Mr. Castro's fingers tighten uncomfortably around my shoulder. He was looking beyond me with narrowed eyes.

David? I said. Um, your hand is—

He released my shoulder and folded his hands over his heart. You too will transcend this moment, Mr. Castro said and bowed. Good luck, Darcy. We'll miss you.

It took me three days to exit the condo. I packed my clothes and personal effects into cardboard boxes, emptied the fridge and listed a six-month furnished rental on Craigslist. Two hours later I handed the keys over to a BC law student and her boyfriend.

A light snow fell. My eyes were dry. I loaded up my blue Prius and left the condo, left Boston, crawled onto the Mass Pike and drove. There was no need for GPS on this journey.

Where does one go, you might ask, when the world falls apart? When the time-before and the time-after become separated by one dread, unanticipated event? When the immutable facts of your life—the mundane, the trivial, the take-for-granted minutiae that once filled every second of every day—suddenly disappear? When the epiphany strikes that you do not control the most fundamental elements of your existence? When you realize you control nothing at all.

Where does one go in such dire and unexpected circumstances?

I went home, of course.

MURBRIDGE COMMUNITY MESSAGE BOARD

Note from the Moderator—PLEASE READ.

Recently I've seen some questionable posts on our Community Message Board. Let this serve as a gentle reminder of our mission in this virtual sphere. We are here to: first, share neighborhood-related PERTINENT information; second, sell, trade or donate APPROPRIATE goods and services; and third, generally IMPROVE our neighborly relations. Our Community Board is NOT: a dating site; a marketing site; a place to air private political views; a place to personally attack or otherwise malign any Murbridge resident. Any such posts will be flagged, investigated and the poster banned for LIFE.

Please remember, we're all in this together! Show kindness to your fellow Murbridgeans. Thank you for your understanding.

Sincerely, your moderator, Pat Pernicky

MURBRIDGE, THE SITE OF MY birth, childhood, adolescence and every Thanksgiving of my life, is a small town in western Massachusetts. It boasts a 7-Eleven, a post office, a library, a corner grocery that sells salami sandwiches and lighter fluid, a manicure place, a dry cleaner. Some parts are old and quaint, others newish and rough. In the fall, the tall maples along Main Street turn startling shades of red and gold. In the summer, hordes of mosquitoes descend between the hours of 6 and 8 p.m. to feast upon short-sleeved citizens. Neighboring towns bear historic markers—this hotel where Hamilton once slept, that grassy knoll upon which Washington once shot an arrow—or contemporary centers for artistic expression. Modern dance flourishes in the small towns of western Mass, ditto experimental theater, architectural extravagance and locally sourced cuisine. But not so in Murbridge. No one famous lives here. No national scandals have erupted here. No remarkable weather event or unsolved crime or suspected supernatural happening distinguishes Murbridge from its neighbors.

Horticulture, however, sets the town apart in one interesting way. Long ago, when Murbridge was just another tract of fertile virgin forest and unspoiled streams traversed by happy animals and native Mahican tribespeople, a group of starving Pilgrims stumbled through the woods. The year was 1677. Our hardy band had departed Plymouth Colony due to a personal dispute between two men, the specifics of which remain unsubstantiated in historical documents but were rumored to involve, naturally, a woman. The woman and her chosen partner remained at Plymouth while the spurned man, a Mr. Gideon Tinker, and his closest buds took off in search of open land. The trek did not go well. After three weeks of bear attacks and bad berries, our Pilgrims were weak and disheartened.

This brutal, fickle land! cried Gideon. Why the hell didn't we stay in Plymouth? It was stinky and rainy but at least there was a pub.

At that very moment, Gideon felt his feet grow wet. He looked down and found himself standing directly atop a miraculous burble of fresh water spurting from a mossy and rock-strewn spring. Gideon, giddy from thirst, threw himself atop the spring, scooping up water with his hands and, in the process, disturbing a sizable group of mushrooms that sprouted beside the spring. In his haste, some of these mushrooms made their way into Gideon's mouth.

Gideon did not retch or vomit. He swallowed the mushrooms down and said: *Hmmmm. Good eating.*

Soon enough, every member of the party was drinking fresh spring water and chewing on woodland mushrooms. Unbeknownst to them, these mushrooms contained significant amounts of the hallucinogenic psilocybin. Within the hour, all the colonists became wondrously, supremely happy, visions of friendly bears and gigantic potatoes dancing before their eyes. They agreed: here is where we should settle, right here, beside this fresh spring and these delightful mushrooms.

When the Pilgrims awoke the next day, they saw the error of their fungi-induced decision: the land was too mushy and murky to support wooden structures. Did they despair? No, they merely backed themselves up onto sturdier land within spitting distance of the spring. There, they felled trees, constructed a handful of houses and, as a matter of high priority, built a bridge over the marshy land to allow for easy access to the spring and those miraculous mushrooms.

The "mushroom bridge" became, in time, *Murbridge*, and, well, here we are. Murbridge is notable as the only New England town founded not by religious missionaries but by recreational drug users. In those early years, Murbridge established itself as a place of peaceful communion between colonists and members of the Mahican tribe, who were well aware of the local psychedelics. Neighboring Mahicans often visited the spring, plucked a mushroom or two and sat around the fire with the Murbridgean colonists, shooting the shit and trading wolf pelts. These friendly evenings continued until the mid-1830s when a series of one-sided land deals left the Mahicans bitter and hungry. In the end, colonial land lust proved stronger than hallucinogenic bonding, and over one brutal weekend in 1844, the Murbridge townspeople slaughtered all the Mahican men and ran the women and children out of town, forcing them to march west to their new "home" in northern Wisconsin.

Today, there's a plaque in the middle of town to commemorate the Mahicans and thanking them for their service. Long ago, the original bridge fell into the muck but others followed. A stretch of aluminum now extends over the marsh, which in 1985 was designated the Western Massachusetts Wetland Bird Protection Zone. The spring itself is a burbling water feature fronted by a viewing platform and surrounded by uniformly round river stones imported from China. I've never seen a mushroom anywhere in the vicinity, and believe me, I've looked. Every May, graduating seniors from Murbridge High venture into the marsh to search for the famed fungi. It's a local rite of passage, our own little vision quest. No one has ever found a local mushroom, as far as I know, although plenty of specimens purchased elsewhere have been consumed on-site.

Murbridge now boasts a population of just under three thousand souls, an economy based on tourism (old houses, rare birdlife, leaf color), a private residential mental health facility, a nearly defunct paper mill and the provision of goods and services to the white-collar city professionals who want to raise their kids in a picturesque small town and don't mind a hellish two-hour commute to and from Boston. It's an interesting mix of people, let me tell you, a true melting pot of socioeconomic, cultural and racial differences. A place of penny candy and Protestants, low crime rate, middling property taxes, Somali grocery stores, kosher butchers, fantastic Peruvian food, high-speed internet and amiable postal workers. An oasis of calm and decent public schools. A place so apparently peaceful and prosperous that, growing up here, I sincerely believed in the continuing vitality of the American Dream.

As I drove the Mass Turnpike, past Chicopee and Holyoke and Westfield, the thought never once crossed my mind that Murbridge may have changed.

ISO Nanny ASAP! Our au pair Szabova decided to return home to Poland after just three weeks of work. We very urgently need a full-time nanny for our twins, Jett and Viggo, 38 months old. Please respond with experience, availability, CPR completion certificate and at least four personal references. Thanks! BestBoyMommy22

•

Our cat Beyonce went missing last night. We found her, but someone shaved her legs. What kind of sicko shaves a cat? See attached photo. Reward offered.

•

REMINDER: use your own goddamn garbage can for your own goddamn pet waste. I'm looking at you Peter Luflin.

•

Thanks to the four town residents who attended last night's Board of Selectmen meeting! We swore in our newly elected members and you may recognize some familiar faces: Hildegard Hyman as Treasurer, Pat Pernicky as Secretary, Lydia Aoki as Town Clerk, with Rosalia Gonzalez, Allston Highbottom, and Pearl Odette as members at large. An extra special welcome to Jake Zdzynzky, owner of Zdzynzky Gems-n-Things, our newly elected Board Chair and first-time Select Board member. Congratulations to Jake!

•

Are you my good little soup boy? Who's my good little soup boy?

LET ME TELL YOU ABOUT me. I, Darcy Clipper, am the product of two magnificent parents, Mom and Daddy, Jeanine and Stan Clipper, happily married now for thirty-two years. Theirs is a union of impeccable timing and taste. They both abhor anchovies, horror movies and snobs. They share affinities that started small and now, in the golden days of retirement, have blossomed into full-time pursuits. Mah-jongg, sudoku, crafting with yarn and joining Facebook groups regardless of interest or suitability. This last appeared on the scene only recently. Mom says it's important to stay relevant. Daddy said he wanted to make some furniture. The furniture-making group resulted in no actual furniture, but membership did give him some new friends with whom to share information about tools and semi-offensive political cartoons.

As a child, I viewed Stan and Jeanine's togetherness as an immutable scientific fact, like the existence of the sun or breathing. There was no conceivable world in which their marriage did not flourish. Of course, I now recognize my naivete, Skip's departure notwithstanding. Marriage requires commitment, compromise, acceptance, plus a high threshold for boredom and squeamishness. My parents must have suffered along those lines at some point, although I never saw it. Any marital discord happened quietly behind closed doors, late at night, or possibly while I was practicing my French horn. And if there were any fights, no one ever held a grudge.

I am an only child because, as Mom explained to me when I turned five, I was an impossible act to follow. Later, she elaborated that her ovaries waved the white flag after my birth. No warning, no fanfare, just kaput. But with one perfect egg named Darcy, Mom said, why would we ever need another?

I honestly never wanted a sibling. My parents filled every role—playmates, study partners, dance partners, movie-watchers, popcorn-eaters, gigglers, gossipers. Not everyone enjoys so solid a relationship with their parents, I readily acknowledge, but I never viewed it as odd. My parents are truly my best friends. My childhood glows in my memory, all hot chocolate and *Fantasy Island* reruns and pillow fights. Mom was an able, albeit uninspired, cook who churned out lasagna and kale casserole on the regular. We all loved to watch *Jeopardy!* My childhood bedroom was the largest in the house, east-facing to catch the morning sun, with a lovely view over the front-lawn elm.

Here's a story I like to tell: Once, when I was eight, I stepped smack into the middle of a beehive. As enraged bees flew up my legs, up my shirt, into my hair, I screamed: *Daddy! Help! Killer bees!* I remember a searing pain and then, salvation: Daddy barreling toward me across the lawn. He scooped me up, slung me over a shoulder fireman-style and ran into the house, batting bees off my legs and torso, sustaining quite a few vicious stings himself. He slammed the door hard on the trailing swarm and then attacked the ones that had gotten inside. I cried and cried as he banged his foot down and slapped the air with an old *Consumer Reports,* swearing prodigiously all the while.

In the middle of this chaos, Mom returned from the grocery store, her arms full of bags that she dropped—*bam*—on the kitchen floor as soon as she saw me. The welts! I looked like a pink and white Dalmatian. I sat on the kitchen floor and let my parents fuss over me, cooling down the stings with ice water and baking soda, stroking my hair, letting me lick Popsicle after Popsicle as I hiccuped and emitted the occasional little sob. That night, I slept in their king bed, smack in the middle. I have never felt safer or more protected than I did then.

In other words, my parents take care of me. My parents accept me, no questions asked. I rely on my parents completely, without hesitation, because they are the only two people in the entire world genetically required to love me.

AT 12:09 P.M. on February 5, 2019, I pulled into the driveway of my childhood home, 18 Longtree Lane, the blue house with white trim on the north side of the block. I love my house. Have I mentioned that? I love the two front steps and the little shed area where you put your muddy boots and the front door with the little glass circle so you can see who's knocking. I love the brick fireplace with its sooty, cavernous opening and the flue that sticks. I love the stairs. They go up straight from the back of the house, just off the dining room, and squeak on steps numbers four and seven. I love those squeaks!

That day, exiting the car, taking stock of the shingled roof, the dar-ling mailbox, the snow-covered shrubs, I would like to say that I no-

ticed something amiss. I would like to say that I wondered why the
front steps were encased in ice, why the bird feeder swung empty in
the breeze, why the windows were dark. But I did not.

I bounded up the stairs, opened the door with my key and said:
Surprise! I'm home!

No reply.

Daddy? I called as I wandered through the dark downstairs. Mom?
The shutters were shut, furniture draped with sheets. All the houseplants, gone. The heat, turned down. The refrigerator, bare. The land-
line, disconnected.

I stopped at the base of the stairs. Where the hell were Stan and
Jeanine?

I called Mom's cell phone. She picked up, her voice breathless.

Darcy, sorry, dear, I'm just doing an exercise video.

A video? I said. You mean, at home?

Yes, dear, I'm watching an exercise video at home. Today is abs
day.

No, you're not, I said. I'm at home. *You* are not at home.

A few moments of heavy breathing followed. Oh, I knew we should
have told you, said Mom. Your father—he thought it was best if we
didn't say anything. But I told him—Darcy should know about this!

About what?

We're in Arizona, dear. A retirement community down here called
Little Valley. It's actually very nice. They have a delightful crafts instructor. I'm learning macramé.

You moved to Arizona and didn't tell me?

We're trying it out. Just for a year, Darcy, that's all. At first we
thought only the winter season, but we want to see how the summer
goes. You know your father can't stand humidity, but it's really a dry
heat down here. At least that's what we've heard. My mother's voice
became half muffled. Stan, talk to her. She's in Murbridge.

I heard my father grunt and then: Oh brother, here we go. He got on the phone: Darcy, Bunny. This was my decision. Your mother thought we should tell you, but I know times are tough for you right now and I didn't want you to get all upset about this. You're so attached to the house.

Wait—are you selling the house?

No! See, Bunny, that's why I didn't want to tell you. We're definitely not selling the house, at least not right away. They say it's a dry heat down here, but, well, we've got to see for ourselves.

I was so mad I started to cry. The fern that usually sat near the big picture window was gone. When I was four, I'd named that fern Fred.

Where's Fred? I sobbed.

Fred? Oh—the fern is with your mother's friend Louise. She's got all the plants, I think. Jeanine, who's got the plants?

Shuffle shuffle, whispers.

Darcy? It was Mom again. Darcy, I'm sure you can go visit the fern if you want. Louise wouldn't mind having you, dear. I'm sure it would be a treat for her. And for Fred.

But—but—it won't be the same. I began to wail.

Or—I know! Find a new fern on the Community Board. That message board is a godsend, Darcy. You wouldn't believe how many people use it for all sorts of things. Baby gear and selling old stuff and finding dates to the prom. I'm sure you could find a new fern, Bunny. You can call it Fred Junior.

I don't want another fern. I want *my* fern.

Oh Darcy, come now. There are lots of ferns in this world. Fred is not the only fern.

I didn't answer. I was too busy blowing my nose.

Oh, and Darcy, I almost forgot—we canceled the Wi-Fi and cable, but you can piggyback on the Dykstras' next door. Their password is easy as pie to guess.

The Dykstras?

They moved into Mrs. Rogers's house last year. I'll warn you—they are not the friendliest people in the world. But they do have incredibly fast Wi-Fi and their password is 1234. How stupid is that? Our little block is changing, Darcy. There are the Joshis across the street, a lovely family of five, and Patty and Linda on the corner, a newly married couple. Very nice lesbians. Ramona and Axel in the yellow house. Their first home together! Between the two of them, they've got more tattoos than a drunken sailor, but don't be alarmed. They run an Etsy shop out of their home. The prettiest little roach clips and bongs. Axel is a very talented potter.

Bongs?

Marijuana is legal now, Darcy. Don't be so shocked. Not down here in Arizona, of course, but your father has some connections.

Mom, I don't want to know.

Please don't be upset. We were going to tell you about the house. Eventually. But we just didn't know how.

How long? How long before you sell?

Oh Darcy. At least a year. And we're still not set on it. It's a process.

Again I began to cry. For Fred, for my old neighbors, for Skip, for everything that had changed without my notice or consent.

When will you be home? I asked between sobs. How soon can you get here?

A throat clear. A significant pause. A cough.

Well, Darcy, Mom said slowly, we signed a year lease on the unit. We'll have to see it through.

Immediately my tears stopped. *What?* I said. This is no time for jokes, Mom.

No, Bunny. We need to stay.

Put Daddy on.

I heard a muffled conversation, Daddy's deep baritone and Mom's higher tenor, their voices joined in the unmistakable tone of agreement.

Then it was Daddy speaking. Darcy, he said. We're going to tough it out here at Little Valley. But you are welcome to stay at the house. Some peace and quiet will do you good.

I was too shocked to reply. Even my parents had changed. Marijuana, Arizona, macramé. Who would make me muffins? Who would scratch my back? I felt utterly abandoned. How could my parents desert me in my time of need? It was a Skip repeat, but I couldn't blame Bianca for this one. I was baffled. I was also extremely pissed.

You and Mom can stay in Arizona for all I care, I said to Daddy. I don't want to talk to you or see you or think about you.

Oh Bunny, please.

I hung up the phone.

All these years I'd expected my parents to provide a safety net whenever I needed one. Why had I expected this? Because, for my entire life, they had *allowed* me to expect it. In fact, they'd encouraged me to believe in their ubiquity. I'm not saying I blame my parents for all of my failures. I'm just saying I blame them for *some* and probably, on balance, *most*. I blame them for providing me with so much support and love that I never learned to stand alone.

When I first started dating Skip, Daddy said: He reminds me of a young me. The choice of words, thinking back on it now, was a little weird, but at the time I had welcomed them. I needed Daddy's approval. I wouldn't have continued to see Skip without it.

Oh yes, Mom had agreed. Skip does remind me of a young you, Stan. Even his crooked left incisor! I remember that tooth knocking up against mine when we first started going steady. Remember that, dear?

Gross, I said. But I felt a deep peace knowing my parents approved of my boyfriend. The fact that they liked him was almost as important as me liking him.

And dear, if things don't work out, Mom had added, we're always here for you.

If things don't work out. They said these words when I went to sleepaway camp in Poughkeepsie; when I joined the volleyball team in high school; when I first started at South Boston Junior College; when I was studying for my actuarial exams; when I left school to work for Mr. Castro; and even on my wedding day. The reminder that things not working out remained a distinct possibility suggested to me, in a fairly strong way, that my parents *expected* things to not work out. This refrain might also be called the unintentional but implicit undermining of a daughter's self-confidence. If my parents believed my efforts would fail, was I a fool for trying? My parents expected failure because they knew, deep down, that I wasn't smart, ambitious, pretty, charming or funny enough to succeed at much of anything. Therefore, I needed my parents absolutely and forever because, at some point in time, I would fail at every single thing I tried to do.

And so it came to pass: On day three of sleepaway camp, I got the sniffles and my parents came to take me home. I failed my first actuarial exams. They took me out to dinner to celebrate. I was cut from the volleyball team. Mom made a cake. I decided not to transfer to a four-year college, even though I got straight As in junior college. Daddy hugged me and said: Atta girl.

At my wedding reception, just moments after Daddy's teary speech, my mother leaned over and whispered in my ear: *Don't forget, Darcy, if Skip doesn't work out, you can always come home.* I was twenty-one years old with an associate degree in actuarial science, a savings account I'd started in the third grade, a brand-new 401(k) courtesy of my brand-new employer, and a husband who told me every night how much he adored my breasts. What was my mother so worried about?

But that was what my mother did: worried about me. My parents remained on perpetual full-time parental duty. Is this what they wanted in their golden years of retirement? To always prop me up? They could be sailing the Greek islands or touring the national parks in one of those fancy trailers with flush toilets and a waterbed. They could be joining a swingers club in Berlin or finding themselves at an ashram in Big Sur.

A realization struck me: This is why they hadn't told me about Arizona. This is why they'd felt the need to flee, secretly, like members of the political opposition fleeing an oppressive regime. In this scenario, I was the regime. My parents, Solzhenitsyn and Ai Weiwei. At last, my parents had recognized the error of their perpetual, boundless love and support. They'd finally seen with clarity the bloodsucking emotional leech I'd become and had moved across state lines to escape me.

Standing in the cold, dark kitchen, I decided that I did not want my parents. I did not want my friends. I did not even want Skip. I did not want anything or anyone to remind me of my past mistakes, my glaring inadequacies, my poor decision-making skills, my occasional bad breath. I wanted distance. I wanted space. I wanted to wall myself away and do nothing, speak to no one, contemplate nothing more onerous than when to nap and what to heat up for dinner. More than anything, I wanted a life devoid of meaningful human contact and the risks associated with emotional entanglement. Everything necessary for life, I surmised, could be accomplished without personal investment or interaction. In other words, everything necessary for life could be accomplished on the internet.

This was the year 2019, for crying out loud. What else did we have but technology?

URGENT: Does anyone know how to do the Heimlich?

•

FREE: 500 cans of corn. Accidentally ordered them online. I really hate corn. Happy to help load.

•

A reminder for all (and especially Willie Mangina): garbage cans
are intended for garbage. In my book, pet poop qualifies as garbage. If you don't want garbage in your garbage can then move
to another country. Yours truly, Peter Luflin

•

Our Havanese Lulu wandered off today. Easily caught with
Cheetos or pepperoni slices. Please let us know if you see her!

•

REMINDER: monthly Select Board meeting this Friday. Agenda
items: 1) sludge removal; 2) upkeep of chime tower; 3) ice rink
monitor thank you gift. Questions? Contact Hildegard Hyman,
HHMurbridge@gmail.com

•

Someone left a thermos of tomato soup on my front porch. I
ate it, but the whole thing weirds me out. Thanks for the soup,
I guess.

WHAT FOLLOWED WAS A PERIOD of despondency and complete
ennui. Dietary breakdown and sedentary lounging. I survived on the
canned and packaged foods my mother had squirreled away in our
basement during those turbulent weeks before Y2K. I remembered,
vaguely, some talk back then of building a bomb shelter. My father
had objected on the grounds that it would make the house less mar-
ketable. Where, he asked, would new owners put an in-ground pool,
should they ever wish to do so? After a steady diet of public radio
pronouncements and cable news hysteria, my mother strenuously
disagreed. A pool is a luxury item, she argued. In these extraordinary
times, a bomb shelter is essential.

Compromise came in the form of a re-jigged basement. My father installed a freezer large enough to hide an adult body. His
tools moved to one sad shadowy corner of the garage. Where once

Daddy had sawn and whittled, he now brought in a set of aluminum shelves, which Mom promptly filled with canned goods. On the last night of 1999, we huddled around the television, our stomachs clenched in fear of Armageddon or complete civic breakdown or at least a few flickering lights, a burnt fuse. Maybe a mysterious scream? We held our breath, *5-4-3-2-1*. And . . . nothing. Only a collective exhale that reverberated through the streets and alleyways of little Murbridge and indeed the entire Eastern Seaboard.

Mom shrugged. Well, that was anticlimactic, she said. And then we all went to bed.

Every generation thinks they'll see the end of the world, Daddy said that night as he tucked me in. Everyone thinks their time is the worst.

For the next nineteen years, my parents waged the Battle of the Canned Goods. Daddy, believing in the goodness of people and the rightness of the universe, would surreptitiously throw the old cans away. Botulism, he'd tell me. Forget nuclear holocaust or zombies or whatever. Your mother will kill us with food poisoning. And my mother, just as sneaky, would read an article about tsunamis or Saddam or radiation from a dying sun and replace the old canned goods with new canned goods. Always the same kinds—my mother is nothing if not consistent. Peas, carrots, chickpeas, Chef Boyardee pasta, Green Giant creamed corn. Rows upon rows. My mother stocked the shelves well. She had selected foods (inadvertently, I'm guessing) with just enough nutritional value and starchy heft to fill my stomach some two decades later and leave me, more or less, in good health. My sodium levels were a bit elevated, no doubt, but what did I care?

I wrote draft emails to Skip but did not send them. I wrote nasty emails to my parents and did send them. I stared deep into my navel and contemplated the wreckage of my twenty-nine years on the planet. My professional life had focused on risk calculation and modeling matters of uncertainty. What is the life expectancy of a sedentary fifty-eight-year-old male with twelve cavities and an otherwise clean health history? A thirty-eight-year-old childless, unmarried female with a self-reported three-drinks-a-day habit? An eighty-year-old sexually active, never-married female yoga instructor who ate vegan and smoked only the finest weed?

Predictions were my forte, accuracy my superpower. And yet Skip had blindsided me. In a year of global unrest and government shutdown, the Syrian civil war and #MeToo, the institution most at risk of destruction was my own marriage and I hadn't suspected a thing.

Draft email files

Dear Skip,

When I first met you, I thought you were a real snooze. Remember when we went to that new Korean place and you said you'd never heard of kimchi? I mean, who's never heard of kimchi! You only put the tiniest bit on your fork and then glugged that huge glass of water like your tongue was about to fall off. Talk about drama. That night you managed to demonstrate both your boring-ness and your knack for fabricating scenes of personal torment. I thought we would never last another date because you were so insufferable. But then you sent me that super-long email and it was so long and so complimentary. You said you liked the way my hair smelled and the short socks I wore and the way I walked with my shoulders pitched a little forward like I was always excited to get where I was going. I'd never noticed my walking style before, but you pointed it out so favorably, like it was a magical attribute only I possessed, and it was all those observations—as though you had studied me without me even realizing it—that made me feel special. You made me feel beautiful and amazing. And so I decided to overlook your total boring-ness and your overbite and we didn't break up the next day or the next or the next. But I never should have let you study me because now

Hi Bunny,

I hope you enjoyed the package of Arizona treats I sent last week. See all the natural wonders available down here? It's a true paradise of spices, sunshine and local handiwork.

You ended our last phone conversation so abruptly that I didn't have a chance to remind you of a few items. DO NOT, and I mean NEVER, put your hand down the garbage disposal. Even if it's turned off, use a long-handled wooden spoon if you must go digging around in there. You never know when a power surge might hit and your hand would become hamburger. Also, remember to lock ALL doors and windows before bed. I know crime in Murbridge is incredibly rare, but you can never be too safe. And also remember to wear the orange glow vest if you go walking after dusk. There's a new one hanging by the back door that features flashing lights and a glow strip down each arm. It's darling, you'll love it.

I'll let you know if anything else comes to mind. I know you're a very safety-conscious person, Darcy, but reminders never hurt.

Love,

Mom (and Daddy)

P.S. I've asked Mrs. Pevzner, Todd's mom, to check on you. I remember Todd so fondly! You two were cute as buttons all dressed up for the prom. He's in Utah now, father of five. Five! Apparently he had some kind of religious awakening in college, that's what his mother told me, though I'm still a little vague on the details. Maybe you can get more out of her when she stops by. Tell Mrs. Pevzner I send hello from Arizona!

P.P.S. I'd like to continue following Skip on Facebook. He posts the most charming cat videos from time to time and I'd hate to miss out. Do you mind?

——————————————

Dear Mom and Daddy,

Thank you for the Arizona care package. I enjoyed the southwestern spiced nuts and perhaps will someday find a use for the Hold-on-to-your-boots Hot Sauce. I'm surprised you sent me armadillo earrings because I rarely wear jewelry, as you should know by now after twenty-nine years of being my mother. Ditto the smiling cactus figurine. Cacti don't smile and I have no desire to look at a fake representation of supposedly cheerful plant life. I thought immediately of Fred the fern and got all tearful, so thanks for that.

Regarding your safety reminders: I am perfectly capable of looking after myself. If your concerns were genuine, you would come home and remind me in person. This I would tolerate in a good-natured and easygoing way, especially if you baked some banana-nut muffins for us to eat while we talked through your apology. However, I cannot abide the long-distance alarmist warnings. I can certainly envision a scenario where I would indeed put my hand into the garbage disposal, and wouldn't you be sorry then.

Regarding Mrs. Pevzner, I will not answer the door for any friend of yours, and particularly not my ex-boyfriend's mother. Are you insane? I will stay away from the windows and wait for her to leave. Or I may be bludgeoned and dead in my bed from an intruder and therefore unable to answer the door. You will never know.

Regarding Skip's cat videos, I'm shocked and saddened to learn that you prioritize a few moments of passing amusement over your daughter's emotional well-being. Skip has decided to unfollow me from life. Surely you can unfollow him on one social media platform.

Yes I'm still mad at you. A box of cheap souvenirs won't help.

Sincerely yours,

Darcy

Did someone hear gunshots? It sounded just like gunshots.

•

Please could people stop touching my dog? I don't want your germs and neither does Napoleon.

•

ISO: hourly babysitter. As we sift through nanny applications, now looking for temporary care for Jett and Viggo (39 months). Anywhere from 2 to 90 hours per week. Must know toddler CPR and avoid all gluten while working for us. Email me BestBoyMommy22@gmail.com

•

Warning: I saw a gang of about five teenage boys, all with "hoodies" and those ill-fitting dungaree pants, walking towards the town basketball court. Be careful out there.

•

Who named their wi-fi network PeterLuflinSucks? It's mean and upsetting my grandkids. Grow up, Mangina.

•

For my good little soup boy: do you like chowder?

IT WAS 11:32 A.M., DAY 15 of my period of self-imposed isolation and canned food consumption. I lay in bed and stared at the ceiling. A dream from the night before appeared like smoke, a shifting ghostly vision that faded even as I struggled to keep it intact: a giant bird flying against a gray, cold sky and me, watching from below, as the bird approached. I knew that the bird meant me harm, I knew I should run, but my limbs were leaden, my entire body paralyzed. As this horrible creature stretched out its razor-sharp talons to grab me or gouge out my eyes or slash at my face, I saw that its nails were painted lavender.

Fred! I called to my absent fern. What happened? Where did I go wrong?

I sat up and pulled my laptop onto my lap. Why Bianca? Why my Skip? I did what any self-respecting twenty-first-century jilted lover with free high-speed internet would do: I began to cyberstalk my husband's new girlfriend.

I scrutinized Bianca's accounts: Facebook, Instagram, TikTok, LinkedIn, Twitter, Pinterest. Bianca was a woman who liked scented candles and axe-throwing. She cooked a mean veggie chili and belonged to the Association for the Prevention of Pet Obesity. On Facebook, she followed James Blunt and Angela Merkel. Late last year, per Pinterest, Bianca considered renovating her basement into a mother-in-law-apartment unit. Rental income. I gathered from her numerous public posts and queries re knockoff Gucci that skydiving did not place Bianca at the income level she desired and believed she truly deserved.

Fred, I called from my bed, do you think Bianca wants Skip for his money? Skip doesn't make much, but I'm guessing more than a skydiver. Recreational industries tragically underpay their employees. You're better off as a kindergarten teacher.

I looked again at Bianca's online Pinterest boards. What's that you say, Fred? More research needed? I think you're right. Let's get on it.

The scenario made perfect sense. Skip had fallen victim to a scheme. Instead of an email from a Nigerian prince requesting a wire transfer, Bianca struck in the flesh. She appeared in a silken jumpsuit and presented her case. Was it illness? A lost inheritance? A hostage situation? All sorts of people fall victim to the clever shenanigans of financial tricksters. Very intelligent people, members of Mensa and the United Nations and whatnot.

I moved from my bed to the couch, bringing the comforter with me. No, I am not suggesting that Skip is a member of Mensa. Far from it. I believe he's of extremely average intelligence. He never told me his SAT scores, though I certainly asked, and we both got straight As in junior college, but Skip generally copied my work, so there you go. What he *does* possess is a high degree of dopey innocence and a trusting nature that undoubtedly would play right into the hands of a person like Bianca. Or a person like the kind of person I imagine Bianca to be.

But Pinterest, in the end, proved me wrong. If you were to spend the better part of a day perusing the Pinterest boards of a twenty-something single woman with a job and domicile (rented or owned, doesn't matter), no kids and a pet smaller than your average handbag, you would learn all there was to know about her. Every desire, every plan, every preference, every budget range, every clothing choice and favorite muffin recipe—there for all to see. It was here I found that in addition to the mother-in-law unit, Bianca had also posted boards for a spa bathroom and newfangled kitchen with hand-built cabinets. And, most recently, a child's nursery complete with elephant wallpaper and a mobile of tiny crocheted skydivers. Bianca, it seemed, had sufficient funds to remodel her home in true Joanna Gaines fashion without Skip's contributions. Even worse, she must truly envision a future mother-in-law someday residing within that mother-in-law apartment.

Oh Fred, I mumbled. This is horrible.

As an image of Skip's mom, Eunice, living in Bianca's basement rose in my mind, I closed my eyes. Tears, which I'd managed to avoid for at least thirteen hours, returned. Some images are too painful to sustain. Eunice and I always got along famously. That's how Eunice put it: *famously*. She was a grand dame who smoked long thin cigarettes and ate peanuts out of the shell. Her teeth, not so great. But her hairdos! She visited the salon every week for a shampoo, blowout and style. Every week, a different sort of updo or twist, long luscious waves or corkscrew curls.

I missed Eunice. Why hadn't she called me? I imagined the fun she must be having with Bianca. I imagined the two of them sitting side by side at the nail salon. Eunice, red; Bianca, lavender.

Now, *you* are a delightful daughter-in-law! Eunice exclaims. Thank goodness Skip got rid of that downer Darcy.

Oh Eunice, Bianca replies. You are the best. Already I love you like a mother. And I promise to give you oodles of grandchildren.

At the thought of children, my tears turned to full-on weeping, snotty-nose blowing, asthmatic lung heaving. Eunice had wanted nothing more than to be a grandmother. I'd tried, I'd tried so hard but—

And then, I heard a voice calling my name. I wiped my eyes.

Fred? I whispered. Is that really you?

A knock at the door.

Darcy, dear, it's Mrs. Pevzner, said the voice. Your parents asked me to check on you.

A shock ran through me. Paralysis struck. I remained on the couch, moving not one muscle.

Darcy, your parents are very worried. Please let me just get a look at you. They want to make sure you're not bludgeoned. Oh, and Todd says hello! His kids are so darn cute dressed all alike—I brought photos. Darcy? Dear? Are you bludgeoned? Darcy?

A pause. I grabbed a tissue and silently wiped my nose. The need to avoid Mrs. Pevzner immediately and completely eclipsed the need to weep dramatically over my personal predicament. I could not, under any circumstances, face my high school boyfriend's mother at this moment.

The pause lengthened. Outside, snow began to fall in slow, fat flakes.

Had she left?

No. Mrs. Pevzner was just gathering strength.

Darcy, dear, I know you and Todd didn't end on the best of terms, she shouted through the door. He told me about the parking brake incident. I'm so sorry, Darcy, it sounds just terrible. And on prom night! But that was so long ago. And look how you both turned out! If I could look at you, that is, I could see how you've turned out. That's all I need, Darcy, just one look. Remember, I'm not here to ask questions. I'm only here to verify that you're still among the living. No bludgeoning. No sudden asphyxiation or hair dryer in the tub. Poisonous spiders. Carbon monoxide. Undiagnosed heart condition. Darcy, you know how your mother worries.

Another pause. I held my breath.

And Darcy? I've brought you some blondies. Coconut caramel, which honestly is too sweet for my taste—five cups of sugar in every batch!—but Todd just loves them. They always sell out at the school bake sale and I send boxes out to the grandkids in Utah.

Darcy? Please come to the door.

Darcy? Please.

Please, Darcy.

Darcy!

Finally Mrs. Pevzner's voice grew hoarse and I heard the distinct sound of a mildly overweight, incredibly annoyed sixty-five-year-old stomping down my front steps. Slowly, I removed myself from the couch and peeked outside. She'd left two things: a path carved in the snow from front door to sidewalk, and a round pink Tupperware full of blondies. I ate them all in one sitting.

Tara Conklin

Draft email files

Dear Skip,

 I just wanted to let you know that things are going great in Murbridge. It's so nice to be back here after all these years. I know you always admired how quaint the town was and yet also how conveniently located to the major northeastern metropolitan centers. I bet you wish you were here too. Well, you're not! I love sleeping alone! Love it! I was looking at the Fly Away Fly website again and must tell you that Bianca looks distinctly like she has a mustache in the third "action shot" photo, under the last tab on the second page. It looks like she's got a real handlebar going on, I mean serious facial hair. I find this an interesting choice because you yourself are so hairless. I wonder about friction issues, skin burn, etc. Also, in addition to being hairless, and I think you already know my views on this, I believe you are clueless and without any idea of what you truly want because if you did then

Hi Darcy!

 Mom here. I want to apologize about my cat video question. Of course I'll unfollow Skip. It was an insensitive request. Plus, my new friend Roberta is a whiz at cat videos. She always finds the best ones, far superior to Skip's in fact, so I won't even miss him.

 I'm so sorry about the whole Skip business. Have you heard from him? I had a thought: maybe he's suffering from a bout of temporary amnesia. Memory loss is more common than one would think and can be triggered by the most unusual circumstances. I read about a young woman who tripped at the dentist, just a stumble, but her head glanced the side of one of those metal tables they cover with a blue cloth, where the hygienist keeps her vicious little tools. And that was that.

She couldn't remember her own name, the poor dear. Thank goodness she was in a place of healing. The dentist asked her to lie down and recite the presidents from Washington to the present as they waited for the ambulance. And that, apparently, proved very helpful in reconnecting her brain nerves or neural pathways or whatever they're called.

Darcy, maybe something similar happened to Skip? And maybe no one was there to remind him of the presidents and so his neural pathways remain detached, just blowing loose in the wind of all that skydiving. Have you given that a thought?

I don't mean to raise a painful topic, Darcy. If you'd like me to just forget Skip's existence, I'm quite happy to do that too. I've never told you this before, but Skip was atrocious at loading a dishwasher. Truly one of the worst I've encountered. I tried to teach him, I did, but he seemed deficient in spatial awareness. And following instructions.

Mrs. Pevzner is planning to check on you again. Could you please leave her Tupperware on the porch? She'll drop off another batch of blondies.

Okay dear, I've got to run. Daddy and I miss you SO MUCH. We're sending you buckets of kisses and hugs and cuddles. Please reply and let us know you're not bludgeoned. And do you need any money? Daddy said he's happy to send money to get you through this difficult time.

Love, Mom

Dear Mom,

Skip does not have memory loss. He certainly remembers who I am and the extensive plans we made for our future life together. The problem is that he has rejected those plans in favor of the new plans he's now made with Bianca.

No, I do NOT need money.

Yes, I'm still mad about the house. I hope the crafts instruction is worth it.

Sincerely,

Darcy

I pressed send on the email, sat back against a pillow and sucked on a chickpea. Maybe my mother was right. Maybe Skip did have some sort of brain injury or condition. It seemed unlikely, but then again the idea of me sitting in my childhood bedroom still wearing pajamas at 3 p.m. on a Tuesday, eating legumes straight from the can, would also have seemed unlikely just a few short weeks ago.

Bianca's motives were pure. Pinterest proved it. She wanted Skip, wife be damned. And I respected that, in a strange fatalistic way. At least I understood it.

But Skip? He had demonstrated no signs of unhappiness, no requests for marital counseling or better blow jobs, no signs of boredom or annoyance with our life together. Aleeyah was partially right in her frat boy assessment. Skip was not a guy who liked to talk about his feelings. I'd seen him cry only twice, first when the Red Sox won the World Series in 2013 and second when his childhood bulldog, Rocco, died from overeating. The animal weighed 130 pounds, with a thirty-four-inch neck, and had managed to pull a fifty-pound bag of chow off the kitchen counter and eat the entire contents in under an hour. Eunice had returned home from the post office to find him splayed on the kitchen floor. Poor old Rocco.

But that was it for crying. Skip never seemed depressed. Not much complaining, very little whining, no insomnia or stress eating, never any talk of hopelessness or hate, no fascination with tall bridges or household poisons. Skip was cheerful, a glass-half-full kind of guy, each and every day of our time together.

Something must have happened to drive him into Bianca's Prius. If not traumatic brain injury, then what? I searched my memory for arguments, incidents, forgotten errands, burnt dinners, grudges or resentments. What had I done wrong? How could I have been a better partner, lover, friend? Identifying my core failure would lead me to answer the most urgent question: What can I do now to win Skip back?

Cyberstalking had failed me, so I decided to apply my actuarial skill set to the problem at hand. I poured myself some coffee. I found a pen and put it behind one ear. I opened my laptop, cracked my knuckles and then clicked on that mystical, magical green icon for Excel. My jaw unclenched, my foot stopped its mindless tapping. Logic, data and a well-constructed spreadsheet always made me feel at peace.

Fred, I called to my absent fern, here's the structured scenario we'll be using today: 1) healthy but child-averse twenty-nine-year-old female; 2) healthy but already balding twenty-nine-year-old male; 3) two equally time-consuming and yet ultimately unsatisfying professional careers; and 4) a relationship based on shared activities and daily sex but little to no intellectual or emotional intimacy.

Of course we need our core assumptions, Fred, can't forget those. Assume the male travels for work eight days out of the month. Assume the male said once in passing: I guess you'd call me an ass man. Assume the female possessed a booty that most would consider meager. Assume the male often breathed loudly from his mouth, particularly when reading. Assume the female believed that the perfect life consisted of calm, quiet reading, careful consideration of the day's events and a total absence of travel. Assume the male placed "visit 100 countries" at number one on his bucket list.

You would expect any marriage to experience loss over time. Decreased sex life, sure. Increased irritation with spousal snoring, to use one completely random example, yes. But the sudden and total breakdown of my marriage suggested the existence of severe, unanticipated operational risk.

To analyze the failure of any institution, a good actuary needs an organizational chart, a map, so to speak, of the institution in question. But how to map a marriage? I racked my brain. I considered the major notable events: gifts he'd given me (random); the vacations we'd taken (few); the public declarations of love (one). Third-party statements were too difficult to come by, seeing as they'd require me to communicate with other people and, more important, walk downstairs and retrieve my phone. What else did I have?

Words.

All the communications exchanged over the course of our relationship still existed out there in the cloudosphere, ready and waiting for examination. And so I began reading.

I created a spreadsheet that cataloged and analyzed every email, text message and voicemail ever exchanged between me and Skip. I noted word frequency, choice of sign-off (ranging from *see ya* to *LOVE*), length of message, tone, time of day and every other pertinent factor, major and minor, of each correspondence. I charted use of the word *love* over time. I charted the number of *xo*'s over time. I assigned a value to each correspondence based on the frequency of words that connoted positive affection: dear, honey, sweetie, like, amazing, charming, funny, wine, yes, movie, jiggy, sexy, love.

Just you wait, Fred! I called as I pored over voicemail transcripts and typed in data. The reason for Skip's departure will be abundantly clear. Even you, a sedentary plant life who currently resides with my mother's third closest friend, will recognize my mistake and support me as I work to fix it. The love between me and Skip will endure. Our resilience and ability to reconcile will shock you to the very root, the very last tendril of every root in your pot!

Data input and modeling took me approximately twenty-seven hours. During this time, I did not sleep. I chatted occasionally with Fred, listened to nineties music, ate one can of chickpeas and two of Chef Boyardee.

Finally, I sat back and printed out the spreadsheet. The results were unmistakable. Email and text message values declined steadily every year of our eleven-year relationship. The data suggested no major shock event, no error, either human or environmental, that caused our marital breakdown. Skip and I began dating at twenty-nine positively affectionate words per correspondence and, in the last year before Skip's departure, we averaged a measly four. Four! And in the last ninety days of our marriage, we racked up zero. In fact, I would venture to say that we entered negative territory. Rather than dear, honey and movie, we wrote: busy, late, work, sorry, can't, won't, no.

I guess Skip did try to warn me, in his own half-assed way, I told Fred. The clock said 3 a.m. I was gassy from chickpeas, dehydrated, unwashed, ungroomed.

The writing *was* on the wall, I said. My voice wavered. I am indeed a fool. I did nothing wrong other than exist as myself, Darcy Clipper, year after year, email after email. And how can I fix that? I asked. What sort of precautionary measures could I have put in place to save our marriage? Not a one. Because it was the very act of me being me that drove Skip away and now nothing would bring him back.

AFTER MY SPREADSHEET endeavor, I lay in bed for two days. Or was it five? The time blurred, my dreams churned with lavender claws and vicious axe throwers and dancing spreadsheets full of swear words.

In a rare moment of lucidity, I called to Fred: I've hit rock bottom, my dear fern. I cannot possibly sink any lower.

And then, I received an email:

Dear Darcy,

I hope time at home has helped your mental health. We miss you in the office. Gordon was saying just last week that you were always the one to make the afternoon coffee. We miss our afternoon coffee, Darcy! Now Linda makes it.

Anyhow, I am writing to inform you that unfortunately I can no longer offer you a guaranteed job upon your return to Castro Insurance. I'm a businessman, Darcy, and that means my eye must remain firmly fixed on the bottom line. Granting a sabbatical of mercy to one employee sends the wrong kind of message. What if everyone wanted to run home and surf the internet for six months after their husband left them? Or a loved one died? Or they ate some bad potato salad? Or they just needed a break from the soulless 9–5 grind? Do you see my point? You're a smart girl, Darcy, I'm sure you understand that one sabbatical inevitably leads to many sabbaticals and that places my bottom line in a precarious position. Furthermore, I'm under no legal obligation to offer you anything at all because, unfortunately for you, we did not memorialize our discussion in writing.

I wish you the best, Darcy, truly I do. If you ever recover from the clinical depression you exhibited during those last weeks of work, please get in touch. If I have any open positions, you're certainly welcome to undergo the interview process, reference checks and aptitude tests I administer to all prospective employees.

Sincerely yours,

Mr. David Castro, CEO and President, Castro Insurance Agency Inc.

I read the email once and then again. I considered drafting a reply, something along the lines of: *Dear David, you're a horrible human being—*. Or maybe: *Dear David, you can take your job and shove it up your—*. Or perhaps even: *Mr. Castro, I was surprised and hurt to receive your communication. I've spoken to my lawyer and—*.

But any response would have required me to sit upright in bed, to type, to think. I couldn't possibly summon the strength for any of these activities. Fred—I began. But even speech proved too taxing. I closed my eyes. I drifted into a restless and fitful sleep.

Tell your kid to quit drawing smiley faces on the sidewalks with chalk. The dust gets all over my shoes.

•

Willie Mangina, did you poison my Elvis? He's a very healthy lab but today he won't stop puking. I know it was you, Mangina. Watch your back.

•

Reminder: Our monthly Board of Selectmen meeting takes place Sunday, 7:00 pm. This is the body that governs our town and keeps true democracy alive in the good old US of A. Remember those Chinese students standing in front of tanks? No? Well, google it and you'll see. People die for a democracy like ours, people bleed for it. Surely you can skip Game of Thrones for one night? Our agenda items this month are: 1) clearance of sewage backup at 32nd & Columbia; 2) purchase of new kayak racks for Lake Quinnikiki; 3) repainting of Town Hall handicap parking spaces. Do your civic duty and show up to vote! Your town secretary, Hildegard Hyman

•

Hey parents, did your kid get ahold of my cat? Jojo came home yesterday with her claws painted hot pink. I don't want anyone giving my cat a manicure. If this is your kid, deal with it.

•

To whomever it may concern, soups in order of preference are: Lentil, turkey rice, cream of broccoli, clam chowder, pho, tomato, potato leek. Thanks a ton.

Draft email files

Dear Skip,

I've been thinking a lot about the crappiness of other people. Recently I've come to the conclusion that the effort of meeting people, talking to them, befriending them, working with them, living with them, loving them is more work than it's worth. Without other people, I can do what I want all the time. I don't have to listen to anyone, I don't have to compromise any aspect of my own personal wishes and desires. I am entirely free. Freedom! It's the American way. It's what everyone wants. I am free as a bird, free as a humpback whale swimming in the ocean, free as a darting little bee going from flower to flower, drinking all that sweet nectar, free as a—you get the idea. What could be better than freedom? You probably have to share a bathroom with Bianca and, as noted in previous correspondence, she is one hairy lady. I bet she leaves hair in the shower drain, on the sink, on the toilet seat. Yikes. You were always fairly squeamish when it came to feminine hygiene so I imagine that a hairy toilet seat does not factor high on your list of most desirable home attributes. Do you know what I love most about living alone? When I put something down, I know exactly where to find it. Nothing moves unless I move it. What a treat! I can't believe I've never lived alone before. It was Daddy and Mom, Larissa and Hui-Chen in junior college, and then you. Never a moment without a shared shower. Not a single day of complete and utter solitude and silence. Now I enjoy day after day of solitude, weeks of solitude, a full month so far of nothing but solitude and it's wonderful, it's mind-blowing, stupendous, it's

MY DAYS FELL INTO A routine. I changed into different pajamas every third day; I did laundry every Sunday, sometimes. I limited my consumption of caffeinated beverages, preferring instead to exist within a bleary state of perpetual near-nap. I remained perfectly still during Mrs. Pevzner's visits to the front door. I ate two meals per day culled from the canned stores downstairs and supplemented by Mrs. Pevzner's blondies. Chef Boyardee, creamed corn, chickpeas, green beans, blondie. Repeat. I did not watch television of any kind, due to the risk of unsavory news, preferring my entertainment to arrive instead via the Murbridge Community Message Board and my parents' stacks of decades-old *National Geographic* magazines.

Those magazines had been permanent fixtures of our home décor for as long as I could remember. Yet, I'd never once cracked open an issue. Now, during my period of self-imposed isolation and canned food consumption, I remedied the oversight. Did you know that horsehair worms are parasites that turn their host insects into zombies? Did you know that a Viking ship found in Roskilde Fjord, Denmark, contained an entire cargo of honey?

Consider Friedrich Nietzsche. *National Geographic,* February 1981. Cover story on the old rascal, a man born before the age of Prozac and mustache trimmers. Nietzsche loved to be alone. He saw the risks involved in human interaction, the pitfalls of walking along a city street, the mental anguish of caring. He proposed to Lou Salomé three goddamn times, and she always said no. It was rumored that he'd had sex only once, at a brothel, and contracted syphilis in the process. Poor guy. Without a spouse or children or a sex life, he certainly enjoyed ample time for thinking and philosophizing. Sure, he had friends, but his legacy, his life's work, occurred in solitude.

One must avoid chance and outside stimuli as much as possible, said Friedrich. *A kind of walling oneself in belongs among the foremost instinctive precautions of spiritual pregnancy.*

I dog-eared the page. Spiritual pregnancy? This was a new and intriguing concept. I knew all about the other, regular kind of pregnancy. Or rather, I knew about trying to get pregnant.

For the last two years of my marriage, physical pregnancy had eluded me. Skip and I tried. Boy, did we. Clomid, Femara, primrose oil, raspberry seed, acupuncture, meditation, fertility tracking, membrane testing, vitamin B6, B12, folic acid, fish oil. My geriatric OB, Dr. Able Ahmed, had two tufts of gray hair above his ears but otherwise was bald as a coot. He liked to turn most every conversation into song. *Priscilla, Queen of the Desert,* he told me at my first appointment, was his favorite musical.

Skip got tested first. A simple affair, at least somewhat enjoyable. We waited a week and then Dr. Ahmed called. He began by humming "What's Love Got to Do with It" and then told us the results: healthy sperm count, healthy motility. The blame for our lack of offspring lay firmly with me.

I underwent test after test: scans, blood draws, swabs, palpitations. Nothing remarkable presented. On one such examination, with Dr. Ahmed's hairless head between my legs, I heard a throat clear, a foot tap. He began to sing:

Why, oh why, is this lovely vagina
inhospitable to life?
Inhospitable
inhospitable
inhospitable
To life!

On my back, feet in the air, I felt the need to respond to this query. I began to speak: In the summer sometimes, when I was a kid, I wore my bathing suit, like, all day long . . . Do you think maybe . . . ?

Dr. Ahmed rolled back his stool, unpeeled his gloves, snapped them off with a dramatic flourish and shook his head. He opened his mouth and sang:

My darling Darcy, you are a mystery!
There's nothing to see here. Nothing at all
You're ripe as a peach, dear. Slick as a pearl!
Now go forth and propagate
Go forth and unfurl!

Once I was wearing pants again, I sat in Dr. Ahmed's office and received his advice in speech. Do not attempt pregnancy, he said. Trying to get pregnant has, in fact, a prophylactic effect. Wanting a baby is the world's best birth control. Put pregnancy out of your mind. Banish it from your thoughts. Babies are grotesque, messy, noisy little pests. Repeat that to yourself as a daily mantra. Let's give it a go. Dr. Ahmed gazed at me, eyebrows raised. Come on, he said.

Babies are, I began slowly, grotesque, messy, noisy little pests.

Wonderful! he cried and clapped his hands. Just wonderful. Now, what you must do is simple—and here he closed his eyes and assumed the affect of a lean, tan Buddha—Darcy, you must *relax*. Do not want. Do not anticipate. Let your mystical feminine power take the lead. Relinquish yourself to the sacred wisdom of the ovum. He opened his eyes and smiled.

I was not smiling. Trying to get pregnant had occupied at least 72 percent of my waking hours for the past two years. How were my ovaries to lead if I wasn't tracking my temperature? Or googling prospective baby names?

I know, I got it. Of course the whole pregnancy-attempt factor— heretofore unexpressed by myself in this narrative—influenced Skip's decision to leave our marriage. Bianca qua Bianca was largely irrelevant. But Bianca the metaphor, the feminine ideal, was another thing altogether. Her cunningly wide hips, her lush black eye-lashes, her naked ring finger with that long lavender nail—all blended together to compose an irresistible milkshake of feminine wile and fertility. Those hips were childbearing hips, as Mom would have said. Those hips showed my husband how to free-fall and, just like that, my marriage ended.

Draft email files

Dear Skip,

I saw your most recent Instagram post: you and Bianca at Del Vecchio's in Back Bay. God, I used to love that place. How they made the Caesar salad right at the table, cracking the egg, grating the parm. Did Bianca order the Caesar salad? I hope she choked on an anchovy.

I know I've been playing the high road here. I know it may seem like I'm over it. But I'm not. I miss you. I can't sleep very well. My mind is always distracted. I check emails about 100 times per day and then do the rounds on all the sites where I might catch a glimpse of you. I even look at that god-awful LinkedIn photo, the one where your head tilts weirdly to the left. Why did you pose that way? It looks like you suffer from some sort of spinal condition. But you're still cute. Here's the thing, Skip: I still think you're cute and quirky. I thought we were similar like that. I didn't realize that you really wanted some adventurous, athletic, mustachioed woman who throws caution to the wind. Bianca is literally the opposite of who I am. Bianca is

I FOUND RELIEF IN MY isolation. Admittedly, I grew sick of chick-peas within that first month, but there was an ease to my days, a haze of indifference that I had never experienced before. I went no-where. I saw no one. Other people, I decided, were superfluous. Other people were loud and caustic. Cranky. Also, unsightly and grating to the ear. People with kale in their teeth. People who spoke in over-anxious tones or coughed directly into your unsuspecting face. Body odor and road rage. Rudeness at the checkout counter. Line cutters and open-mouthed breathers.

Within the confines of my house, I experienced true peace. Or at least a stasis so complete that it could reasonably be mistaken for peace. Solitude removes virtually all unknown, rogue elements of daily existence. The weather outside your window, perhaps, still exists beyond your control. But who cares? You're wrapped up tight in a blanket, reading a *National Geographic* magazine from July 1976, drinking weak tea and eating creamed corn. You're warm, fed and entertained. What could be better?

CONSIDER ZENO OF Elea, *National Geographic,* January 1989. Zeno was an old-school Greek philosopher, pre-Socratic, his beard as long as his schlong (so they say). *Little is known of Zeno's life,* the article begins, and then continues for twenty-two pages. And there he is! A marble bust of a man with formidable brows, a monumental nose, a long sad face and empty eye sockets. Not exactly a looker, but still, I smiled: I'd found an old friend.

As a child, I stumbled upon Zeno one night while my parents were out for Thursday night fondue. My babysitter, Tiffany, suffered from a generalized boredom so acute that she usually fell asleep as soon as my parents walked out the door. This allowed me the freedom to spend the duration of fondue nights reading Tiffany's college text-books and eating peanut butter out of the jar.

On one such evening, Tiffany began snoring and I opened a text-book on ancient Greek philosophy. To be honest, I was hoping for some good war stories or weird sex. Instead, I found Zeno and his fa-mous paradox. Zeno surmised that motion is nothing but an illusion because distance is infinitely divisible. Think about it: You must travel the first half of any distance before reaching the second half. And that second half can be divided into two, and that quarter divided again, and so on and so on ad nauseum. The ability to reach any destination is therefore a hoax. A sham. You'll never get anywhere.

After that one fateful fondue night, I became obsessed. I viewed all distances as marked by this never-ending division. Walking to the end of the hall, reaching a hand to touch the wall, setting one foot onto the floor, removing my body from the bed.

For weeks or maybe months I refused to let my parents touch me. They wanted to bring me to a doctor but I wouldn't leave my room. We'll never make it! I told them. We'll be trapped, stuck on a path of perpetual advancement but never reaching the destination. Don't come near me!

I sobbed. I screamed. I was eight years old.

I'm not telling you this to brag about my precocious obsession with Greek philosophers. Please. I mention Zeno because he seems a harbinger of what my life became during my self-imposed period of isolation and canned food consumption. My natural tendency to solitude predated Skip by decades. Did Skip see that in me? Did he find it impossible to touch me, and by that I mean touch in a deeper, metaphoric sense? Touch my soul. My spirit animal. The true Darcy.

Zeno developed his theories primarily to defend his friend Parmenides. And by *friend* I mean "friend," aka lover. At least that's the gossip Socrates later reported. Parmenides was seen as a bit of a kook so Zeno put his admirable intellect to the task of taking down Parmenides's critics. It's interesting, don't you think, that a theory of stasis originated from a love relationship? I imagine a lovestruck Zeno holding a hand above Parmenides's stomach. I imagine the hand lowering bit by bit by tiniest bit. The heat of skin. The navel. The gently curved abdomen. Perhaps a gleaming sheen of sweat. Tender pale hairs. But Zeno cannot touch his beloved. He cannot bridge the distance between them.

Draft email files

Dear Skip,

Once I had a dream about a baby and in the dream the baby was ours. It wasn't a girl or a boy, it was just a generic chubby baby, and we loved it so much. In the dream I was holding the baby and you were sitting very close to me, so close that I could feel your hair on my cheek. We both stared down at the baby and then it started talking to us. It said, *Whatever,* and hopped down off my lap and started walking! This was really strange because obviously this baby was too young to walk. But the baby looked over its shoulder and said, *You guys suck,* and it walked away. The baby left us. The baby rejected us as parents. And we just sat there and watched it go, we didn't even try to convince the baby to stay, because deep down we knew the baby was right. We did suck. A baby wouldn't want you as a father because you're so goddamn self-righteous and inconsistent and also selfish and self-serving. What kind of baby would put up with that? And no baby would ever want me as a mother because I can't

ON DAY 29 OF MY self-imposed isolation and canned food consumption, I heard a knock on my front door. It was a Tuesday afternoon, I believed, though without much conviction. I was still wearing pajamas and had eaten Chef Boyardee for breakfast and lunch. I peeked through the peephole: not Mrs. Pevzner bearing more blondies—bummer—but a policeman of average height and commendable shoulders. I considered, briefly, tiptoeing away from the door and back upstairs to bed, but I was, and remain, a rule follower and so I opened the door.

Hello, Officer, I said.

Good afternoon, miss. I'm sorry to bother you but we've had some calls concerning a possible squatter residing here. What's your connection to this property?

I snorted. I grew up here. My parents own this house. Everyone in Murbridge knows my parents. Stan and Jeanine Clipper? Stan, the engineer? Jeanine, with the crazy hair?

The policeman shook his head. Sorry. I'm relatively new to the area. His name tag said *Omar* and his shoes were very clean.

Listen, Officer Omar, I said. Who called you? Was it those Dykstras?

He looked to the ground and then back up. I'm not at liberty to say who put in the call. Can I see some ID? Do you have proof of your parents' residence here? Utility bill, mortgage statement?

I have a driver's license, I said. But your guess is as good as mine where I put it. I haven't left the house in a month.

I invited Omar inside while I searched for the documents that would prove I was myself. He hesitated by the front door, but I insisted he sit on the couch, although first I had to move the blankets and the bowl I'd used for chickpeas the night before and a printout of the Skip Excel spreadsheet and my book, a tattered copy of *Jane Eyre,* and the tissues I'd used while crying over *Jane Eyre.*

Upstairs I retrieved my driver's license from under the bed and then searched and searched for some kind of utility bill, but of course my parents had redirected their mail.

I descended the stairs. I now wore a cardigan over my pajamas, to appear less like a squatter.

Officer, I said. Let me explain the situation. I showed Omar my driver's license, which naturally listed the Back Bay condo as my residence, and so I told him about Skip, and then I mentioned Bianca, and then I launched into the whole sorry tale, and at some point I began to cry, only stopping when I noticed the look of concern on Omar's face.

Maybe we should call your parents? he said gently. To verify your residence here? And you should probably talk to someone.

No! I said. I told my mother I'd never speak to her again.

Never is a long time, Omar replied.

I began to cry again. My parents just love me too much, I explained in between sobs. They give me too much support. It's totally unfair and it's turned me into a person destined to fail at everything. I began to hiccup uncontrollably.

I need to sit down, I said, falling onto the couch. I might be sick.

Omar stepped back. Ms. Clipper, why don't you give me your parents' number in Arizona. Once I'm back at the station, I'll call them to confirm your identity, verify property ownership in the town records, and then I won't have to bother you again.

Okay, I said in between hiccups. Do you have a pen?

Once Omar and my hiccups had both departed, I found Daddy's binoculars in the upstairs closet, lifted a west-facing curtain and stared into the kitchen that now belonged to the Dykstra family. I saw a shiny chrome espresso machine, a double-door refrigerator, some kind of breakfast nook thing. A breakfast nook, I muttered. What a bunch of assholes.

And then I saw a female figure holding binoculars to her eyes, peering back at me.

Dear Daddy and Mom,

I write to report some problems at the house. There's a flushing issue with the downstairs toilet—it sounds like Niagara Falls every time I push the handle. The microwave is also acting weird. If I open the door before the bell, the table still turns and I feel a rush of heat. Is this normal? Maybe I'm microwaving myself?

Also, what do you know about the Dykstras? They seem incredibly nosy and odd. But you're right—their wi-fi is fantastic.

Also, Officer Omar Abdullah will call you soon to confirm my identity. Please tell him I'm not a squatter.

Also, I've decided to paint my bedroom black. I know you'll hate it, but tough nuts. I need a safe, dark, non-distracting space in which to nap and read. I find the current taupe-y beige overwhelming. Black will better suit my emotional state.

Sincerely yours,

Darcy

ISO: paint supplies. Black paint, preferably matte. Also brushes, etc. Cannot pick up but will pay extra for delivery.

•

ISO: canned food (anything but chickpeas)

•

ISO: houseplants, preferably large expressive ferns that respond well to human voice and early Taylor Swift

•

ISO: *National Geographic* magazines, any issue after March 1992

IN AND AROUND 2015, IT became popular to give away all the things you'd spent your entire adult life accumulating. Thank you, Marie Kondo, and your declarations of joyful sparking. Paint supplies arrived silently on my front porch after a few short email exchanges.

Re: paint supplies: Yes, I have a drop cloth and brushes gathering dust in my shed. Take them all, please, take them!

I've got 32 sample pots of interior paint in different shades of black. None of them was the right black—maybe you'll have more luck.

The drop cloth didn't quite cover my bedroom floor, but good enough. The larger paintbrush was too stiff to use, but the small one worked just fine. I dumped all the paint samples into Mom's big spaghetti pot and stirred to create a wonderful shade of the inkiest black. It was perfect.

Painting your bedroom with one tiny paintbrush is an exhausting task. One coat took all day and well into the night. Afterward, I lay on my back on my bed and pulled the drop cloth over me like a blanket.

Good night, Fred, I called and then I fell asleep in my painting clothes, which were the clothes I'd worn for three days straight, which were pajamas.

I ACKNOWLEDGE NOW that spending your days inside a room painted entirely black is not the best for one's mental health. Nor is staying abreast of the news cycle via all-cap headlines culled from accidental stumbles onto the MSN homepage. My anxiety pulsed like a second heart. Day after day I stayed in bed and watched my black ceiling. Day after day I contemplated the wreckage of my twenty-nine years on the planet.

Isolation, I can tell you now, breeds paranoia. I began to suspect that my old boss Mr. Castro joined forces with Skip and Bianca to cause my emotional breakdown. Mrs. Pevzner became involved in the scheme, as did the entire roster of the women's rec softball team I'd joined last year and then promptly quit when I learned that practices began at 5:30 a.m. Why did they all conspire against me? What had I done to prompt such dislike? Did I deserve their acrimony? And how did Mr. Castro know about my brief and ill-fated softball career? The details never fully lined up, but whatever.

My conspiracy theories proliferated like fruit flies around a dying banana. After I exhausted Mr. Castro and the softball team, I moved on to Mom and Daddy (which, let's be frank, wasn't such a stretch) and their plot to sell the house out from under me; then those spying Dykstras (also not a stretch); then the new east-facing neighbors who I swear had a telescope pointed right into my kitchen; and then the UPS guy who always lingered longer than seemed appropriate on my front porch. Was he casing the joint for points of entry? Was he planning to bludgeon me?

I ordered a pallet of two-by-fours, one heavy-duty hammer and a box of very long nails. When the UPS guy arrived, I was waiting for him.

I opened the front door. It's you, I said. This was day 37 of my self-imposed isolation and canned food consumption. My voice felt a little rough from underuse, but I rather liked its hoarse new smoker's tone.

The UPS guy jumped. Whoa, he said, you scared me.

And why's that? I growled.

I wasn't expecting someone to open the door.

You mean you weren't expecting someone to figure out what you're up to. *That's* why you're scared.

I'm just the UPS guy, ma'am.

What's your name?

Jared. He pointed to the name stitched on his brown uniform.

You always spend a lot of time on my porch, don't you, Jared.

Not any more time than usual, ma'am. He began to back down the stairs.

You're always looking around out here, lingering longer than you have to. I've seen you.

I just deliver the boxes. I try to find a safe, dry place to put them. That's all.

I've even seen you take pictures with your phone. How do you explain *that*? I was following Jared down the steps as he backed toward his truck. He did in fact look scared and it gave me a small but delicious thrill.

Lady, we have to take pictures of all deliveries now. UPS policy.

I honestly hadn't thought of that.

But you—you take a lot of pictures, I said.

Two or three. He held up his hands and added, UPS policy.

He was standing beside his truck now. I have to get going, he said. Busy day. Amazon, they rule the planet. He laughed nervously. Anything else I can do for you?

Well. Just. Don't try anything funny.

He laughed again, this time with a little more gusto. No worries there. You have a good day, ma'am.

He slung himself into the truck—those seats are awfully high— and put-put-putted away. This truck was an old wheezy one and Jared drove slowly. No way he could ever sneak up on me in that thing. No way, nohow.

I felt silly standing on my front lawn in pajamas and fuzzy slippers, but I also felt empowered. I'd looked my conspiracy theory straight in the face and I'd come away the winner. I still believed what I wanted to believe, even if it flew in the face of all available data and observations, and yet I would sleep well tonight because I'd neutralized the threat. That's the great thing about unsubstantiated conspiracy theories: it takes very little effort to solve them. If your enemy is an imaginary monster, you can imagine yourself victorious no matter how weak, stupid or crazy you are. And that was why I skipped back into the house, fixed myself some Chef Boyardee and felt my pounding heart slow itself down for the first time in weeks.

Plus, Jared had delivered all the materials I needed to board up my kitchen window to stop those psycho Dykstras from spying on me.

ALERT: I saw a highly suspicious man (possible gang member?) walking very slowly down Maple Ave this morning. Physical description: African-American, tall, wearing an odd vest-like garment (gang attire?). Stay safe out there.

•

Yikes, I just found a baked potato on the hood of my car. Shit you not. Why would someone leave a potato on my car? It's freaking me out. Is this a gang thing?

•

Neighbors, if you suspect gang activity, it's important to notify the police. Don't be shy. I call them at least once per week to report suspicious activity. The officers are all very nice young men and women, not the rough types you read about in the news.

•

ONE MORE GODDAMN REMINDER, PETER LUFLIN: STOP putting your dog crap in my garbage can. You adopted the four-legged shit factory, so you deal with the shit. Got it?

•

Dear Soup Lady, my friends think maybe you're trying to poison me. I've really enjoyed your gifts (especially the chowder) but no more soup. Thanks for understanding.

CONSIDER VALERY POLYAKOV. *NATIONAL GEOGRAPHIC,* January 1987. A human can survive alone in space for a very long time. At NASA, scientists experimented with astronauts, volunteer civilians and conscripted chickens to ascertain the outer edge of the survival envelope. The Russian cosmonaut Valery Polyakov spent 437 days in space, orbiting the Earth along with space dust and meteors, no fresh air or real food or touch of skin. Completely and utterly alone. He ate freeze-dried shrimp cocktail and sardines, poor guy. He suffered nausea and bone loss. Radiation sickness too. His wife, Nelly, was gorgeous. Slavic cheekbones and a teeny-tiny waist. Along with their three kids, she waited for him in a Moscow suburb until he returned. Reportedly she told him she was so proud and would support another trip, if he were asked by the great Soviet state to make one. But honestly, who overheard that conversation? Imagine them on that first night at last the two of them in bed together, darkness, but a different darkness than the one in space. This darkness is full and warm with hazy undefined shapes. The dresser, Nelly's discarded shoes, the faint outline of a window. Valery remembers the cold dark of space, the starkness of it, the never-ending arc of time, and he begins to nod off. He's so relieved to be warm under a blanket, a warm body beside him. He doesn't have the energy for sex, not yet, but he reaches for his wife's hand under the covers and she grips it. You fucking asshole, Nelly whispers. I don't care what they say. You are not going back up there. You are not leaving me alone again.

Dear Darcy,

We miss you, Bunny. How are you? We haven't heard from you in over two weeks and frankly, Darcy, I'm beginning to worry. I gather you're still upset about the move and the house, but are you ill? Any flu? Cough? Nasal drip? Muscle pains? Chest pain? Difficulty breathing? Bloody stool? Stinky discharge? Remember to take zinc, vitamin C, fish oil, castor oil, stay away from bees and don't put your hand in the garbage disposal.

Arizona is truly an astounding place. There is simply no such thing as the sniffles down here. Cancer, yes. Kidney failure, heart failure, stroke, shingles, yes, yes, yes and yes. We're in a retirement community, for crying out loud. But those are age-related! Those are not germs! Down here the germs just heat up and die. I think it's a good thing for me and Daddy. We can live more freely, knowing that our health problems are pretty much inevitable. You can't do much about cancer, not at this particular stop on the tour bus of life, but sniffles are equally irritating and those we've been avoiding nicely.

I miss you and hope you're not still mad about the moving thing.

Love, Mom

Dear Mom,

I'm taking my zinc, vitamin C, kombucha, goop energy
supplements, probiotics, quaaludes and vodka shots before bed.
I should be fine. I'm glad to hear you don't have any sniffles
but are you trying to tell me something about cancer? I thought
Daddy's colonoscopy left him in the clear? If you're trying to
express something horrible, I suppose I'll pick up the phone when
you call. But please no dirty tricks. I'll hang up if you start talking
about a reconciliation. Yes, I'm still mad and plan on being
mad for a very long time. You disappointed me, Mom. You and
Daddy left me at my moment of need. You, Skip, my best friends,
everyone has let me down. I'm going to stay inside, alone, germ-
free, 100% safe until some undetermined future date. Please
respect my decision.

Sincerely, Darcy

CONSIDER POOR DR. IGNAZ SEMMELWEIS. *National Geographic,*
October 1998. Ignaz was born in 1818, a Hungarian physician with an
epic mustache, one almost as impressive as good old Nietzsche's. No
one listened when he said wash your hands. No one listened when
he talked about cadaverous particles, aka germs. People thought
Ignaz was a quack. Worse, people thought he was trying to blame
other doctors for making patients sicker. Other doctors wanted the
freedom to take their blood-soaked hands and stick them into another patient's oozing wound. Gross, I know, but that's what they did
back then. Ignaz tried to warn them, but no dice. At the washed-up
age of forty-seven, he landed in a mental asylum and died two
weeks later of sepsis, an infection in the bloodstream that is easily
prevented by—wait for it—handwashing. Irony's a bitch.

The lesson here is that touching other people makes you sick.
Don't let anyone tell you different. Touching in any sense of the word
causes the transfer of germs and emotions. Physical skin to skin,

breath to breath, feeling to feeling. Don't kiss or hold hands or listen or love or share air with a person who might simply decide to transfer cadaverous particles from one body to the next or to ride off in a Prius of a different color. You will never safely bridge the gap between point A and point B, so don't even begin the journey.

WHY WAS I so afraid? I don't really know. My fears were diverse. Dying and running out of canned food and the polar ice caps melting and Ebola and plastic in the oceans and mean people and dying and hurricanes and Facebook and student debt and Brexit and Ivanka and Venice underwater and plastic in the microwave and cruelty and my split ends and America and dying and would anyone ever love me again?

Draft email files

Dear Skip,

Sometimes I wonder why people get married in the first place. It seems impossible that any two people could find enough common ground to last a lifetime. We all have brains, spines, stomachs, hearts. But that's where the similarities end. We're all just simmering little pots of our own private complaints and insecurities and shame. Why do people even bother? Is it sex? Money? Propagation of the species? Your sister is never having children, that's for damn sure, so I can see why you'd feel some pressure. Skip, let me remind you of a few things: you consistently told me there was no pressure to provide your mother with grandchildren. But there was indeed pressure! How would you like to get stuck with needles every single day? And blow up like a game day blimp? And cry because a cute dog food commercial came on TV? That first IVF round was fairly quick and painless, but the second and third? Not quick and painless. I took all the supplements, followed the diet, meditated, hypnotherapy, acupuncture, etc. etc. etc. and look where it got me.

At the time, I convinced myself that I wanted a child. And perhaps in convincing myself, I may have also convinced you. But I now believe that some women aren't meant to be mothers. Some women lack the maternal instinct. And one of those women is me. Here's the flat-out truth: I don't like babies. Too many sticky digits and sudden loud noises. Bodily fluids and mysterious demands. How do you know what a baby is really thinking? How do you know what a baby needs? How do you keep a baby safe? There is no way to keep a baby absolutely safe. Danger exists everywhere. Fire and car accidents and drowning and guns and tsunamis and rabies and so many things that scare the crap out of me. I'm so relieved, Skip, so very relieved that I never

---

Someone made a snow penis on my front yard. It's tacky and disgusting. Next time I see someone playing in my snow, I'll call the police.

•

POLL: (age 18 or older) do you enjoy live nude burlesque? ☐ very ☐ somewhat ☐ maybe ☐ yes

•

To the noxiously noisy jogger who came through at 7:00 am today. Stop breathing so hard! People are trying to sleep.

•

WARNING: I've wired my garbage can to deliver a mild but painful electric shock. If I see anyone opening the lid who's not a town-certified garbage collector, I'll let her blow. How do you like that, Peter Luflin?

•

ISO new good little soup boy

JESUS, FRED, I CALLED FROM my place on the couch with my laptop. People are so weird. And so *mean*. I've been spending too much time on the Community Board. When did people begin to suck? And why do they suck so much?

It was day 52 of self-imposed isolation and canned food consumption and my patience was wearing thin.

Fred, how can people do what they do? Say what they say? People, it turns out, are despicable. There is so little kindness and mercy in the world. Mass shootings and North Korea and this one teenager who went blind from eating nothing but potato chips and French fries for ten years. Where were his parents? Where were his friends? Why did no one say: *Hey, maybe eat an apple today?* Or, *How about we lay off the potato products for a spell?*

I closed the laptop and lay back against the cushions. *Ouch.* I removed an empty can of creamed corn and got comfortable.

But then again—I paused in my soliloquy and wondered briefly if I was in fact going insane. The sun poured in from the window with that yellow buttery look that only happens in late winter in New England, a light that announces itself as strong and getting stronger. Dust motes painted with brilliance moved wavelike in the air. My coffee mug sat precariously on the arm of the sofa. I pinched the thin skin on the back of my hand.

I felt that, I said aloud. I'm still here. I'm speaking aloud to an absent fern, but I recognize the lunacy of what I'm doing and *that* is an unmistakable sign of sanity.

Fred, I resumed, I am an island. Here, inside my house, inside Murbridge, Massachusetts, inside the great old US of A. I have declared my independence. I am free from the tyranny of personal relationships and expectations. Free from anyone and anything that might impose upon my personal desire to sit on this couch and talk to a plant. No, Fred, it's not that I hate people. I certainly do not *hate* people. I certainly *adore* ferns. But I've come to realize that life without the actual, physical company of other people is possible. In fact, it's preferable.

Misanthropes get a bad rap, Fred. Socrates said that a person will end up hating everyone only after her optimistic expectations are repeatedly thwarted. The misanthrope starts off an optimist. People forget this. It's not the misanthrope's fault that she hates people. Experience leads her to this conclusion. Life beats the optimism out of her. Other people show her that other people suck.

Misanthropic isolation is as American as apple pie. Go West, young man! No one ever said: Go West, neighborhood! Or Go West, group of kind and supportive friends! No, the cowboy rode alone. Or with a few other lonely cowboys, but they were always shooting each other in the back or getting lost in the woods when they wandered off to pee. Those western young men stomped on native cultures, with their interdependency and traveling villages and complicated lineages, and showed everyone what the single-minded pursuit of self-interest might accomplish. They built cabins in the middle of goddamn nowhere. The Puritans crossed an ocean just to get away from other people. They didn't want anyone telling them what to do. Although the Puritans *definitely* wanted to tell other people what to do, especially if the task was difficult and joyless. The Puritans were the first true misanthropes. No idolatry, no alcohol, no adultery, no witchcraft, very little sex, no fun. Only God, self-denial, self-flagellation, corsets and hair shirts.

Oh my goodness, Fred, I called, all this talk of hair shirts is making me itch. I could do with a nice bubble bath.

Upstairs, I ran the bath hot until steam clouded the room, fogged the mirror, wreathed my skin with damp. I undressed and stretched out in the claw-foot tub of my youth and considered my naked body. It was no longer a child's body, of course, but it looked nothing like my mother's. Mom tended to pear, with a wide comfortable rear and bountiful hips and a small-ish waist that she often accented with a brightly colored sash or belt. My body combined narrow hips, a meager though decently formed chest, thighs that, truth be told, had expanded a bit during my sedentary isolation, strong solid calves, feet with high arches that I always considered rather fetching. Beneath the bathwater, my skin turned pink and my belly button turned in on itself.

Was this body safe and strong? I wondered. Did this body need to protect itself from danger, to cower and hide and cover itself in warm fuzzy blankets? Or could this body survive in the cold, unforgiving outside world full of unpleasant strangers? Would this body bridge the distance? Or was she better off alone?

CONSIDER PABLO NERUDA. *National Geographic,* July 1978. Neruda was a poet and a true romantic; also, a politician. Word on the street was that General Pinochet ordered a doctor to poison Neruda while he was in treatment for prostate cancer. Can you think of a dirtier trick? Pinochet forbade any public recognition of Neruda's death, but crowds defiantly lined the streets regardless. Emotion will defeat guns any day of the week, General, check your history books. Neruda wrote about solitude and about love. He loved love. He loved women and children and men and Chileans and Argentines and pretty much anyone who wasn't General Pinochet. Neruda had seen some tough times. He was the original country-western singer, the lonesome cowboy with charming dimples and the saddest eyes.

There is no insurmountable solitude, Neruda wrote. *All paths lead to the same goal: to convey to others what we are.*

Here I stopped reading and put the magazine down. My fingers were still puckered from the bath, my hair wet and cold against my scalp. What, exactly, was *my* goal? Was I trying to convey to others what I was? I didn't think so. I thought in fact that conveying anything to anyone, other than conveying extreme annoyance to my parents, ranked pretty low on my priority list. But perhaps that was because I didn't know the answer.

Darcy Clipper, what are you?

Damned if I know, I said aloud. I'm not a fern, clearly, but anything more specific than that, and I go a little fuzzy.

I kept reading. *First we must pass through solitude and difficulty, isolation and silence in order to reach forth to the enchanted place where we can dance our clumsy dance and sing our sorrowful song— but in this dance or in this song there are fulfilled the most ancient rites of our conscience in the awareness of being human and of believing in a common destiny.*

Solitude, difficulty, isolation, silence—I've certainly got those covered. If anyone needs me, I'll be right here, isolated and difficult. Alone and silent. Except for you, Fred. You're the only one who hears my voice.

Was I aware of being human? Did I possess an ancient conscience? I sure as hell didn't believe in a common destiny. Bianca's destiny was all hers, and hopefully it involved a faulty parachute and lots of excess air time. But, I realized now, sitting alone in my black bedroom, a forty-year-old magazine open on my lap, I wanted to believe in Neruda's enchanted place. I wanted to believe in a common destiny. But how to find it?

ON DAY 65 of self-imposed isolation and canned food consumption, my heart began hammering so hard I believed I was having a heart attack. I felt my breath shorten, my chest tighten, my feet tingle. I reached for my phone and, without thinking, I called Skip. His number remained right there at the top of my speed dial list. My medical emergency person. My just-in-case person. My person.

But as the phone rang and rang, an interesting thing happened. My thudding heart and existential anxiety faded and were replaced, for a few brief but significant moments, by aggravation. Skip was not answering his phone. I could picture him staring blankly at the screen, just as he would when his boss or his mother called, tilting his head as he listened to that inane ringtone—a digitized "Eye of the Tiger"—and then rolling his eyes and silencing the ringer.

I mean, what a dick. Me, his wife whom he left without warning or marital counseling or explanation, who hasn't contacted him once in eighty-nine days, calls at six in the morning and he lets it go to voicemail?

Hi friend, you've reached Skip Larson—

I threw my phone across the room. It struck the black wall with a dull thud and left a whitish dent in the plaster.

I got out of bed, opened my window and yelled, *Fuck you, Skip Larson* until my throat was raw and I thought I heard sirens.

Then I took a shower.

HELP butter: I need some butter but I can't find my keys and I don't want to see anyone. Please can someone leave a stick at 34th and Peachtree. I love butter. Please.

•

Thank you for all the kind referrals! We found the perfect caregiver for Jett and Viggo (40 months). Andy, our new manny, starts full time next week and we couldn't be more thrilled. With gratitude, BestBoyMommy22

•

Our cat Jojo came home yesterday and looks like someone gave her a bath. Thank you, kind stranger! She'd been pretty funky since a tussle with a skunk last week but now our sweet Jojo is back.

•

Has anyone come across a potbellied pig? She chased after the garbage truck yesterday and we haven't seen her since. She's very fat and answers to Stella. Thanks neighbors!

•

Reply to the butter poster—I just left a box of salted on the corner. Enjoy and take care

•

Darling, are you there? Can you hear me?

•

Darling, the tulips are coming. The red and the yellow. Soon, darling, soon.

Spring

AFTER MY SHOWER, I DECIDED it was high time for a walk. The temperature hovered at a balmy forty-six degrees, snowdrifts had melted, lawns now sported calico spots of dead brown grass that looked quite hopeful. Spring had arrived. I smelled it as I opened my bedroom window to dispel the odor of Chef Boyardee and sadness. *Sniff sniff.* There it was: dank, water-logged, possibly moldy, with just the slightest hint of crocus.

I pulled on my boots, slipped into my parka and arranged a neck gaiter to cover as much of my face as possible. I wanted to travel incognito. No accidental run-ins with nosy neighbors or friends of my mother. I particularly wanted to avoid run-ins with socially superior old high school classmates. At least I assumed they were still socially superior. Those minute gradations of adolescent popularity and attractiveness still loomed large in my mind. Peter DeBacki was still Most Likely to Succeed and Most Attractive and Most Likely to Appear on *The Bachelor.* Georgina Oliver was still Most Attractive and Sweetest Smile and Most Likely to Marry Elon Musk. Garston Copaheck was still Class Clown and Most Likely to Fart in Public and Most Likely to Be Divorced by a Supermodel.

And me? I wasn't Most Likely to anything. Those high school achievers reached a level of personal development in their teens that I still hadn't managed to score in prime adulthood. Compared to Georgina Oliver, I was a grub, a fat wriggly caterpillar eating her way through canned food and sofa upholstery, more likely to get squashed underfoot than transform into any kind of butterfly. But Georgina had achieved butterfly status roughly around the same time she began wearing a bra. I shuddered at the thought of where she might be today. Had she moved to L.A.? Or Paris? Was she running a tech startup? Or a fashion franchise? Had she actually married Elon Musk? It seemed a distinct possibility.

I pulled my gaiter up over my nose. The likelihood that anyone from my high school intelligentsia still resided in Murbridge seemed remote, but I didn't want to take any chances.

It was Sunday. My legs felt weak at first, shaky from so much lounging, but then they remembered how to move. My street was empty, so too the next block and the next, and this suited me just fine. I didn't want to talk or nod my head. I only wanted movement and fresh air and to see scenery that wasn't the interior of my house. After a good ten minutes of what I believed was aimless wandering, I realized that in fact I was walking the path I'd once walked every day to my grade school. Muscle memory, my subconscious leading me, call it what you will but there it was: Murbridge Elementary School, K through sixth. It's a strange thing as an adult to look at a space that appeared monumental to you as a child. The ten (*onetwothreefour-fivesixseveneightnineten*) concrete steps to the front entrance, the huge heavy red door, the sweet little scalloped overhang that gave a good six inches of rain cover to anyone whose parent was late picking up.

The building was quiet, empty, peaceful. I saw my grade-school self flying up those steps, backpack bumping against my rear, hair all in my face. Back then, I knew what I wanted. I knew who I was: Darcy Clipper? Here! I felt part of a common destiny. What had happened to that girl?

It was then I heard a shout: Fuck you, asshole!

Yeah—

Then sounds of scuffling, and one large crack.

I followed the noise to the back of the school where the playground was located. Next to the swing set were two boys and they were beating the crap out of each other.

Hey kids—cut it out! I said.

They did not stop.

I said cut it *out.* I pulled the littler boy off the bigger one, who appeared to be losing. The little one wore a *Hello Dora* T-shirt.

What the fuck, lady? he said. Mind your own business. This asshole owes me five bucks.

Do not, the bigger kid said. On his T-shirt: *Sorry, Ladies, I Only Date Models.*

How old are you? I asked.

I'm seven, he's eight, answered Dora.

Where are your parents?

Both boys shrugged.

Look around you! I said, spreading my arms wide. You should be playing, not fighting.

Dora said: Listen, lady, the swings are all broken. The merry-go-round is a death trap.

Only Date Models said: And who wants to go down a lousy slide? *Wheee!* He fluttered his fingers and wiggled his shoulders to show the ridiculousness of this scenario.

I looked around and saw that the boys were right: the place had seen better days. I remembered the Murbridge school playground as a wonderland of fun, dizziness and exploration, but the yellow police tape and cracked concrete definitely ruined that vibe. And where was the climbing structure shaped like a caterpillar?

Hey, what happened to the caterpillar? I asked.

What caterpillar? said Dora.

Only Date Models was nodding his head. I know what she means.

My mom told me there used to be, like, a caterpillar thing here to climb on but some kid fell off and cracked his skull open really bad, like, blood everywhere and brain tissue, and so they decided to take it down. Dude, a *serious* safety hazard.

Oh yeah, said Dora, slowly nodding his head. I heard about that. The kid was totally brainwashed.

Brain-*dead*, dude.

Yeah, brain dead.

Or maybe he's *dead* dead, like, totally dead? I can't remember what my mom said.

Wow, I replied. That's a really sad story. I had so much fun on the caterpillar when I went to school here.

You're lucky you didn't die, Only Date Models said.

Shit, my mom is texting me. Dora whipped an iPhone from his back pocket. A smile spread across his face as he read the screen. Epic. She made lobster mac and cheese for lunch. She knows it's my favorite.

My stomach grumbled loud enough for us all to hear.

Lunchapalooza, said Only Date Models. Time to load some carbs before lacrosse. Let's bounce.

I RETURNED HOME winded from the walk, confused by youth these days and ravenously hungry. My interaction with the boys revealed two startling truths about my period of self-imposed isolation and canned food consumption. First, my lungs enjoyed fresh air, and second, my tolerance for canned food had reached its natural end. My stomach needed food, real food, and lobster mac and cheese sounded like the food they served in heaven.

That night, in the basement, I reviewed my dwindling supplies. Only two more Chef Boyardees, one more creamed corn and three more chickpeas. No mac. No cheese. And certainly no lobster. To add variety to my diet, and also to avoid starvation, I needed more food, better food, and for that I needed money. But herein lay the kicker: without a job or a husband with a job, money was not forthcoming.

Of course I couldn't ask my parents. They would have given it to me, no questions asked, thus perpetuating our cycle of mutual codependence and we'll-always-be-there-for-you-Bunny malarkey. No, I'd canceled that bad sitcom after season 29. Plus, asking my parents for money would have required me to call them, which they would interpret as an implicit apology. And I wasn't ready to apologize for anything yet. Withdrawing from my paltry retirement and saving accounts went against every practical, data-driven bone in my body.

I decided to sell some of my belongings via the Murbridge Community Message Board.

FS: vintage Vans, circa 1999, black and white check, size 7. Well-loved, only a few holes and one medium-sized ketchup stain, but still full of life. $175

•

FS: vintage fondue set, circa 1980, metal bowl, Sterno holder, five little forks with long handles. Will include recipe for world's best and cheesiest fondue. A steal at $315.

•

FS: five skirt suits, size 6. Originally bought at Filene's Basement. Worn in professional capacity for 3 years, 2 months. Without holes, tears or stains. Asking $250 each or $1,245 for all.

•

FS: NSYNC CD collection, full catalog, 1995–2002, together with Justin Timberlake life-sized cardboard cutout (slightly damaged, see photo). $499.

My ads attracted no buyers.

I did notice, however, numerous desperate posts for plumbers, electricians, handymen, people with skills of that sort.

URGENT: plumber with availability this year to fix broken toilet

•

Looking for someone to install motion sense camera. Must have own tools and complete extensive background check.

•

Desperately need a handyman to complete DIY my husband began but now cannot finish. Wiring five overhead lights, re-tiling bathroom, installing dishwasher, refinishing wood floors, the list goes on.

Briefly, I considered a radical career change. Plumber Darcy, why not? But upon further discussion with Fred, we decided that some jobs are best handled by the experts. Plumbing involves a multitude of disgusting germs, electricians have been known to accidentally catch on fire and tiling looks really hard.

And then I found one post that required skills I already possessed:

WANTED: someone to jump on my trampoline. Must stand approximately 5' 3"–5' 6" in height and weigh less than 200 pounds. Please wear socks. Additional part-time work possible in construction of children's adventure playscape.

Hi, I'm calling about your trampoline post?

Oh great! said a male voice. I have an incredibly sensitive stomach, so trampoline jumping is strictly verboten. Unless you want to see my breakfast.

My stomach is ironclad, I assured him. I'm also interested in the additional part-time work. What, um, sort of work is it?

It's a little hard to describe. Probably best if you just come over and I can show you. Are you flexible?

Flexible? In what way?

Flexible like bendy. Like, can you touch your toes?

Sure, I can touch my toes, I said, although in truth I could not remember having ever touched my toes.

Great! You sound perfect. Wear comfortable clothes. Don't forget socks. And feel free to google the hell out of me. Marcus with an *M*, Dash like the fifty-yard, hyphen, LaGrand like the LaCanyon.

Excuse me?

My name. Marcus Dash-LaGrand. Google me. I want you to feel comfortable that I'm not creepy or a registered sex offender. I am asking you to come to my house, after all.

Yes, right. Thank you for the consideration. I'm a whiz at cyberstalking.

Aren't we all? said Marcus

We made an agreement to meet the following day. Our place is easy to find, Marcus told me, it's got scaffolding out front and this week there's a red crane too. I'm totally stoked—we're installing the zipline.

IT IS ASTOUNDING how much online information you might find about a random individual knowing only the correct spelling of their name and place of residence. Not only did I assure myself that Marcus was no sex offender, I was the one who began to feel creepy. When Marcus's second-grade teacher's funeral notice popped up, I decided I'd seen enough. Marcus Dash-LaGrand looked rich, handsome, nice, generous and fun. He was a college graduate, parent, homeowner, taxpayer, non-felon, registered to vote and I was going to just leave it there and turn off the laptop.

The house was indeed easy to locate. In the front lawn, a zipline dangled in midair from the end of a crane. A bright orange backhoe shifted between piles of raw earth while a small crew of men in hard hats and dirty jeans worked busily. As instructed, I wore clothes designed for comfort: gray sweatpants, a gray hoodie, purple socks and the old Vans from high school that had failed to sell.

Marcus Dash-LaGrand had short, neat dreadlocks and long long legs.

Hey, Darcy, he said, thanks for coming by. He was wearing board shorts, a black hoodie and hiking boots with purple socks. Nice socks, he said, nodding in the direction of my feet.

Marcus explained that he and his husband, Dan, were installing a state-of-the-art, environmentally sound and energy-efficient playscape for their three sons, Xanther, Ludovic and Phineas.

Kids need to play, Marcus explained. There's too much rote memorization, too much sitting in one place. Too much structure, too much pressure. Too many frigging screens. Imagine if kids could run free and teach themselves, teach each other, experiment, find their joy. Free play is an antidote to our times. Plus, he continued, we're planning to open it to the community. I mean, parents need some options to keep their kids entertained and we've got three acres just sitting here. Our awesome nanny, Harriet, is totally on board. Our home insurance is bulletproof. And last month, our building permit was approved by the town selectmen. Have you seen the public playground? It's like a scene from *The Walking Dead*.

It wasn't that bad when I was a kid, I said, shaking my head.

My background is in design and architecture, Marcus continued. This town needs someone who knows about synergies and can play with form and fenestration. I've always adhered to minimalist principles, but a children's playground cries out for some brutalist influence, biomimicry and a whimsical folly to focus interest.

Um. Yeah, I said. I agree, I think.

Sorry. Architecture-speak.

Marcus then began talking like a normal person and told me about buying the house and the adjoining empty lot. The owner had inherited the property from a childless aunt who'd built the house with her husband over sixty years ago.

The place hadn't been touched in all that time, Marcus told me. You should have seen the avocado bath fixtures. I made a fortune on eBay. And no dishwasher! That woman handwashed dishes her entire life. Yikes. I would have died young.

Do you know her name? I grew up here. Maybe my parents knew her.

The niece wasn't much of a talker, Marcus said. She just wanted to cash out. This property had no mortgage. We got into a bidding war. Some shell LLC wanted it—an anonymous developer. But Dan likes to win. He manages a hedge fund so, well, you know what I'm saying. After we closed, the niece took off for the Bahamas.

A pause as we pondered the poor dead nameless aunt and her lottery-winning niece.

Now let's test this epic trampoline, said Marcus with a grin.

My job was to jump, using the force and enthusiasm of an extra-sized preteen, to assess the safety of the trampoline's net and ceiling. It's built for kids, Marcus said, but kids these days are gigantic. Our Ludovic is eleven years old and he's already five nine. Organic milk. He drinks it by the gallon.

I zipped open the mesh safety net and crawled onto Marcus's enormous trampoline. The surface felt jiggly but firm, a pleasant combination of instability and rubbery pushback. At first I jumped very gently. Then with more force. And then I really got into it. I high-kicked and jumping-jacked and cannonballed and even attempted a (failed) flip that left me with a slightly bruised ego but an intact bottom. I found it thrilling to hurl myself into the air, feel the push as the trampoline propelled me upward, air against my skin, my own miraculous buoyancy. All that creamed corn, all those chickpeas and Chef Boyardee found their outlet. My body was in motion, in flight! For the first time since Skip's abrupt departure, I laughed.

Then I stopped.

I was dizzy, from the activity and from the overwhelming immediacy of synchronous communication. I spoke, Marcus answered. He spoke, I answered. Thanks to my extended period of solitude and internet stalking, Fred monologues and navel-gazing, I had become a woman incapable of speaking to another human being.

I have to go, I said. Sweat beaded on my upper lip. My pits felt clammy.

Okay. Cool, said Marcus, though he looked a bit sad. I've got more equipment, he added quickly. Some really cool stuff. I could use a regular test-jumper, test-hurdler kind of person. Paintball too. Would you be up for it?

Not sure, I mumbled. I'm, uh, busy with other projects. My skin felt x-rayed, my face too prominent and exposed, my voice strange to my own ears. I longed for my black bedroom, my duvet, inside air and soft interior light.

It's only part-time, Marcus continued. I'm personal chauffeur, chef, secretary and shrink for my boys most afternoons, but Harriet helps out two days a week. And I offer a competitive employment package. I can give you Harriet's number—she'll vouch for me as a stellar boss. Marcus flashed me a grin so winning that I almost— almost—said yes.

Sure, I'll think about it, I mumbled, backing away fast. I gave Marcus a little wave, turned and walk-ran all the way home.

SKIP LIKED TO say that I was a person without a point of view. He said I was too eager to please others. He said I worried too much about the world and was afraid to live fully. In the last months of our marriage, he often wore a T-shirt that said *Every Day I'm Alive Is the Best Day Ever!*

I think that shirt is grammatically incorrect, I said once.

No, it's not.

But *every* day can't be the best day ever.

Yes, it can.

But if being alive is your only requirement—that seems like a low bar.

Why are you so negative?

I'm not.

You are. You really really are.

Where'd you get that shirt anyhow?

Um, a friend gave it to me.

Now, of course, I wonder who this friend might have been. Had the radically optimistic Bianca given my husband this radically optimistic T-shirt? Maybe every day alive with Bianca *was* the best day ever.

Skip misunderstood me, I realize that now. I'm not afraid to live fully. I simply recognize and respect the multitude of risks that encircle us all day, every day. What's wrong with that? Maybe it's boring. Maybe it's limiting, to a degree. But absent an awareness of risk, a person might just rush forward willy-nilly into danger and live the rest of their days, however short those may be, burdened with regret. And wouldn't that be the worst possible fate?

CONSIDER POOR MICHAEL Clark Rockefeller. *National Geographic,* November 1991. He wasn't *poor* poor, of course. He had oodles of money thanks to his billionaire grandfather, but all this wealth led him to believe in his own invincibility. At the ripe age of twenty-three, Michael Clark fancied himself a world explorer. After assisting on one measly expedition to record birdsong in southwestern New

Guinea, he decided to embark on an adventure. The Asmat of Papua, Michael believed, created art so astoundingly beautiful that it could only be properly understood and appreciated by Westernized people gazing at it within the hushed and clean confines of a museum in, say, New York City or Cambridge, Massachusetts. So young Michael, together with a Dutch anthropologist named René Wassing, took off in a canoe to find some Asmat and relieve them of their art. Roughly midway through a river crossing, their dugout canoe overturned and Michael decided to swim ashore. A mere twelve miles in choppy water with a treacherously strong current. See what too much money and courage can do? Now, if Michael had properly weighed the risks of adventuring in New Guinea (distance, language problems, unknown terrain, poor access to medical care, cannibals) he most certainly would not have found himself tying two empty gas cans to his body and setting off for shore, leaving poor old René to cling alone to the canoe and wait for help. Help found René. The Asmat, regrettably, found Michael.

Of course, the dangers indigent to equatorial New Guinea in the 1960s outweigh those found in twenty-first-century New England. But I believe one's perspective toward potential dangers should remain steadfast—whether in jungle or city, mountain or stream. You cannot simply assume your world is a safe place because your neighbors look presentable and manage to wave at you in the morning. Who knows what's going through their heads? Or their bloodstreams? Don't forget our poor Dr. Semmelweis and his cadaverous particles. Sickness pervades invisibly. Hunger does too. Those Asmat artists didn't have *cannibal* tattooed on their foreheads. Perhaps they greeted Michael Clark on the banks of that river with open arms, a dried gourd full of fresh water, a few berries or a dried piece of monkey to eat. Michael drank the water and felt cool relief run down his throat. Not only had he survived the river, he was on track to score a major haul of primitive art. Visions of statuary and carvings, twigs woven together with dried grass, clay softened with rainwater, molded by hand and left to dry for weeks in the sun. Good old Michael believed himself lucky. He believed himself saved.

Hey Darcy, thanks for coming by yesterday. I was stoked to meet you. Wondering if you've given any more thought to my offer? Seriously, I need someone to help. My husband Dan works long hours and stays in the city during the week. I'm a little light on adult conversation tbh here. My sons are the bomb but sometimes I need more than preteen humor to keep me sane. Know what I mean? Marcus

Marcus, thanks for showing me the trampoline. I'm glad I could help, but I'll have to decline your offer of further toy-testing. I believe I've come down with a case of acute social anxiety. Or maybe panic attacks related specifically to trampolines? Regardless, more face time just isn't in the cards right now. And, to be frank, even at my best, I'm not that chatty. Providing conversation under pressure will only aggravate my condition. Furthermore, I don't think I can get on board with your program. The playscape is too dangerous! Kids will get hurt. I might get hurt. I'm sure you'll find a very talkative risk-taker to fill the position. From my experience, those types of people pop up when you least expect them. Sincerely yours, Darcy

Darcy, I've heard all this before, believe me. But kids who become comfortable with risk, experimentation and failure grow into resilient, brave, independent adults. Really, it's true! There's boatloads of research—I'd be happy to show you some of my favorites. Lady Marjory Allen of the U.K., for example, was the original badass. She built these amazing playgrounds of garbage and rubble from bombed-out WW2 buildings and let kids run all over the place, start fires, swing into streams, tear down shit. Now compare that to our coddled generation, kids who can't even walk two blocks to school alone without someone calling the cops. Give me postwar London any day. Those kids knew how to have fun.

Interesting comparison, Marcus. I'll google your Lady. But I'm unswayed by your argument. I'm no parent, but letting unsupervised children set fires seems like a bad idea. Call me crazy. Good luck!

Okay, maybe postwar Europe was the wrong case study. I'm not going all grunge in Murbridge, don't worry. Our space will be techy and state-of-the-art but fundamentally Lady Marjory had the right idea about play, independence and growth. I can talk your ear off about privilege and socioeconomic disparity and learning deficits and a boatload of other pedagogical socioeconomic theories but I'll spare my sermon for another day. Listen—you strike me as someone who gives a shit about this community. Will you help? I sense you're going through some kind of personal psychodrama. Trust me, I get it. But this is bigger than you, and me. This is worth your time. Please? Signed, your (future) friend, Marcus

---

Marcus, I applaud the impassioned plea. Ditto your enthusiasm and your totally uninformed comments on my psychological state. But I can't do kids. Inanimate objects and plant life, totally. Animals, usually. Adults, rarely but optimistic for the future. But kids? Nope. Good luck to you! Best, Darcy

WARNING: I've seen numerous slow-moving and illegally stopped cars, all with blue lights on the dashboard. Undoubtedly another gang custom—perhaps members signaling to each other? Drug deals or the like? Please call police if you see similar activity.

•

Board of Selectmen meeting, agenda items: 1) additional tater tot purchase at Murbridge Elementary; 2) stoplight refurbishment project; 3) salary increase of 2% for town tax steward.

•

SUBSTANTIAL REWARD for our potbellied darling Stella! Where are you, Stella? Any pig sightings? She's been missing for over two weeks. Please come home, Stella. We love you.

•

Reminder: Mushroom Festival organizational meeting this Wednesday, April 16, at Murbridge High! We need volunteers for: face-painting, axe-throwing, the all-you-can-eat-mushrooms contest and one lucky person to wear the Marv the Mushroom costume. (Sadly after 7 years as Marv, Pat Pernicky has developed an allergic reaction to the latex lining in the suit so we need a new volunteer.)

•

To the folks on Aurora who let their guinea pigs run around their backyard: we know it's exciting when spring arrives, but we've had enough with the squealing. Please bring them inside.

Dear Darcy,

Just a quick note to say we miss you and please return all the Tupperware to Mrs. Pevzner. According to her, you're hording at least 24 containers she left on the porch full of blondies. Darcy, she understands why you never came to the door, but please show some common courtesy with the Tupperware.

How's the weather? Is it spring yet? Don't be fooled by the crocuses—they are sneaky little teasers. Spring hasn't really arrived until the bluebells pop. Have they popped? It's very nice down here. I'm wearing a darling sundress and sandals as I type this to you. No long underwear in April in Arizona! Although I admit I do miss the seasons. I miss watching the trees turn green, those buds bursting out. It's like Christmas morning when spring arrives, but without the financial ruin of buying all the presents. But we're so enjoying our pool time and Daddy's been golfing like there's no tomorrow. That man won't even sit still for his watercolor portrait. Did I tell you about my watercolors? So much nicer than macramé. The instructor is a delightful young woman with the most pleasing eyebrows. She reminds me of you.

Sending you hugs and cuddles,

Mom

ON DAY 78 OF MY self-imposed isolation and canned food consumption, I was sitting in the window seat of my black bedroom, finishing up my last can of chickpeas and wondering how long I would last before the survival instinct kicked in and I asked my parents for money. One week? Two? Or maybe tomorrow? I placed a hand on my stomach—was I already feeling weak from hunger? At that moment I saw, down below, a pig. It was a small pig, more gray than pink, and it had the tiniest feet. Little hooves, like a horse, and very large nostrils. The pig was snorting loudly and moving around the yard with its head down, searching, it appeared, for food.

Where the hell did a pig come from?

And like a thunderbolt, a shock wave, a seismic shift, I realized:

here, right in my own front yard, was the infamous Stella, the beloved potbellied pig that had been missing for weeks. Stella's owner had posted dozens of mournful messages on the Murbridge Community Board. I didn't recall Stella's exact physical description but surely there was only one wayward potbellied pig wandering the neighborhood?

I put down my coffee and ran—really, it was the fastest I'd moved in nearly three months—down the stairs. At the front door I paused. It was a weekday, I believed, sometime around noon, maybe? I felt a brief tremor of embarrassment that I hadn't showered in several days (a week?) and my right big toe protruded from a hole in my sock. Stepping outside raised the distinct possibility that other people would see me. Mrs. Pevzner might surprise me with more blondies and expressions of deep concern. If Mrs. Dykstra caught a glimpse, she'd undoubtedly call the cops again. I would probably call the cops too if I spied someone like me lurking around the neighborhood.

But, Stella. The pig was right under my nose.

I pulled on my neck/face gaiter, opened the door and walked in my socks toward Stella. *Crept* would be a better word. *Slunk* perhaps even more accurate. I did not want to startle the pig. A chase would be too taxing. My dash down the stairs had left me winded; a run might prove fatal.

Step by step down the driveway. Apparently Stella had found something tasty at the bottom of that last bit of residual winter snow: she was making snorty piggy sounds, her mouth working busily. Pigs, it turns out, are not very vigilant while eating. Had I been a lion or hungry coyote, Stella would have been toast. I saw that she wore a collar, reached out a hand and grabbed it. Stella barely noticed; she grunted and just kept on eating something that looked like sauerkraut and smelled like bad milk.

Stella's owner, Larita, picked up on the second ring and began immediately to weep when I told her who I'd found.

Oh, thank you, thank you, she kept saying. I can't—I can't even—

Larita arrived at my house in fifteen minutes flat. During this time, I sat on my front steps, holding Stella by the collar. Have you ever tried to keep a pig in one place? I don't recommend it. Stella pulled and pushed and whimpered. I let her eat another disgusting unidentified mass she found in the side flower bed, and then Larita's car pulled into the driveway.

To say that I was deeply touched by the pig-human reunion would be over-egging it. But I was certainly touched. Larita shed real tears when she hugged that dirty pig, and Stella, I truly believe, sighed a little sigh of contentment as she rested her head ever so briefly on Larita's shoulder.

I can't thank you enough, Larita said, and, before I could protest, she hugged me. A long, firm hug that partially suffocated me, but in a good way. It was the first time I'd touched another human being since arriving in Murbridge. No haircuts, no manicures, no accidental brushing of fingers at the grocery checkout, no friends to hug, no parents to kiss. The embrace left me feeling very odd: a hot flash, a cold flash, a flittering in my stomach, a flicker of the same jitters I'd felt at Marcus's place when testing the trampoline. Thankfully, Larita didn't notice my awkwardness. She was just happy to have her pig back.

Here's the reward—you really earned it, she said and pushed a wad of bills into my hand. Obviously it would be bad manners to count the money then and there, so I mumbled thank you and pushed the bills into my pocket as I waved good-bye to pig and owner.

It was chilly out, a tad gusty, but I remained standing on the front lawn for a good while after they'd gone. The clouds shifted and a spot of sun fell onto my face. The warmth felt almost like the hug with Larita. I closed my eyes. I was cold, my socks were wet, my pajamas stunk of pig, but I stayed right where I was. My house, my beloved safe house, the place I knew back to front, up and down, every corner, every closet, every nook, offered nothing new or interesting, tasty or exciting.

I reached into my pocket and counted my reward money: $250. It seemed an enormous amount for catching a distracted pig on my own front lawn. I held tightly to the bills as the wind pulled at my pajamas and scoured my cheeks.

How many other distracted pigs were out there? I wondered. Or wandering weenie dogs? Cavorting cats? Pets disappeared all the time in Murbridge and, judging from the volume and tenor of Community Board posts, most owners would pay handsomely to get their beloved furballs back. Who needs a real job when there are fortunes to be made in finding lost animals? The answer to my food problem and fresh air deficiency lay before me. Today, I realized, was the dawning of a new auspicious era: this would be the age of lobster mac and cheese.

I OPENED THE Community Board and scanned for animal references. Finding them was not a difficult task. There were dozens, each more plaintive than the last. And really, how did people pick pet names these days? Where once you'd have a Fido or Boomer or Spot, now you found Greek gods or the cast of *Downton Abbey.*

Have you seen this cat? Aphrodite slipped outside around 2:11 pm on Mercy Avenue. Please call immediately! She's a house cat on anxiety meds and needs her dose!

•

Hamish our golden lab is missing! My kids are heartbroken. Photo attached. Reward!

•

Criminal ALERT: My two purebred Siamese, Rosalind and Alistair, have vanished . . .

•

Our darling Zeus is LOST . . .

•

HELP my ferret Rupert . . .

•

Have you seen Samson the snake . . .

•

MISSING bulldog, answers to Fergus . . .

•

MISSING calico . . .

•

LOST lizard . . .

•

WAYWARD westie . . .

•

VANISHED vizsla . . .

•

LOST: a stuffed squirrel with one eye . . .

I stopped counting after thirty ads. Lost pets represented an untapped market, particularly in the feline department. Cats disappeared at an epidemic rate in Murbridge. I would have assumed that dogs would more commonly go missing, namely due to dog-nappers looking to make some money from reselling that purebred pit bull Rosie or wackadoodle Lulu. But cats? There's no money in cats. People give away cats for free. If you sneeze in the right direction you'll open your eyes to find a cat staring at you with a look of mild disgust, licking its paws with a dainty pink tongue. I never liked cats, truth be told, for all the usual reasons. Their selfishness. Their inability to catch a ball. Their barely disguised disdain for the human race. The hissing. Also, they are exceptionally good at hiding.

I decided to focus on dogs. Cats could fend for themselves.

Hamish was a big, meaty golden retriever, a lumberjack of a dog. He looked dim-witted and slow-moving. The attached photo showed old Hamish wearing a cowboy hat, surrounded by three blond children, their hair nearly the same color as the dog's. The youngest was perched on the dog's back, gripping handfuls of fur and wearing his own little cowboy hat. Cute, sort of. It looked like a photo from a Gap ad, both heartwarming and slightly sinister. Did I want to return Hamish to an environment like *that*? But I couldn't blame the kids for their parents' idea of a delightful family memory. They'd work that out in therapy later. And Hamish certainly wasn't the kind of animal who'd do well on his own. Some dogs are survivors and some need their organic chicken cut into cubes. Hamish clearly fell into the latter category. Plus, he looked easy enough to catch. My guess was those big haunches hadn't sprinted for a squirrel in five years at least.

I loaded my backpack with tennis balls, a Frisbee, a flashlight, Oreo cookies, a good length of rope and a hunk of unidentified meat I'd found in the freezer. I figured it would defrost as I searched the neighborhood, trailing the scent of wet meat behind me. I could throw it at Hamish as a peace offering if he seemed hostile.

The day was beautiful, one of the first true spring days with sunshine, bird twitter, crocuses and daffodils pushing up all over the place. Although I'd ultimately enjoyed my pig-related foray outside the house, I was nervous about traipsing all over the neighborhood in search of Hamish. Who knew where Mrs. Pevzner might be lurking? Or Georgina Oliver, home for a brief respite from her luxurious life with Elon? I wore my trusty neck gaiter to hide my face, kept my head down and crossed the street at the first sight of anyone on the sidewalk ahead.

Hamish! Here, Hamish! I called, waving an Oreo and keeping my eyes open for flashes of lumbering golden fur.

For two hours, I cased the neighborhood. The smell of damp meat (pork shoulder was my guess) grew stronger and, as the morning progressed, I became a dog magnet. First it was a sweet raggedy mutt, then a sleek pointer, a pair of Yorkies, another mutt, this one bigger and shaggier than the first. I began to worry: What if the dogs decided to pounce all at once? I could fend off one, maybe two of the smaller ones, but I'd be a goner if they organized.

I walked faster, my calls grew louder and then, just as I decided it was time to turn around and head home, I saw him. Hamish. He was bouncing along at the end of my dog train, a jolly golden caboose. How long he'd been there, I had no idea, but it was unmistakably the dog from the photo. I recognized the dumb rheumy eyes, that particular buttery shade of fur, his sturdy haunches. Even without the cowboy hat, I knew I'd found my dog.

This time, I dropped Hamish at the owner's house. Otherwise, too much capacity for emotion and lingering. I'd learned my lesson from the pig venture. I tied Hamish loosely to the front porch railing of the Lemster family home, rang the doorbell and retreated to the sidewalk to watch the reunion.

The door opened slowly and one blond boy—I'm guessing the oldest—looked confused for a moment. Then his eyes fell on Hamish. Hamie! he cried. Other blond people followed, both short and tall. There were squeals, cries of surprise, some real wailing as the youngest clutched the dog around the neck. I was worried about choking, to be honest, but Hamish didn't seem to mind.

Finally the mom searched the street with her eyes and found me. Thank you! she called and held up a finger. Wait, she said, wait right there! She ducked inside the house and returned with a stack of cash.

You're an absolute angel, she said as she handed me the bills. An angel.

That day, I earned $300 for a measly two hours of low-impact walking. Fred, I said to my absent fern as I counted out the bills at my kitchen table, I've found my calling.

• • •

AND SO BEGAN my tenure as neighborhood angel/pet finder. Through those early spring days when mud replaced snow and sodden replaced frozen, I trudged down alleyways and ducked under cars and discovered that I had a knack for finding domesticated animals, particularly those who were cold and hungry enough to remember the positive aspects of a life spent locked inside a human's home. I worked alone, obviously. I avoided pedestrians and owners, except for the payment part.

Each pet presented diverse challenges, led me down different paths and showed me new parts of the town I thought I knew. Dame Judy, an Irish setter. Rupert, a three-legged ferret. Lola, a gigantic shaggy mutt with a bark like a foghorn. One rat—an exceedingly tough find, never again. One very fat hamster named George who, sadly, was crushed to death upon reunion with his enthusiastic youthful owner. Four cats, I forget their names.

The rewards varied, from a tenner to one whopping check for $500. I accepted them all graciously, with a nod of thanks. No handshake, certainly no more hugs. The owners generally cried, which I found both embarrassing (for them) and distressingly moving (for me). To avoid my own unpleasant emotional reaction, I took the onset of tears as my cue to leave ASAP. Yet no matter how diligently I tried to protect myself from accidental human contact, each pet-owner reunion left me feeling wistful and nostalgic and sad, missing something I couldn't quite put a finger on.

Growing up, I never owned a pet. Mom is allergic to animal dander, dust and saliva, and no pet—save a boring goldfish, which I promptly killed by bringing it into the bath with me—was free of those threats.

The nostalgia, I'm trying to say here, did not derive from my own memories of pet ownership. This was a yearning for something that never was, something that might have been. Pets love their owners with such blind devotion, such slobbering enthusiasm, such guileless innocence, the innocence of a creature that has never been burned. Or, if it has, it doesn't care. Animals don't hold grudges. I wondered if humans were capable of such earnest commitment. I wondered if the pets fed the humans, rather than the humans feeding the pets. A pet understands instinctually that humans make mistakes and yet each animal loves its human regardless.

Draft email files

Dear Skip,

I know it's been a while since I've written, but I've been busy with a new business venture. Plus, I no longer think of you and Bianca every second of every day. Now it's more like every minute of every day. Her Facebook profile changed again. Your hair is getting long. It looks good. Scruffy, but still hygienic. I never realized you had curls. Did you know that I had an auto-reminder on my phone for your haircut appointments? I never asked if you wanted a haircut, I just called Randall at the salon and forwarded you the date. And you accepted it. Every other month, that same haircut with the same shaved sides and shaved neck and little ridge up at the top. You always reminded me of Tintin, who, I will admit now, was the subject of my very first sexual dream. But maybe you didn't want a Tintin haircut? If we were to meet and marry today, I would apply the wisdom I've gained during these last few months of quiet consideration and solitary internet stalking to build a better relationship with you. I would listen more. I might even consider taking that skateboard class with you. Life is scary, Skip. Life is terrifying. Do you feel it too? I sought only to protect you and protect myself from all unforeseen circumstances, all the dangers that lurk, car wrecks and plane crashes, floods and tornadoes, disease and pestilence, dog bites and spiders. But sometimes, despite every precaution, a rogue element just pops up from behind and bites. I can't protect you or me from the whole wide world. Skip, do you ever wonder what you might do differently now if we met? Do you ever think maybe

LET ME TELL YOU ABOUT Barnum. Oh Barnum! He remains my most memorable animal catch, the one who nearly moved me to become a pet owner myself. Barnum was a conure parrot with brilliant green wings who whistled like a construction worker and had a particular fondness for crispy bacon. His owner, a childless woman in her early thirties with a BMI that looked, from the attached photos, tending toward the underweight, was named Clementine. She had a long thin face that matched her long thin hair and a bony shoulder upon which Barnum often sat.

A bird presents unique challenges, as I'm sure you can imagine, particularly a bird with unclipped wings belonging to a species known for its innate adaptability to urban and semi-urban environments. Conures prefer life outdoors, be it jungle, forest, city park or leafy suburb. There's a flock in northeast L.A., another in Long Beach, hundreds living in one small urban park in Seattle. There might even be a conure outside your window this very minute, eyeing that BLT you're eating and wondering when you'll open the back door.

And that in the end was how I got him. Not an open door, which seemed a long shot even for my lazy self, but the bacon. After efforts at call and catch in both Longtree and Fink Parks and underneath the big maples on Main Street, I developed a strategy to save my larynx from so much calling and my neck from so much craning. I affixed a piece of nicely cooked bacon to my head and strolled slowly through town. I will say that waiting for a hungry bird to land on your head is not the most relaxing day out, but the bacon was highly effective.

After about an hour of loitering beneath tall trees, I heard a distinct *mine, mine, mine* from above and—*whoosh*—Barnum dove. It took a few tries before he managed to connect with the bacon and by that time I was ready for him. I reached up, plucked him off my head and carried him home under one arm. Despite not knowing me, the bird was remarkably friendly. I held him in one hand, bacon in the other, and he chatted and clucked in between bites. I found it difficult to follow his train of thought, but his singsong bird voice was deeply comforting: *hey mama, hey mama mama, mine mine mine, dizzy feeling dizzy, spin me round round baby round round, like a record player baby, round round.*

Barnum rode on my shoulder during the drive to Clementine's house, murmuring *bacon bacon bacon* into my ear and trying to eat my hair. Clementine met us in the drive. This delivery was not a drop and depart, for obvious reasons. As soon as Barnum caught sight of Clementine he let out a long, low whistle, followed by *hey baby*, and lost all interest in me.

I rolled down the window. Clementine was crying, big rolling sobs of the kind seen at boy band concerts and the funerals of dictators.

Oh—oh—oh Barnum, she wailed. She reached into the car and Barnum hopped immediately onto her extended index finger. She brought the bird to her face and he snuggled up against her cheek and then hopped onto her shoulder and snuggled some more.

You—you silly bird, Clementine said in between sobs as Barnum tickled her cheek. He appeared—and I know how this sounds, believe me—genuinely concerned for his owner's mental state. *Why all these tears?* he seemed to be saying with his angled head and a little *tut-tut* bird sound. *I'll always come home, you silly human.*

Wow, he's very affectionate, I said.

Conures are known for their snuggles, said Clementine and she heaved a shuddering sigh and wiped her nose with her sleeve. I'm so grateful to have him back. I thought I'd never see him again. Thank you so much for bringing him home. How did you find him?

Bacon, I said. You mentioned it in your post. I put some on my head.

Clementine looked at me quizzically and I realized then I was wearing my usual pajama bottoms and a ratty old sweatshirt from high school. I'd pushed down my neck gaiter so she could see my face. I felt exposed, discovered. What kind of weirdo goes around with bacon on her head, searching for a stranger's lost bird?

Wow, said Clementine. I never even thought of that.

You gotta think like an animal to catch an animal, I replied for some reason. Why did I say that? What was happening to me?

Sure, she said, backing away from the car. Well, um, thank you. And Barnum thanks you too.

It was my pleasure, I said. Barnum's quite a bird. You're a lucky woman. It was as though my mouth had decided to operate on a different frequency than my brain. The words just arrived, inappropriate and nonsensical. Perhaps this was the next step in my social decline, I thought. With Marcus, I'd started to sweat. With Clementine, I couldn't stop talking. My condition had morphed from social anxiety to social humiliation. And I was powerless to stop it.

I barreled ahead: If I'd known Barnum was a cuddler, I said with a wink, I probably would've kept him. He seemed pretty happy when we were together. It was brief, sure, but I felt good with him. We definitely had a connection, a deep soulful connection.

I saw the look on Clementine's face. I was proving too weird even for a woman who rode her bicycle with a bird on her shoulder.

Okay, bye now! I called and reversed out the drive, my heart in my throat.

Wait, Clementine called. Don't you want the reward?

But I didn't wait. I drove away.

To the woman who returned my son's stuffed Squirrel—thank you! You're a total angel.

•

FS: bunch of unmatched socks, gently used. I lost the mates but there's life left! $1.00 per sock obo.

•

ISO lawyer: my neighbors are assholes and I want to make their lives miserable. Any reccs?

•

ISO loving home for my 2 pet turkeys, Carmen and Curmudgeon. I'm moving abroad and can't take these cuties with me. Prefer someone with plenty of outdoor space, no other pets, willing to sign document promising not to eat them.

•

Darling, I'm sorry. I will never forgive myself for leaving you alone.

•

Darling, the blooms are yellow, blue and red, a color like a flame. Do you remember how the tulips moved in the breeze? Do you remember their magic?

AFTER BARNUM, MY COMMITMENT TO pet-finding wavered considerably. In fact, I discovered two large and fatal cracks in the foundation of my pet-finding enterprise. First off, the money wasn't reliable. I could spend thirty hours on an aging Westie and only get a measly twenty bucks. Plus, the fear of face-to-face contact prevented me from actually collecting the reward money in a disappointingly high percentage of cases. See Barnum et al.

But most important, I was done being an angel. I didn't want all the attention, all the scrutiny. I didn't want people looking at me, expecting appropriate chitchat. I didn't want people wondering why I devoted hours to the rescue of animals to which I had no attachment. Wondering why I wasn't fully dressed at 2 p.m., or working a real job, or taking care of my own pets or taking a bath. After the initial wave of relief and gratitude, I saw confusion and—worse—pity reflected in those pet owners' eyes, a sort of sideways jab at my life choices and my current state of stasis. Yes, I was an angel, but I was an angel living in her childhood home, unemployed, unloved, underwashed, sedentary. This angel was probably dumb, possibly dangerous, certainly weird. She couldn't make direct eye contact without blushing and she began to sweat when in close proximity to another human being.

So after rereading my favorite *National Geographic* (July 1978), I decided to quit. Neruda, I realized, didn't have pet-finding in mind when he talked about a common destiny. My dance had been sorrowful, sure, but I wasn't showing the world what I was. I was only showing these pet owners that I was creepy and uncomfortable and spent too much time indoors talking to a fern.

The final search of my short-lived pet-catching career involved Aphrodite, a white princess of a cat with a rhinestone-studded collar, the face of a feline Zsa Zsa Gabor and a reward in the gobsmacking amount of $1,000. Just one more, I told myself. Just this one spoiled cat and I'll be set for life. Or at least until Mom and Daddy come home from Arizona.

Aphrodite looked easy. In the photo posted by her grief-stricken owner on the Community Board, Aphrodite sat on a pink satin cushion, paws outstretched, collar all a-sparkle, eyes fixed in dumb wonder at the flash emanating from her owner's iPhone. In other words, Aphrodite looked the opposite of street-smart. This was the kind of lost cat who would cower beside any old BMW for days, waiting to be placed in her own fur-lined car seat. Finding Aphrodite, I assumed, would not prove taxing.

This was day 92 of my self-imposed isolation and canned food consumption, only now I primarily consumed gourmet, all-organic prepared meals delivered to my doorstep by a plump kilt-wearing man driving a white van. I didn't know his name, but I adored him. We never spoke. I'd watch him from behind the living room curtains as he carefully placed his recycled cardboard box with compostable cooling brick on the porch. Generally he skipped down the stairs back to the truck, his kilt flying up to reveal strong manly thighs. But it wasn't just the thighs I admired. The food! He cooked with passion and bravado and flair. Brie and prosciutto on ciabatta, roast chicken with thyme and garlic, fig bread with olives, pappardelle in a creamy tomato basil sauce. Chef Boyardee had become a thing of the past, and thank the sky above and earth below for that.

I usually began a pet hunt within a few blocks of the animal's home base. Contrary to popular opinion, most pets don't go far. The fault for a lost pet generally lies with its owner's overestimation of the wanderlust instinct. An owner thinks: Little Fido isn't in her basket, so therefore she must be hitchhiking to Vegas. No. Domesticated animals are lazy and afraid. And I don't say this critically—I'm lazy and afraid too—but the fact is that Little Fido is most likely shivering and cowering under a car two blocks from home because she got chased by a crow.

As expected, I spotted Aphrodite three blocks south of her owner's address. The rhinestone collar glinted in the sun. It was a Saturday morning, calm, breezy, a touch of spring damp in the air. According to her owner, Aphrodite ate nothing but smoked salmon so I held out a (gloved) handful of the stuff, whispering softly: Here, kitty kitty. She looked at me, yawned and headed down an alley. I followed at a normal walking pace, one block, two, across a street, around a corner, up a hill, down a hill, across another street, through an empty parking lot.

This was ridiculous.

I threw away the salmon and sprinted straight for her dainty white tail, but Aphrodite was faster than she looked. I chased her through the parking lot, down another alley, out from under a car, across the street and through someone's backyard. I thought I had her cornered against a wooden fence, but with a flick of her tail she squirreled through a gap in the slats. That bitch. My knees muddy, my hands muddy, I ran around to the side alley and there sat Aphrodite, daintily licking her paws and cleaning her face. She looked at me with bored eyes: *You again?* She didn't even have the decency to run.

Here, Aphrodite, here, kitty, kitty, I called. I wiggled my fingers, figuring the glove must still stink of salmon. I was ten feet away, eight, five, closing, closing, almost—and then she picked up and ran.

I followed. Down this alley, then another, under a hedge, through a field, across one street, then another—this one busier, dodging a minivan and a Subaru—over a hedge, down a neglected sidewalk heaving with tree roots, through a taller, thicker hedge and then—sweating, out of breath, hating all cats for all eternity—I rounded a corner and—

Blammo.

I collided with a man.

Oof, I said and stepped back. The man was tall, brown skin, handsome face, a shaved head. He wore binoculars around his neck and a vest with many pockets. In one hand he held a book; in the other, a whistle.

I'm sorry, I spluttered. I was trying to catch a—

The man held up a finger. Shhhh, he whispered, and then pointed to the sky.

My eyes followed the line of his finger. Perched in a tall bare maple sat an extraordinary bird. It was small, round as a sparrow, but the colors! A bright purple-blue head, red breast, yellow and green wings.

A painted bunting, male, whispered the man. The famed rainbow bird.

The bird dipped its head, hopped farther along the branch and then began to sing, a high, bright, chirpy sound that seemed full of purpose, like a cartoon character trying to make a point. It was silly and charming and completely entrancing.

Together the man and I silently listened and watched for one minute, two, and then without warning the bird lifted off and flew away in a tiny swirl of color and wind.

Wow, I said. That was intense.

They don't normally come this far north, the man replied, his eyes still trained on the place the bird had been. This is a real event bird. I'll have to notify the blogosphere.

Event bird?

Once in a migratory season, if you're lucky. He winked. Today, we're very lucky.

There was a gentleness to the man, a way he moved and spoke, slowly and with grace, that temporarily hypnotized me. I blinked. I opened my mouth to speak and then shut it again, not because I felt anxious, embarrassed or self-conscious but because I wanted to prolong this wondrous encounter. A moment of shared contemplation and reverence. The famed rainbow bird. This was an event.

Well, the man said, have a nice one. And he walked away.

For a few moments I stood, staring at his retreating back.

Wait! I yelled, just before he turned the corner.

The man turned. Yes?

Who are you?

I'm a birdwatcher, he said. We are many. You'll see us around. Bye now. And he turned and was gone.

Today, we're very lucky, the birdwatcher had said. I examined the empty tree, bare but for little green buds beginning to sprout all over. I had never in my life felt lucky. In fact, deep in my soul I imagined myself the unluckiest person who had ever lived. I never won contests, raffles, card games, prizes at the fair or tic-tac-toe. I often stepped on bees, got stuck in traffic, picked the slowest line at the grocery store, missed the plane or train or bus I was trying to catch. Of course, objectively, I was a very, very lucky person and it was important to remind myself of this fact or else risk a self-absorption so complete that I might actually disappear into my own navel.

I am not unlucky, I said aloud. I have a home; I have parents who love me, despite their recent abandonment; I have food; I have strong legs and a brain that works (usually) and my teeth are fairly straight thanks to four years of painful orthodontics, and my breasts, while small, manage to remain perky even at my advanced age and tendency to not wear a bra.

Reciting aloud the list of items that made me feel lucky—bedroom slippers, fond memories of Fred, an electric toothbrush—I wandered down the street. Comfortable purple socks, a snow globe from that trip to San Francisco, a mesmerizing little scar on my right thumb, a jar of pennies, my knack for crosswords—

Aphrodite.

She was sitting on the northwest corner of Del Ray Avenue and Marino Drive. I'd never been to this part of Murbridge before and to my list of lucky things I added: the capacity to enjoy a good surprise.

There you are, I said. Are you waiting for me?

Aphrodite meowed, picked herself up and, with a twitch of her tail and a backward glance, walked into a bush.

Cat, you are killing me, I said. At that moment, I did not care about returning Aphrodite to her owner. But curiosity got the better of me. I followed her through the dense undergrowth, spiky branches scratching my shins, a leaf in my mouth, a mosquito up my nose. At last I emerged into a placid, verdant landscape.

I pulled up. An expansive lawn stretched gently upward toward an imposing stone mansion flanked by longer, lower, more modern buildings, painted white. The ground beneath my feet was squishy from the spring thaw, but the earth closer to the house must have been firm because across it sat a dozen wheelchairs and in those

wheelchairs sat elderly women. One woman appeared to be snoozing, another read a book in her lap and the remainder cooed and
clucked and stroked the cats surrounding them. There were a
dozen felines at least, different colors and sizes, curled up around
the wheelchairs or sitting placidly in the women's laps. I saw a calico,
a tabby, another tabby, one black with white ears and, of course,
Aphrodite. She was sitting in the lap of a white-haired woman who
was hand-feeding her sardines from a can.

So this was where they went, all the cats. A grassy den of treats
and cuddles. A feline Shangri-la. The women didn't appear to notice me; they were too busy petting, cooing and feeding. I wondered:
What is this place? A hospital? A home for wayward elderly women
and wandering cats? I didn't remember any kind of senior citizen
facility in Murbridge. My parents had never mentioned one. Why go
all the way to Arizona when they could have camped out here? Besides, I didn't see any nurses. Didn't nursing homes generally employ
nurses?

Slowly I wandered up the lawn. Aphrodite most definitely noticed me now. Her ears stiffened, her eyes widened. She assumed
a sphinxlike pose on the white-haired woman's lap. The woman
was very small and wore a bright pink top and the vividness of the
color made the woman's body seem out of place against the hard,
cold lines of the chair. She was looking down at Aphrodite, stroking
the cat's head and murmuring in soothing tones.

Good morning, I said to the woman. Aphrodite hissed.

The woman looked up. Her eyes were a golden, hazel-y color, as
bright as the pink of her shirt. Golden but rimmed in red. Oh dear,
you startled me, she said. Gloria here doesn't seem to like you.

No, she doesn't, I replied. And isn't her name Aphrodite?

The woman laughed and shook her head as though I had said
something deeply embarrassing for both of us. Oh no, this here is
Gloria. I'm her favorite.

It certainly looks that way, I said. Gloria/Aphrodite continued to glare at me, but the purr intensified as she swallowed another sardine.

Are you searching for someone, dear? the woman asked. She was compact, like a gymnast or Glinda the Good Witch: wrinkled and wizened, but strong. I had a strong urge to pick her up along with Aphrodite and take them both home.

No, I said. I'm looking for this cat.

Well, she's right here. She's already been found.

Did any of these pets need finding? I wondered then. Perhaps all the lost animals of Murbridge were getting cuddled by nice old ladies in wheelchairs. Absence in one place means presence in another and who's to say which one is home?

My name is Fanny, said the woman. Take a seat. Let's have a chat.

And so I sat on the grass. I felt damp soaking through my pajama bottoms, but I didn't care. Following Fanny's order—and it was most definitely an order—seemed the easiest, best thing for me to do at that moment.

I asked Fanny about the mansion and she said, yes, it was a nursing home, the Marian Sisters Home for Elderly Women, here since the 1930s but operations had been winding down for some time. They'd stopped accepting residents nearly ten years ago. The nuns who ran the place were getting on in age themselves and the state diocese had decided to close up and sell the property.

But we're taking longer to die than expected, Fanny explained. And the nuns don't want to leave. This is their home. The sisters are very stubborn. Do you know, they have never had sex. Isn't that sad?

It is.

Do you have sex, dear?

I cleared my throat. Not anymore. My husband left me. He had an affair.

Oh, said Fanny, I'm so sorry. That is atrocious behavior. You are a lovely person, I can already tell. But a little lost. Not like Gloria here.

Gloria/Aphrodite was now asleep, having realized that I no longer posed much of a threat. Fanny had neutralized us both.

My Barnaby never cheated, Fanny continued. Maybe he wanted to, but I don't think so. He adored me. And we had a very adventurous sex life. Massage. Handcuffs. This thing with feathers. I miss all of it. She smiled.

Me too, I replied. I wanted to tell Fanny that it wasn't only sex, or even primarily sex, that I missed but touch and taste and the smell of another human being, one you loved and who loved you too. Even more than that, I missed having an idea about the future, an idea that the future might be good; it might be everything I hoped for. What did I hope for now?

I sat at Fanny's feet, my butt well and truly soggy, the chill creeping up my spine, Fanny's *all of it* playing in my mind. A new feeling spread through me. Not anxiety of other people's judgment or grief over Skip's departure or anger at my parents' abandonment. This was an emptiness, a lack, a longing.

Fanny stroked Aphrodite's fur. She picked a bit of lint off her sleeve. She looked at the sky as if reading the clouds for signs of change. She turned to me and smiled, showing her sweet pink gums.

Dear, Fanny said, will you help me jump this joint?

Excuse me?

Escape. The Marian Sisters. We aren't allowed to leave on our own and I need to leave. There's no one left who will take me. They're all dead. My husband, my friends, my sister.

But where would you go? I asked.

Home.

Isn't this your home?

It's not my real home, said Fanny.

But what about your wheelchair? I asked.

This? said Fanny. It's just because I'm a wee bit lazy. It's nice to be pushed around. You should try it. But my legs work just fine. So, shall we make a run for it now?

I don't think—I began. I'm not sure—

Dear, just start calling me Granny. We can fool those nuns. Half the time they're napping.

Granny?

Excellent! See how easy that was?

No, Fanny, I can't.

Yes, you can, dear.

No, I can't.

Yes.

No.

Yes.

No.

Fanny rolled her eyes. You're as stubborn as the nuns. Tell me, why won't you help?

I paused. Well, for starters, I'm a rule follower. And also a risk-averse, highly anxious personality. And also we've only just met. And also I suspect that breaking an elderly woman in a wheelchair out of her religious living situation would probably get me arrested.

Hmmmm. Fanny was watching me. So, she said, once we become better acquainted, *then* you'll help me? Is that right?

Well, there are a few other hurdles we'll need to jump, as I mentioned. But that would certainly be a start.

Fanny smiled brightly. Okay, then, she said. If you won't pretend I'm your granny, then let's become friends. Please come whenever you can, but at least once per week, and bring chocolate, preferably dark, at least seventy-five percent. None of those sickly add-ins. Just straight-up, or the tiniest bit of sea salt. Shall I write this down?

No, I'll remember. Dark chocolate, straight up, once per week. Got it.

Wonderful. Well, dear, I believe it's time for my nap. Fanny yawned. You enjoy the afternoon. It's a rare and beautiful day. How lucky that we've met. I can tell already that you and I will have a most auspicious friendship.

Me too, I said.

I left Aphrodite where she was: asleep in a swirl of fur on Fanny's lap.

CONSIDER THE ISLAS Desventuradas, *National Geographic,* October 2002. Geologists call these four islands the most changeable place on Earth. They sit off the southwestern coast of Chile, unprotected against the elements, lone bits of rock, soil and sand pounded by the Pacific, battered by wind and rain. Punishing, persistent destruction. Erosion occurs here faster than anywhere else on Earth. You should see the limestone! Formations like question marks and clouds, rivulets formed by wind, caves that flood fifty times per day. Entrancing and frightening, like a movie set in some distant, horrible future. The scientists sent there to take pictures and crawl through the caves look rain-soaked and scared in all the photographs. They measured water levels, photographed in darkness and driving hail, camped out in a forest of moss, ate rehydrated food by a flickering fire. One of them broke his foot midway through the trip and spent the second half in a windswept tent, trying not to cry. After four weeks, a mammoth research vessel picked them up and brought them home to their central heating and Wi-Fi. I wondered about those islands today, if any marks of that expedition remained. If the islands remembered. My guess was no. Anything those scientists did to the land would be long gone by now, blown away by Pacific gales, washed into the churning surf.

I studied those photos for a good couple hours, until it was dark and I was sleepy. These precariously placed bits of land, battered and

thriving, made all our human endeavors seem puny and imperma-
nent and, in a way that did not depress me, futile. I let the magazine
slip to the floor. I turned off the light. That night I dreamt of riding
a giant wave onto the pebbly shore of a deserted island and finding,
among the strange rock formations and mossy earth, a tiny white
kitten.

I WAS TELLING Fred about the Birdwatcher and the event bird,
Aphrodite and Fanny and my decision to quit the pet-finding business, when I heard a knock. Mrs. Pevzner hadn't visited in a month
at least, and while I missed her blondies, I didn't miss feeling like a
jerk about her Tupperware. I loved those plastic orbs. I loved their
soothing colors and smooth surfaces. I couldn't bear to part with
them.

Very very quietly, I tiptoed to the door and peeped through the
peephole. Standing on my front porch was Officer Omar. It had been
eight weeks since the first time we met and, truth be told, I wasn't
entirely unhappy to see him again. I opened the door.

Hi Ms. Clipper.

Hi Officer Omar. A pause as we considered each other. I was waiting for my awkwardness to kick in, to begin sweating profusely or
talking incoherently, but instead I asked, with an implicit wink and
only the tiniest bit of flirtation: So did my parents tell you I wasn't
their daughter?

No, you're good, he said and smiled. I'm here because there was
a call about a lurker. A Peeping Tom was the concern. I wonder if
you've seen anyone hanging around?

Hm. What did the Peeping Tom look like?

The caller has made numerous complaints along these lines. Usually she says it's a suspicious-looking bla—

Here Omar stopped. He was staring at my pajama bottoms, which were white with large red polka dots. But this time, Omar continued, she provided a very detailed description of the suspect's clothing. White pants with red spots on them.

Interesting, I said. You mean like these? I held out a leg.

That looks like a match, said Omar. And have you been, um, you know—he circled a finger in the air to indicate the porch, the lawn, the general vicinity.

Lurking? I rolled my eyes. Mrs. Dykstra and her goddamn binoculars. That woman needs a life. Seriously. I was only looking for lost pets.

And did you at one time have a bird on your head?

Jesus, can't anyone in this town just do their own thing?

I'll tell Mrs. Dykstra not to worry, said Omar.

Please reassure her that I absolutely do not want to peep through her window at any time of the day or night. And besides, I'm finished with my lurking.

No more pets to find? asked Omar.

I'm throwing in the towel, I said. I'm really busy at the moment with . . . other things. I gestured vaguely behind me toward the living room couch and the coffee table, which contained all the detritus of the past three months: tissues and *National Geographic*s and dirty forks and empty food cartons from Mr. Kilt Man.

Omar gave me a dubious and yet good-natured smile. I once again noticed the solid width of his shoulders. He was no kilt-wearing genius chef, but it was nice to experience that feeling of pull toward someone. It was nice to feel anything at all.

Ms. Clipper, this is my cell. He scribbled a number on the back of a business card and handed it to me. You call me if Mrs. Dykstra gives you any more trouble.

I saluted. Aye aye, Captain, I said and stood in the doorway as Omar drove away.

Just before turning back inside, I noticed movement in my peripheral vision. Up and to the left, a sudden jerkiness. A whirring noise. A smattering of green leaves fell without warning like confetti to the ground.

What the—I said, watching the area for more movement. And there, dodging a branch of my beloved elm tree, hovered a black and silver drone, its cold camera eye trained directly on me.

I played coy and continued to scan the sidewalk and surrounding trees. Oh, what could be making that noise? I said loudly. Is there a bald eagle living in my elm? A tree sprite? An incredibly nosy raccoon? Or could it be ... that ... goddamn ... Mrs. Dykstra—

And I sprinted toward the drone, jumping up to bat it out of the air. The drone rose just beyond my reach, navigated past the elm and zoomed up and away over the Dykstras' roof.

I yelled in the direction of the house: Keep that drone away from me! Turn on the TV if you're so frigging bored!

I took out my phone and called Officer Omar.

It's me, Darcy Clipper. The non-lurker?

Wow, he said, that was fast.

You need to come back. I'd like to report illegal drone activity. Mrs. Dykstra, in fact, flying her drone in my yard.

Hang tight, said Omar. I'll be there in five.

I briefly considered putting on some makeup and maybe changing out of my pajamas, but whatever.

I waited for Omar on the porch, on the lookout for more drone activity, but the Dykstra house was quiet. Sneaky fuckers, I thought.

Omar arrived, unfortunately without his siren blaring, and I explained the situation. So the drone was right there—I pointed to the tree—and then it went over there and then it zoomed over there. It was watching me the whole time. And she thinks *I'm* the lurker.

Omar was listening with his head angled to the side.

You're not taking notes, I said. Don't you need to take notes before you file a report and arrest someone? I've watched a lot of *Law & Order.*

Darcy—may I call you Darcy?

I nodded.

Darcy, here's the thing. This is out of my jurisdiction. Drones are regulated by federal aviation law. I know, I know, it doesn't make sense, but that's what we've got. There are a few limited scenarios where I might be able to help. Would you say there's a pattern of repetitive and harassing drone activity?

Um, no.

Did the drone hover directly over your head?

Not really. But it could have!

Omar grimaced. I'm really sorry, but there's nothing I can do. He looked genuinely regretful. I almost wanted to give him a squeeze.

If the drone activity becomes a regular occurrence, he continued, then we could make an argument for harassment. Let's keep a record of any drone sightings, date, time, duration, any other info you think is relevant. Just call or text when you see something. If we start to see a pattern, then I can help. Sound good? He smiled and his eyes crinkled up at the corners.

I liked watching Omar speak. He had a lovely voice and a lovely mouth and I hadn't touched a man in over a year. Those last six months with Skip didn't count, because honestly I was never in the mood: the scenario was of the grin-and-bear-it variety. Actually, thinking about it now, maybe the grin-and-bear-it period had lasted longer than six months. A year of grin and bear it? Could that be right?

Omar was looking at me expectantly, eyebrows raised.

Darcy? he said. Does that sound good?

Oh . . . yes, Omar. Yes, that sounds good. Really, really good. I'll keep track of Mrs. Dykstra's peeping-drone activity.

Okay, then. Take care, Darcy.

You too, Omar.

REMINDER: Board of Selectmen meeting this Friday. Agenda items: 1) stormwater runoff debate; 2) retirement party for Fire Chief Ernie Buffoni; 3) open forum on Mushroom Festival musical act—Riverdance or Kiss tribute band?

•

It's past Easter and I still see one house with holiday lights. Honestly, it's embarrassing. You're bringing down the whole neighborhood with your laziness. Remove the lights or I'll take legal action. You know who you are.

•

POLL: (age 18 or older) choose your favorite gambling activity □ poker □ blackjack □ roulette □ yes

•

FOUND: hey parents, if any of your teenagers are missing a backpack full of cheap beer and hot cheetos, let me know. I've got it!

•

Hi, it's BestBoyMommy22 here (mom to Jett and Viggo, 42 months). We're looking to buy some toddler-sized boxing gloves, full training headgear and a freestanding punching bag. Anyone looking to sell? Thanks!

WITHOUT MY PET-FINDING INCOME, I found ways to limit my spending. I began to ration my toilet paper, I canceled the organic meal service and switched to supermarket TV dinners delivered by a revolving cast of UPS drivers, none of whom wore a kilt. I turned off the heat. I limited my toothpaste use. I reused my tea bags until the water was the color of weak pee. But something had to give.

On one particularly chilly night, day 106 of my self-imposed isolation and erstwhile canned food consumption, I piled every blanket in the house atop my bed. I fell asleep and woke up a few hours later, blazing hot and gasping for air beneath the weight of all that duvet and wool.

Fred, I called into the darkness, no more. I need a job.

On the Community Board, I blew by the lost pet posts without a tremor of feeling. Even the all-cap, desperate ones failed to provoke me.

SAVE my darling turtle, Tom! He's wandered off in Drexel Park. I turned my head for a minute and lost him in the grass. PLEASE HELP!

Not a flicker.

Our dear girl Sunshine has been MISSING since last night. She's a golden labradoodle, answers to sunny-pooh, sun bear, sun-kissed, sunlit, sunny sunny Subaru. Our family misses her terribly.

Yawn.

And then I saw a post that did give me pause.

Help wanted: someone cool to assist with toy testing and light construction work. Good conversationalist preferred. Generous hourly wage, plus awesome snacks.

I felt a pang of remorse. Marcus Dash-LaGrand and his playscape. Why had I said no? Why was I such a bitch? I could help him test some toys. True, roller coasters made me vomit, and paintball had always scared the wits out of me, and studies have shown that monkey bars result in more broken bones than any other outdoor activity apart from slalom skiing. But I was sure there were other, less risky items that needed testing. And I could be a good conversationalist, when prompted. Skip had always tended to quiet. Every night, he liked to watch one movie, then segue straight into sex and then immediately fall asleep. Not much room in there for conversation. Mornings he tended to be chattier, but I was always busy getting ready for work, flossing my teeth, shining my shoes and so my attention was diverted. I remember a few good morning chats with my husband, one about the strange influx of squirrels, another about our health insurance and what cataclysmic health events would certainly bankrupt us. Leg amputation, I believe, was on the list. Ditto rabies.

Now I wondered what sort of conversations Marcus liked to have. This employment scenario, I realized, would provide the perfect arena for practicing unemotional, arms-length, socially appropriate communication. I would not be subjected to tearful expressions of relief and joy from pet owners, there would be no cute animals to stroke and adore. I could conquer the awkwardness that now struck whenever I was within spitting distance of another human being. Except, I noted, Omar. And the Birdwatcher. And my old lady friend Fanny. But the world contained multitudes. Unless I wanted to live forever in my childhood home and become the weird, sad lurker Mrs. Dykstra believed me to be, I would need to branch out beyond three human acquaintances. I would keep matters with Marcus professional, appropriate, polite, firmly focused on money and meaningless chitchat.

Yes, I could do this. I needed to do this.

THE NEXT MORNING, I made the call.

Hi Marcus. It's Darcy Clipper. From the trampoline testing?

Darcy! Of course. I remember you. You jumped with flair.

I saw your new post on the Community Board.

Super. Can you come by today?

Um, yeah, but I have a few conditions.

Spill. Whatever you need.

I really don't like children.

Yeah, you mentioned that. Listen, my kids will be at school, no worries there. And the space isn't open yet. That's why I need some help.

Another thing, I'm not really one for touching.

Hey, workplace sexual harassment is a serious problem. I wouldn't dream of—

No, I just mean no thumb wrestling or swing pushing. High-fiving. That kind of thing.

You refuse to high five?

Skin on skin makes me nervous.

The swings would be shirt to hand, so technically only one skin layer. Not trying to persuade. Just saying.

Okay, okay, maybe the swings. But in other ways, I need to avoid touching.

I catch your drift. No kids, no touching. No worries, my friend.

And would you say emotions run high in this workplace?

Not quite sure I understand the question.

Is there much crying involved in this job?

Not if I can help it.

Great. And what's your hourly rate?

I was thinking maybe fifteen? It's not strenuous and I'll provide lunch, snacks and all the rosemary-mint iced tea you can drink.

I was thinking more, like, I don't know, fifty?

Marcus cleared his throat. Hmmm. Can you operate a power drill?

Um, sure thing.

What about a sander?

Yep. I coughed. Practically a pro.

Okay. How about we meet in the middle—thirty-five per hour.

Done.

I MET MARCUS an hour after lunch. His playscape was coming along nicely. The zipline was installed, swings set up, two more gargantuan trampolines flanked the one I'd tested.

We decided to go big on jumping, Marcus explained. Our boys each wanted their own.

Around the back, a group of men in orange vests and hard hats stood at the lip of a huge dirt hole.

Hi Burt! Marcus waved to a white guy with tattoos on his forearms and a little gray man bun. He wore a *Namaste All Day* T-shirt and black jeans, plus hard hat and safety goggles. Burt Sweeten was the project foreman, Marcus told me. He worked with his two sons, Brendan and Brandon, and a crew of two Poles and two Mexicans and one Irish guy and one Kiwi.

He's a genius, Marcus whispered. And he teaches yoga at the Y. How cool is that?

Today Burt and the crew were digging out the in-ground pool, lazy river and water pavilion. A gigantic yellow excavator lifted bucketfuls of earth and dumped them into a waiting truck.

I had to convince Dan about the pool, Marcus explained. All he thinks about is liability. Lawsuits, lawsuits, lawsuits. Are we going to pay a lifeguard twenty-four/seven? No, twelve hours per day is enough, I told him. Six in the winter. And we've got fencing, of course, and we'll alarm it. And life jackets, obviously. We'll be totally safe and, goddamn, we need a pool. No one really thinks of heat when they think of Massachusetts but it's like the Serengeti in mid-August. I've never sweated so much in my life, and I've been to Marrakesh. How can we *not* have a pool?

I could see his point. Murbridge got steamy in the summer. *Humid as a fat man's armpit,* Daddy would say even when Mom told him that sort of talk was inappropriate.

I'll start you off with something small, Marcus said, turning us away from the pool excavation and toward a two-story castle, its walls studded with colorful plastic climbing holds. Let's paint!

He handed me a painter's jumpsuit, goggles and a paper face mask. Safety first, he said. Don't want any fumes to trouble you. You can change in the bathroom—first door on the right. He nodded toward the patio doors.

Inside, the house looked just as I'd expected: solid old bones with shiny modern renovations. Wood floors that glowed like honey, moldings painted bright white, tall ceilings, arched doorways. There were high-tech kid toys everywhere and artistic flourishes chosen by someone with excellent and expensive taste. An enormous painting of odd squiggles and bright colors. A chair made of chrome and leather straps that looked very uncomfortable and possibly illegal. A gigantic chandelier of long glass tubes and black wire.

Interesting, I thought. So these are the things that rich people buy.

After changing, I lingered for a moment by the fridge to examine the family snapshots. Marcus and Dan and their three young sons decorating a Christmas tree, lighting a menorah, weaving a mkeka for Kwanzaa, standing in front of the Disney castle, the Eiffel Tower, the Trevi Fountain. Everyone smiling. The images of family togetherness made me miss Mom and Daddy with a sudden fierce ache in my throat. I shook my head and reminded myself of my own rule: no on-the-job crying.

As I turned to leave, I caught sight of a small person. Or rather, he caught sight of me.

Are you Daddy's new project?

The question came from a youngish child with long auburn curls and a fake mustache. He was perched on a tall stool at the kitchen island, eating what appeared to be a raw zucchini.

No, um, I don't think so, I answered. I'm here to help with the play-scape. What's your name?

Phin. I'm the youngest. I'm five and one quarter.

I whistled. Very impressive.

You think? Phin raised one eyebrow. Six will be the *real deal*. He rapped the zucchini on the countertop for emphasis.

I nodded. Six is a great year. You have a lot to look forward to.

Please don't get mad at my daddy. He can get pretty intense.

Do I look mad?

No, but one time these other ladies got really really *really* mad at—

Phin, what's going on in here? Marcus had slipped into the kitchen. I see you've met Darcy.

I don't want her to yell at you, said Phin. He took another bite from the zucchini and said through the mouthful: Daddy, can you be chill?

Marcus rolled his eyes. Why is everyone in this family so worried? Did Papa put you up to this?

No, silly, Phin replied. Papa's in Croatia all week, remember?

Of course I remember. And shouldn't you be on the way to jujitsu with Harriet?

Daddy, tell her. Phin pointed the half-eaten zucchini at me.

Tell me what? I asked Marcus.

Daddy.

Okay, okay, I'll tell her, said Marcus, rolling his eyes. Geesh. Now go find Harriet. You'll miss the opening chant.

Phin scampered out of the room and Marcus turned to me. Don't be scared, he said. Phin made it sound much worse than it was.

Than *what* was?

Marcus sighed. Let me open some wine and we can discuss my crimes and misdemeanors like rational adults. You should know the background to this project. It's near and dear to my heart and if you do anything to mess it up, I may have to—Marcus stopped and smiled. Well, we don't need to go into specifics right now.

I giggled nervously. Clearly I'd need to brush up on my sarcasm to work with Marcus.

We sat on the patio with glasses of pinot gris and Marcus told me the tale of his family's ill-fated year in Darien, Connecticut. The details were, to be honest, somewhat tedious but in short involved an outright social war between Marcus and the dozen or so Ivy League–educated, unemployed stay-at-home moms who ran the PTO at Crossley-Shep Academy, the private school where the boys were enrolled for one short, tragic term.

Those liberal manicured trophy wives couldn't stand a dad with ideas, Marcus explained. They didn't want nuts in the brownies, fine. I can't wear board shorts to the meetings, fine. A college prep night for third graders, fine. But a separate committee just to approve Instagram photos? And the president appoints all PTO officers based on an IQ test, administered by *herself*? What's that about? *We're all such freethinkers,* they'd say, *we don't shave our pits, we'd vote for Bernie, we love people of all genders and colors and zip codes and blah blah blah.* They ran that PTO like some rich lady, feminists-for-social-media private club.

Despicable, I said.

Despicable is right. The kicker came at the annual fundraising gala. They specifically kept me off the organizing committee. You're too intense, they said. You need to calm down, they said. But that night, I realized why they'd been so secretive. Those ladies thought it would be a hoot to *auction off the teachers* as a fundraising stunt. They set up a big block onstage, told the teachers to wear skimpy clothes, parade around, wink and wiggle and then stand on that block as drunk parents waved their bid cards. Can you think of anything more humiliating? Mr. Bledsoe, bless his heart, wore a thong and did a little dance. The man's a middle-aged biology teacher, for crying out loud—no one wants to see him twerk.

Marcus paused to sip his wine.

So, he continued, I decided to put an end to the whole sorry spectacle. I jumped onstage, screamed *stop* and took a golf club to the whole goddamn setup. I grabbed the microphone and made some inappropriate but entirely truthful remarks about the PTO president, treasurer, secretary and a few of the other ladies too. Apparently I did 50k's worth of damage to the Hilton ballroom. Marcus paused. Oops, he said and smiled. So the PTO banned me for life from attending school events. And Dan. Poor Dan. And the kids were ostracized. Teasing, bullying, the whole nine yards. It was awful. And it was all my fault. I had been the one to say we needed out of the city, the kids needed green space. We left a perfectly lovely duplex in Brooklyn Heights because I wanted something different for the kids. And for myself.

Marcus drained his glass and then reached for a tissue. He was crying, I realized.

I mean, our kids are amazing, don't get me wrong, I love them to pieces, but being a stay-at-home parent is tough. Dan is always traveling, always working and sometimes I feel like my adult brain has shriveled up and died. An intelligent and talented person like myself might need a little more than jujitsu lessons and bedtime stories to justify a life. Know what I mean?

Kind of, I said slowly. Though to be honest, justifying my life is pretty far down on my list right now. I'm focused on keeping myself fed, sane and away from the news.

Ah yes, said Marcus, nodding. Well, don't worry—you'll get there. And do you know what's the craziest? I've always felt like an outsider. I'm a dog person in a world full of cat videos, Darcy. And now I find myself in the most ridiculously mundane position imaginable. I'm a 1950s housewife to a workaholic husband.

Do you collect Tupperware?

Not yet.

Well, I think there's reason to hope. And most 1950s housewives don't build state-of-the-art playgrounds in their backyards.

No. Marcus paused. Mind if I share more?

All you, I said. Go.

And boy, did Marcus go. Architecture was his bag. His passion, his raison d'être. He loved building things, loved light and air, function and form. Loved Miles van der Rohe and Hadid and all those Finnish guys. He ended up at MIT, where he was the darling of the program's top professor. Marcus was on the fast track to worldwide architecture dominance. Until he realized he couldn't get out of bed. Or stop crying. He left grad school in the throes of a full-on nervous breakdown, crawled back home to live with his parents just outside Ann Arbor. Both were tenured professors at University of Michigan, had fought hard for their achievements. Failure wasn't in their vocabulary. Marcus's older brother was an uber-successful M&A lawyer in Chicago and poor Marcus felt like the shameful, unstable loser son. His parents tolerated him, but they were all about tough love.

My mom left a tray outside my bedroom door every night, Marcus said. Protein, veg, starch, absolutely no seasoning and a glass of lukewarm water. Not even one ice cube! And always, a Post-it with some asinine self-help slogan. *You make your own luck. Get up and get moving. If you believe, you will achieve.* That kind of thing. It was horrible.

Eventually Marcus started therapy, got on some meds, started making his own dinners, found a job as a Starbucks barista. And there, six months later, he met Dan.

Truly the love of my life, Marcus said. He walked in, ordered a double-tall, double-hot Americano with a whisper of steamed two percent and that was that. Jeez-oh-Pete. A thunderclap. A lightning bolt. All the stars, all the hearts.

Wow, I said. We'd opened a second bottle of wine and I was crying now too. So when do I meet the wonderful Dan?

Maybe in a few weeks? He's usually home every third weekend of the month. Marcus smiled weakly.

Phin and Harriet returned from jujitsu and went inside to work on Phin's Mandarin. The older boys, Xanther and Ludovic, wandered in from lacrosse practice, tossing the ball between them. Shadows lengthened. The first stars popped.

And still Marcus and I sat talking. Or rather, Marcus talked and I listened with the occasional question or request for more potato chips. It had been so long since I'd engaged like this with another human being. I'd forgotten what it was like. Emotional intimacy, truth-telling, self-examination, confession, care. I wasn't yet ready to participate fully, but I appreciated Marcus's willingness to put himself out there.

Wow, Marcus said at last. I'm really putting myself out there.

You are, I said. But don't worry, I'm here to listen, not judge.

Thanks.

By now it was dark, a hazy night sky above us, the kids calling out about dinner and hunger pangs.

Isn't it amazing how much children *eat*? Marcus asked. I feed them and feed them and feed them but they still want more.

It's truly astounding, I said. One of the many reasons I've avoided parenthood.

Marcus looked at me sideways. I sense there's something more here. You, children. Ready to share?

I groaned. Another day.

Deal, said Marcus. And, Darcy, I'm glad we had this chance to talk. Now you know why this playscape means so much to me. I'm also confident I won't fire you in the first week. Although you totally lied about the power drill.

I hung my head. Guilty, I said. Sorry.

No worries, I'll teach you. We start tomorrow with the real work. Don't forget to wear the jumpsuit.

THE NEXT MORNING, I wore the jumpsuit.

Cute! Marcus said when he saw me. You rock a painter's smock.

I curtsied.

Okay, let's get painting. I'm keeping colors gender neutral. Silver, green, orange. Is an orange castle too weird?

I shook my head. Not at all. Orange is my favorite color.

We began and I quickly realized why the ladies in Darien had yelled at Marcus.

Brush straight up and down, he said. Not too much paint. Wait, that's too little. Use long strokes. Not *that* long. Shorter, shorter. It's all in the wrist. Here, let me show you.

Marcus yanked the paintbrush from my hand and demonstrated.

Marcus, I said with as much patience as I could muster. We're painting a kid's rocket ship, not the Sistine Chapel.

He stepped back. Am I being too intense?

I nodded. You hired me to help you, I said. So let me help.

Marcus grimaced. Okay, I'll try, he said, handing back the paintbrush. I'm kind of a control freak.

I've noticed.

We began again. This time Marcus bit his lip. I saw him twitch a few times, and reach out a hand to correct me, and the sound of teeth grinding was unmistakable, and he let out a strangled little cry when I accidentally dropped the paintbrush, but I did not feel over-managed. No one yelled.

We'd been painting for nearly an hour when Marcus spoke again: So, Darcy, can I ask you a question?

Shoot.

What is this Mushroom Festival thing all about?

I smiled. I'm happy to educate you on the weird and wonderful ways of our annual celebration of fungi. It's basically a town fair. We celebrate our history, eat fried food, play games, gawk at livestock and weird vegetables. The chair of the selectmen serves as our Mushroom Monarch. He wears this long brown cape and a crown of papier-mâché cremini and, at the end of the day, he picks the winner of the festival's main event, the FunGuy stand-up competition.

Excuse me, Mushroom *Monarch*? said Marcus. *FunGuy* competition? And people *volunteer* to participate?

You bet. Every year you have to submit your FunGuy application ASAP. Otherwise you might not get a spot. They only take the first fifty people.

Fifty?

Everyone gets five minutes to do their thing. That's four hours of mushroom jokes. It's a long day.

Well. Marcus paused. I honestly don't know what to say. This is certainly surprising. I did buckets of research on Murbridge. You have a Black principal at Murbridge High, a Korean police chief, an amazing Jewish deli, homeownership at equivalent rates for the WASPs and the POCs and virtually no racial income divide. So how did I miss the Mushroom Fest?

I shrugged. Beats me.

Marcus sighed deeply. It's not worth second-guessing myself now. We're here, home of the annual Mushroom Festival. I'm sure the boys will enjoy it. But don't tell them about this FunGuy business. Especially Ludovic. He might actually sign up. He lives for raunchy knock-knock jokes. Marcus grimaced. So my next question for you, Darcy, is: Why the hell did you move back to Murbridge?

I cleared my throat. After the confessional tsunami unleashed by Marcus last night I felt some pressure to spill my guts.

I—Well—Let's see—

My tendency toward self-protection bumped up against my perennial, desperate need to please others. In this case, to please Marcus. He expected some hard, shitty truth and so I took a deep breath and jumped straight in.

Basically, my husband left me for a female skydiver with a mustache and the shock sent me into a tailspin of depression so I retreated home to mend my broken heart.

Wow. That sounds like a country-western song. So has it worked?

Not exactly. I told him about my parents' treasonous conduct, the loss of Fred the fern, the canned goods, my black bedroom, my spying neighbors, my solitude and social awkwardness. The realization that Skip would never take me back.

But do you want him back? Marcus asked. He sounds kinda clueless.

You're not the first to make that observation, I said. But I always *expected* to be with him. Skip was my future.

Ha! The road to lunacy is paved with earnest expectations, said Marcus. Trust me, I'm speaking from firsthand experience. Listen, Darcy, the future is designed to mess up your plans. Don't attach. You gotta roll with the punches. Dip and weave. Dip and weave. Here Marcus mimed a boxer. He threw a punch. Ouch, he said and grabbed his right shoulder. Old barista injury.

Actually, I mused, the one thing that did help my broken heart was finding a lost pig.

You were the one who found Stella? You're a superstar! I know Larita—she works with Dan's sister's best friend's husband. I heard the whole story. Marcus paused. That was a very noble, good deed. You should be proud of yourself.

She was fairly easy to catch. She was eating something repulsive on my front lawn. Never even saw me coming. I told Marcus how I'd embarked on a pet-finding mission. Chewy the Chihuahua, Barnum the bird, Squirrelly the stuffed squirrel.

Even *stuffed* animals? Marcus whistled. Your versatility is admirable.

We were having lunch now, wonderful prosciutto, fig and Brie paninis made by Marcus himself that were almost as good as the Kilt Man's cooking. I paused to chew and swallow.

But then it all started getting weird, I said and took another bite to avoid elaborating. Too much, too soon, I realized. So far, I'd experienced no awkward symptoms with Marcus and I wanted to keep it that way.

The job lacked reliability, I said instead. I need to eat, ergo I need some regular money.

Eating is important, Marcus replied. And then, slowly: So is that the only reason you're here? The money? His expression was wounded in a way that could have been jokey or could have been genuine. Because, Darcy, I really need a friend in this town.

Now I could see that Marcus was not joking. Well, the money *is* important, I began carefully, but I'm not categorically *opposed* to the idea of friendship. Let's just take it slow. And Marcus, I'm genuinely moved by your vision. Children, together, playing and joyful, learning to jump and fall and get back up again. Resilience. Independence. Boy, girl, black, brown, white, green, orange, silver.

Don't forget LBGTQ+ and differently abled. Also gluten intolerant and lactose challenged.

Yes! I said. *Every* kind of kid. Geeks and scaredy-cats alongside jocks and girly girls. Transgender, nonbinary, gender fluid, confused as hell. All of them, playing in harmony, learning to love one another, respect one another. How could that be wrong?

Does anyone know what's going on at Lincoln Ave and Mercer? Looks like a major build. Condos? Parking? Fingers crossed for a Whole Foods! Sincerely yours, Jennifer Gross-Ross

•

NEIGHBORS: that eyesore on Lincoln Ave is getting bigger! Do they have building permits for that? I'm guessing the zipline violates air-restriction ordinances.

•

Who's building over there? Looks like goddamn Disney world. Signed, a concerned neighbor.

•

Every time I drive by that corner, I shudder. Sending my condolences to everyone in the vicinity.

•

Neighbors, please be assured the Board of Selectmen is investigating the residential building project on Lincoln Ave. I'll update the community as I learn more. Honorably, Jake Zdzynzky, Chair of the Selectmen

---

Dear Mom and Daddy,

    Just a quick note to let you know I have not been bludgeoned. Everything at the house is more or less fine. The faucet miraculously stopped leaking after I jabbed a fork into it. You'll also be happy to hear that I found a job. I've decided to take a break from the scintillating world of actuarial science and apply myself instead to the educational-recreation, real estate–carpentry field. It's an exciting opportunity. Maybe I'll tell you more about it later.

    Hope you're not frying down there in Arizona! I hear it's 107 in the shade today. And it's only May! I truly love Murbridge in the spring. Hummingbirds, lilac scenting the air, tulips bursting forth with their joyful blossoms. Sorry you're stuck with lizards and cacti. Be careful not to step on any scorpions. I hear they leave a nasty bite.

    Yes, I'm still mad about the move, but I'm trying to get past old hurts. I'll keep you posted.

Sincerely yours,

Darcy

Draft email files

Dear Skip,

How would you describe your mental and auditory state on
the day of our first meeting? Would you say there were fireworks?
Stars, hearts and so forth? Did you hear a thunderclap, imaginary or
otherwise? Would you use the word *adore* to describe your feelings
for me? Because anecdotal evidence suggests that something big
happens when you meet a wonderful person with whom you are
fated to spend the rest of your life. And guess what? I heard no
thunderclap when I first met you. Not even the distant rumble of
possible light showers. I saw no stars or hearts or anything else,
for that matter. When we met, I was ordering a beer and so
mostly I remember counting my change and calculating the tip and
wondering why this strange guy—that would be you, Skip—was
standing so close to me and maybe I should watch my wallet.
But now I'm thinking that the absence of mental fireworks was
noteworthy, perhaps even prophetic. I'm beginning to suspect that
we never

For the love of God would someone stop singing those Sound
of Music tunes? Raindrops on roses one more time and I will
literally vomit.

•

POLL: (age 18 or older) do you watch tasteful porn?
☐ very ☐ somewhat ☐ maybe ☐ yes

•

Neighbors, our manny Andy is looking for some playdates—
does wrestling, laser tag or parkour sound of interest to anyone
with toddler boys? Thanks! BestBoyMommy22.

•

REMINDER: Board of Selectmen meeting this Friday. Agenda items: 1) corrected spelling of Mah-kee-knack in all town records; 2) corrected spelling of Quinipipi in all town records; 3) consideration of proposal to propose a review of building permit No. 7729.

•

Darling, I miss you every day. When will we meet again? I have stories to tell you, such stories.

•

Darling, are you unsettled? Something feels wrong. I can hear you calling. Where can I find you? Where have you gone?

Summer

AFTER ONE MONTH OF WORKING for Marcus, I'd fallen into a routine of sorts that got me out of the house, kept me in meals from the Kilt Man and forced me to interact with the few people I considered safe. Safe as in: my connection to them was tangential and new enough that, if one were to disappear or reject me, I would most certainly survive. My gang, my circle, my pod, if you will. I still avoided contact with people at large—too many, too loud, too cranky. Ditto for all former friends, colleagues, neighbors, parents—too curious, too successful, too full of pity.

That left Marcus and the boys; Omar, if I needed to report drone activity, which I did often; Fanny, whom I visited every weekend bearing chocolate and a folding chair; and the Birdwatcher, who appeared regularly but unpredictably on my wanders through Murbridge. I felt, in a word, satisfied. I wouldn't venture to say happy or joyful or even content. But satisfied was a start. Satisfied was something I could work with.

Until Jake Zdzynzky, chair of the town Board of Selectmen, decided to save Murbridge.

Darce, seriously. Can you believe this shit?

Marcus was holding a bright yellow sheet of paper printed with *SAVE MURBRIDGE! STOP THE BUILD!* in huge block letters.

I was poised on a ladder to paint the cone of our rocket ship. Last week, we'd started work on a ten-foot-tall rocket with three round windows and two internal floors, the exterior dotted with climbing holds for little hands and feet. I'd decided on turquoise and silver, with highlights of red, and believed it was the coolest rocket ever to grace a children's play area.

I saw some posts on the Community Board, I said, pausing with my paintbrush, but I didn't realize they were actually serious.

Serious enough for neon flyers, said Marcus. I'm worried the Board of Selectmen might try to revoke our building permit. Jake's the new chair, and he's the one claiming the playscape violates town zoning and it's an eyesore and it'll increase traffic. Though he lives six miles away and only drives by here on purpose. Oh, and also we're putting kids' lives at risk and we're only doing this because we're weird and crazy. Marcus crossed his eyes and stuck his tongue out sideways.

I laughed.

Then Marcus got serious. Darcy, I won't survive a Darien repeat. I need the playscape to succeed.

Maybe consider . . . scaling it back a bit? I suggested.

No. I can't scale it back! Don't you remember what I told you?

You mean about the time you saw Liam Hemsworth in Price Chopper?

No! Although it *was* him. I'm talking about my vision. This isn't just about me. It's about my kids, and everyone's kids, and Lady Marjory, and childhood and innocence and joy. It's about resilience and independence. Inclusion and equality and building a better future.

Marcus, I said, that's beautiful.

Don't mock me.

I would never.

Okay, and it's also about me. My parents still see me as the son who had a nervous breakdown. And Dan seems to have forgotten that I exist as anything other than our sons' dad. Marcus paused. Let's just say I need a win.

So what is Jake's problem? It's like he holds some personal vendetta against you.

What's his problem? Come on, Darcy. Dan and I are two dads, pink and brown, with three beautiful golden kids.

But this is New England, for crying out loud! We're so blue we're icy. We're the liberalist of the liberals. If Bernie Sanders hadn't been born, we'd have fashioned him out of pine needles and Yankee Candle wax. Maybe just try talking to Jake?

You, my dear girl, are naive as hell.

Marcus said this with a dead stare, half accusation and half indulgence. I didn't know how to answer. Was I naive as hell? I had never considered the question before. True, I was small-town America. And privileged in the way of security and parental support and food on the table, although no Maserati for my sixteenth birthday, that's for damn sure. And I was straight, more or less, since Tabitha the summer before college. And cute, more or less, since my acne cleared up. And white. I was whiter than Mark Zuckerberg and Casper the Friendly Ghost combined. And I'd believed in Santa Claus, Cinderella and nuclear nonproliferation until at least the age of sixteen.

Bingo, I realized. Marcus was right. I was a goddamn sucker.

Yes, I am naive, I said. I admit it. But I'm trying to learn. And naive or not, I still think most people want to do the right thing. They just don't always know what the right thing is. They need to be told. No one is born an asshole. People *learn* to be assholes. But they can unlearn it too. Marcus, get on the Community Board and explain why the playscape will benefit everyone in Murbridge. The town will support you.

Marcus raised his eyebrows, but then sighed. Oh, all right. I'll respond. Because no one and that means *no* one is taking down my zipline.

Dear neighbors,

My name is Marcus Dash-LaGrand of 32 Lincoln Ave. Last year, my husband, Dan, and I moved to bucolic Murbridge to make a home here for our three sons. To this end, we're redesigning our backyard as an adventure playscape for our boys. Our plan is to open the space to Murbridge kids of all ages, backgrounds and abilities. Last fall, we applied for and received the necessary building permits from the town Board of Selectmen under chair Hildegard Hyman. I understand there are now some neighborhood concerns regarding the project. Let me reassure you: we are currently in the most intense period of construction. The trucks and equipment will be gone by mid-July. The playscape itself will be surrounded by an aesthetically pleasing, redwood-certified seven-foot-tall fence that meets all zoning requirements for children's play areas. The fence will shield the area from view of passing cars while keeping children safely away from the road. The playscape includes state-of-the-art equipment alongside simple, time-honored play structures.

Play is an essential part of every child's development. In the words of renowned child psychologist Susan Linn: "Play is the foundation of learning, creativity, self-expression, and constructive problem-solving. It's how children wrestle with life to make it meaningful." In this age of devices, video games, racial and social division, childhood obesity, overcrowded classrooms and snotty preteens, old-fashioned outdoor play is more important than ever. As you may know, the playground at Murbridge Elementary is woefully outdated and unmaintained. The Sergeant Cooper Day School space is restricted to the privileged few who can afford the sky-high tuition. Dan and I are building the playscape for our family and for all people of Murbridge.

I recently installed a Little Free Library directly in front of our house and stocked it with books and magazines for kids and adults of all ages and tastes: *Hop on Pop,* James Baldwin, Harry Potter, *Catcher in the Rye,* Margaret Atwood, Julia Alvarez, *Maus* and plenty of Oprah, Martha Stewart and *Architectural Digest* magazines. Feel free to stop by, grab some reading material and check out the site for yourself. Or you can email me at TheMarcus@ DLfamily.com with any questions or concerns about the playscape.

I hope you will support our project.

Peace,

Marcus and Dan Dash-LaGrand, parents to Xanther, Ludovic and Phineas

---

We left Marcus's letter to percolate on the Community Board. After a few hours, we checked to see how the responses were shaping up. The shape was not good.

I live two doors down from the Dash-LaGrands. I can only imagine the shrieking that will erupt from their play area in summer. As a property owner, I should be free to sit in my backyard without unacceptable noise levels. What if I want to sleep late? Or go to bed early? While I support in general the principle of children playing and whatnot, such activity does not belong on my quiet residential street. Karen D., 38 Lincoln Ave.

•

It seems weird to me that a couple of guys want to spend money to build a playground just so neighborhood kids will come to their house. Does that strike anyone else as weird? A concerned parent.

•

The playground at Sergeant Cooper Day School is a delight. Completely safe and extremely stimulating for children of all ages. My children adore it. I see no need for this kind of facility in a town like ours. Signed, Jennifer Gross-Ross

•

They think a free copy of Martha Stewart is enough to buy my support for that crazy build? Think again, weirdos.

•

NEIGHBORS: petition attached to SAVE MURBRIDGE, STOP THE BUILD on Lincoln Ave. Sign and pass along to family, friends and colleagues—even if they're not Murbridge residents, they can still support our mission. And note: although I remain chair of the Board of Selectmen, I'm circulating this in my private capacity as a concerned citizen. Honorably, Jake Zdzynzky

•

I'm sick over this so-called "playscape" project. All hours of the day, there's a crew of rough-looking men with enormous tools. I don't feel safe in my own backyard. Is this how we want to live? Hell no. I'm signing that petition as many times as I can. Karen L., 104 Lincoln Avenue

---

Dear Daddy and Mom,

Do you know a red-haired, red-faced man named Jake Zdzynzky? Any information you can provide on Jake (dirty or otherwise) would be gratefully received.

And how do you pronounce his last name? I can't get a handle on all those z's.

But please don't try to call me. We're still not on speaking terms.

Thank you in advance for your help.

Sincerely yours,

Darcy

Darcy Bunny, it's so wonderful to hear from you! How are you feeling? How's the weather? Daddy and I are so glad you haven't been bludgeoned and that you're working! How's the new job?

To answer your question: yes, Daddy and I know Jake Zdzynzky. He took part in Daddy's weekly poker games. I suspect you were too young to remember much about those nights or you may have blocked out the memories due to trauma. So much smoke and foul language! Daddy only kept it up for a few months, it was very draining, financially and otherwise. Daddy, it turned out, was not a very good cardplayer. He couldn't keep a straight face to save his life. His eyes bug out when he's got a secret. I'm sure you've noticed. It's not the most attractive look, but I've become fond of it, in a way. So much of marriage requires becoming fond of things you would otherwise find revolting. Words of wisdom for you, Darcy, if you ever take another trip down the aisle.

How is your love life by the way? Have you met any eligible men? And Darcy, please be careful. I've read about this catfishing phenomenon. Or is it catnipping? Anyhow, don't believe every photo you see online! That hunky hunk is probably a middle-aged shortie with no teeth and a nasty case of crabs. Make sure you get references. And meet in a public place and sit close to an exit. And don't forget your pepper spray.

Anyhow, as I was saying, Jake played poker just well enough

to win a few and to believe he should win them all. Daddy never actually *proved* Jake was cheating, but we found a few extra cards near his chair and—oh, I don't want to go spreading rumors, especially about our old Murbridge friends. I'll just say that Jake has always wanted to strike it rich. And he possesses a moral foundation that is shaky, at best. And his wife adores Disney Cruises, which are surprisingly spendy. I'll just leave you to draw your own conclusions from that collection of facts.

Some other tidbits about Jake that you may find interesting: he suffers from atrociously bad breath. I remember it vividly. I also remember his dislike of Principal Ross at the school. She did push some buttons, but Jake—oh my goodness, he did not take kindly to a woman in charge. And then there were the off-color jokes he'd tell at poker night. Very naughty and not very funny. And once he grabbed my bottom while I was rounding with martinis, although I never told your father about that. Please don't tell Daddy. It would only upset him and he's already upset about his golf handicap. Apparently it's the highest at the club. Poor Daddy. He tries so hard.

But I will say that Jake's wife always made the nicest cheese spread for poker nights. I can't remember her name for the life of me, but that woman had cheese spread to spare. So, in summary, apart from his dishonest, sexist, harassing and mildly alcoholic tendencies, Jake Zdzynzky was a perfectly nice man.

Why do you ask?

Your loving,

Mom

MARCUS AND I WERE PAINTING a mural on the wall that separated the pool from the paintball course. We'd decided on a jungle scene, big leaves and exotic animals. Marcus had bought brushes of various sizes and paint in twenty different colors with delightfully bizarre names.

So I got an email from our vowel-challenged friend, Marcus said.

And? I was busy painting a sky of Emotionally Bankrupt Blue and I paused mid-stroke.

Well, Jake doesn't buy my *innocent do-gooder* stance and he still thinks the playscape is an *eyesore* and he still thinks there's no way we'll operate within *acceptable* noise levels.

What a stinker.

He also still believes our intentions are not *wholly appropriate*, whatever that means, and he'll be keeping an eye on me.

Oh, will he? And what did you say?

I said, Go ahead, bozo, and don't wear out your prescription bifocals.

I smiled and forced out a laugh.

I know, I know. Marcus sighed. I'm never good with the comeback. This petition has me so worked up, Darcy. I just want to bring something positive to this town. Children are the future.

Let them lead the way.

We both hummed the song and then Marcus said: I'm worried my post made things worse. Now everyone thinks Dan and I are weird. Lud said some kids were pointing at him and laughing at robotics camp yesterday. And Phin's playdate got canceled. The mom texted me and said something came up. Am I being paranoid?

Yes. Well . . . No.

No, meaning?

No, meaning that you're spending money to invite strange children to your home. It seems suspicious. Most people don't *want* to meet anyone new. They just want to hang out with people they already know.

The Sergeant Cooper Day School problem, said Marcus. He was

working on a twisty vine of Modern Subterfuge Maroon with leaves of Sophistry Green.

Exactly, I said. People in Murbridge pay a lot to keep their kids in that manicured, fenced-in, private school mansion-palooza. Hell, that place is like Alcatraz. Have you seen their crossing guard?

I have. Ouch. That school has one lousy ADA-compliant swing, an all-white staff and incredibly unflattering uniforms.

That's exactly how it was twenty years ago! I said. I held my face close to the wall as I began outlining a giant gecko in Depression-era Moss. Many people harbor an innate distrust of the outsider, I continued. Especially when the outsider comes bearing gifts.

That's not true, said Marcus. Everyone loves getting presents.

But gifts contain implicit messages of inadequacy. For example, I gifted my mom a hairbrush because she never, and I mean never, brushes her hair. I think she keeps snacks up there. The gift backfired. She didn't talk to me for a week and her hair still resembles an off-the-grid beehive. You and Dan are building a new playground because you think the existing playgrounds are crappy.

They *are* crappy!

Yes, but it's *their* crap. I turned to face Marcus. They made those crappy playgrounds and accepting your gift means accepting their own inadequacy and lack of vision when they constructed the originals. It's why Americans hate foreigners so much. Yes, pad thai tastes better than meat loaf but goddamnit, we made that crappy meat loaf. The same analysis applies to French pop music, Japanese beer and universal health care. See what I mean?

No. I don't. I think people in this town are crazy. They're willing to let kids suffer and be bored rather than accept that maybe someone else can do it better?

Yes. They'll continue to believe in their own greatness.

Even when it's patently clear they're not so great?

Especially then.

Jesus, Dan and I should go back to New York. The pad thai there is way better anyhow.

No! I cried. You can't go back. Just show Murbridge that your intentions are noble. People will relax. I mean, we're talking slides and swing sets here, not international diplomacy. And the Little Free Library was a brilliant touch. Start them off slow. First they'll take a free Oprah, then they'll take a free playscape.

Exactly, said Marcus. Although I do cut out all the recipes first. And did you notice about the library? I stocked it with banned books!

Wait—even *Hop on Pop*?

Violence to fathers, apparently. Marcus shrugged.

Marcus, look what I did! I stepped back to show him the spectacular reptilian eyes I'd been painting in Anthracite Outrage and Golden Chicken Bullion. Originally Marcus had envisioned only jungle mammals, but I'd talked him into some reptiles. Everyone loves a good gecko.

Nice, he said, leaning in to examine my handiwork. You're a real Darcy Van Gogh.

I think you should go back on the Community Board, I said. Respond to the comments. Show them you're pure of heart. Show them how un-weird you truly are.

Un-weird is my middle na—Marcus began, but at that moment a loud buzzing sound filled the air. From behind me, I felt a compact, direct wind of the kind made by a thousand small insect wings flapping with evil intent.

Oh my God, it's killer bees! I yelled. Marcus, *inside*!

I screamed, Marcus screamed, we dropped our paintbrushes and ran screaming into the house, slamming the patio door behind us.

Where are they? I shrieked. Are they in my hair? Are they in my clothes? This same thing happened when I was a kid! Fucking Murbridge and its killer bees!

But Marcus was too busy hyperventilating to examine my person or listen to my traumatic memory. He was gasping like a goldfish thrown from its bowl.

I forgot about my no-touching policy and placed a hand on his back and rubbed, just as my mom would have done. Breathe, Marcus, breathe, I said.

As Marcus struggled to inhale, I looked out the patio doors, trying to gauge the severity of our swarm situation. Should I call 911? But there, staring back at me through the glass, was the blank silver eye of Mrs. Dykstra's drone.

Marcus, you can calm down, I said levelly. We're not in danger. It's just my batshit-crazy neighbor, Mrs. Dykstra, and her goddamn drone.

The drone hovered in place, bobbing ever so slightly as though taunting me, and then zoomed off. Marcus began breathing steadily, taking long, slow inhales and exhales, one hand over his heart.

Wow, that's one committed Nosy Nellie, he said. But I'm so relieved about the bees, I'm not even mad.

THE NEXT DAY was Saturday and so I packed up my chocolate bar and lawn chair—a nifty design that folded into a backpack—and hiked over to visit Fanny. This was my weekly exercise and, boy, did I need it. With Marcus's generous employee pay, I was seeing a lot of my genius kilt-wearing chef.

As I walked through Murbridge, following roughly the same route Aphrodite had first shown me, I pondered the playscape controversy. I also pondered Mrs. Dykstra, killer bees and pet poop. On my route, I crossed paths with a few other early risers: dog walkers, runners, one pajama-clad man retrieving his mail, another picking a newspaper off his front lawn, a small posse of plump women pushing strollers and walking very fast. To a one, they looked like rational, kindhearted humans who loved their families and worried about eating enough leafy greens. But who was Karen D.? Or "a deeply concerned neighbor"? Who had left a baked potato on someone's car? Who believed gangs roamed the streets of Murbridge? Who was stealing packages? Who was racist? Misogynistic? Transphobic? Disgruntled? Possibly violent? With each passing neighbor, my suspicions grew. I was hoping I'd see the Birdwatcher—I usually did on my weekend morning forays to visit Fanny—but not today. Today, I was not lucky.

I made my way through the thicket of shrubs and emerged, sweaty and breathless, at the bottom of the Marian Sisters' lawn. Because my visits did not necessarily coincide with official visiting hours and because I was scared of nuns, I scanned first to confirm the coast was clear. No sign of a sister and so forward I marched, up the sloping grounds, to meet Fanny in her usual spot.

Darcy, how wonderful to see you! Fanny said, smiling brightly. Did you bring Godiva today? Or the Green & Black's?

Godiva, 75 percent, sprinkle of sea salt, I answered, handing her the bar. I unfolded my chair and sat down.

I looked forward to my visits with Fanny not only because she let me eat half the chocolate, but also because I liked her. I liked talking to her, listening to her stories, hearing about old-time Murbridge, her childhood just outside Boston, her nursing career, her little sister Lotty who sang like an angel. Lotty died when she was fifteen, Fanny told me on one of my first visits.

One summer day, she said, Lotty ventured off to swim at Revere Beach with her friends and disappeared beneath a wave. They finally found her the next morning. She was a strong swimmer, no one knew really what had happened. It had been a beautiful day. Lotty left the house full of sun and vinegar, Fanny had told me. And that's how I remember her still.

Today, I was hoping that Fanny might cheer me up or offer me life advice. My thoughts were as dark and dismal as a baggie full of pet poop. If anyone could scare that image away, it was Fanny Scott.

Fanny unwrapped the bar and handed me half. She brought the chocolate to her nose and inhaled deeply. Exquisite, she said and smiled. Darcy, did you see the sunrise this morning? It was stupendously beautiful. Truly one of the best I've seen in the Northern Hemisphere.

No, I did not see the sunrise, I answered, but I have a question for you. Please tell me your secret. Why are you always so cheerful?

You think I'm cheerful?

Yes! You're always smiling. You're always happy to see me.

Dear, you bring me chocolate.

Yes, but that one time I forgot, you were still cheerful. You didn't even seem disappointed!

Well, let me think. Fanny sucked on a square, chewed, swallowed. I'm cheerful because the opposite isn't very appealing. It has nothing to do with you or the chocolate or the world at large. I just hate being in a bad mood. Good cheer is a selfish gesture, now that I'm thinking about it.

So you force yourself to be cheerful?

Fanny smiled. Well, there's always something to be cheerful about. It's not that difficult.

But Fanny, the world is depressing. I'm not even talking about the news. I'm talking about the Community Board and all those aggrieved dog poop people and grumpy driveway hogs and fearful gang spotters. My friend Marcus is trying to build a playground and people are mad about it. Mad! About a kids' playground! And, come on, are there really *gangs* in Murbridge?

Fanny tilted her head. It's been a while since I've walked our mean streets, she said, but my guess is no. People are generally afraid of material and bodily harm. It's the survival instinct, Darcy, don't judge.

If you're too old for bogeyman under the bed, you need another imaginary monster to blame for your fears.

And you don't find that depressing?

I've seen plenty of real monsters, Fanny said. But some people haven't. It's not their fault, exactly, it's the natural limitations of their experience. They don't realize how great they have it. Honestly, I think everyone should face a firing squad or serious car accident. A near-death experience is good for the soul. Then everyone would stop believing in imaginary monsters and find something to feel cheerful about. And *then* they'd be more vigilant about the real monsters. Here Fanny paused. Darcy, I know we usually talk about you and your problems, but perhaps we can discuss me today? What do you think about my escape plan?

Last week, Fanny had handed me an elaborate sketch and outline of her illicit exit from the Marian Sisters. The proposal included bird-calls, headlamps, a length of bedsheet and Fanny scaling three stories down to a waiting car (preferably convertible) with me inside, ready to speed off.

Um, Fanny, I'm not so sure about your plan, I said. It seems a little, well, dangerous.

I am perfectly capable of descending the side of this building. Look at all those toeholds. Fanny gestured to the stone walls. I was always an excellent rope climber in gym class.

But it's been a while since you climbed a rope, right, Fanny?

Fanny rolled her eyes. The one characteristic I cannot abide, Darcy Clipper, is meekness. Do not be meek. Be bold. My body may be weaker than it once was, but my mind remains strong. I remain strong. Why aren't *you* strong?

I did not answer Fanny immediately. First, because the question seemed a bit rude. And second, because deep down I knew she was right. I wasn't strong, I was meek. And I didn't know why. I could blame my parents for loving me too much or Skip for leaving me or

Todd Pevzner for breaking up with me the morning after prom, but if my months of solitude had shown me one thing, it was that staring down your own bogeymen took time and patience and was really, really hard. My imaginary monsters still lurked around the bed. I wouldn't be strong until I'd faced each and every one of them.

I'm trying, Fanny, I said at last. Can you wait for me? I'll get you out of here, I promise, but not yet.

Darcy, you may have noticed, but I'm not getting any younger. Please hurry up with whatever internal soul-searching you need to do, stop being such a snowflake and start lifting weights because you may need to catch me. I measured, and the sheet only gets me to the top of the first floor—I'll still be a good eight feet off the ground. Fanny paused, gazing at me steadily. I'm too tired for a longer visit today, she declared, closing her eyes and leaning her head back against the chair. I'll see you next time, dear.

Her words felt like a rejection and, like most rejections, this one stung. But there was nothing more I could say: Fanny was already snoring.

Dear Neighbors, thank you for the feedback about the community playscape. I'd like to answer some of the questions I've received. 1) Yes, our plans meet all building permit requirements, which is why the Board of Selectmen issued us a building permit last year for the project. 2) No, I don't want anyone to sue me. 3) Unfortunately I can't allow adults weighing more than 250 pounds on the gargantuan trampoline—those safety limits are set by the manufacturer, not me. Sorry! 4) While it may seem "weird" to many of you that Dan and I are investing in a public playground on private property, please remember that we have three active boys who love to run around and play. The town's public playground isn't safe or exciting enough to keep them entertained, so we'd be building our own space anyhow. We wanted to give back to our community and also help children develop the skills so necessary to thrive later in life. 5) I'm a Pisces. 6) Dan and I married in 2010 after four years of dating. He's from Vermont, I'm from Michigan. 7) Dan is a Libra and, yes, what you've heard is true, he manages a hedge fund. 8) We will abide by all town rules regarding noise and activity after hours. We will close the space at 6:00 pm in winter and 8:00 pm in summer to ensure we don't bother our neighbors. 9) The Sergeant Cooper Day School playground is a fine facility. We toured it last year with our boys. However, their playground is closed to all but paying students and has only one poorly maintained swing for differently abled children. We want to build something more inclusive. 10) Yes, our space will be ADA compliant with ramps and equipment for kids of all abilities. 11) No, we won't charge admission. 12) I'd rather not provide my phone number here, and no, we're not open to polyamory, but please drop me an email if you'd like to chat more about the playscape.

Thank you all for your support,

Marcus and Dan Dash-LaGrand, and our sons Xanther, Ludovic and Phineas

•

NEIGHBORS: our petition to STOP THE BUILD, SAVE MURBRIDGE is going strong! Keep those signatures coming! Honorably, Free Leader of the Selectmen, Jake Zdzynzky

•

POLL: how much money would you spend weekly on local leisure activities like gambling and/or amusement park attractions? ☐ $100 ☐ $500 ☐ $1,000 ☐ much more

•

WARNING: the tall gang member is back in town. I saw him this afternoon wandering slowly, wearing his gang attire pocket vest and holding some kind of weapon. I called the police but the line was busy.

•

The Murbridge Mushroom Fest is just around the corner! Volunteers still needed for food prep, set up and break down. Please email Pat Pernicky or Hildegard Hyman on the Select Board.

•

To the gross woman in the white Volvo who stole my contact lenses off my porch: I hope you get pink eye and die. I have a very strong prescription and astigmatism so you can't even resell the lenses, loser.

•

Darling, where have the tulips gone? I'm sorry, darling. Please forgive me, please.

MARCUS, DO YOU EVER WONDER about the tulip lady? I stepped back from the table saw and pushed my safety goggles onto my forehead. Today, Marcus was showing me how to use his favorite power tool. We had started at 6 a.m. because, as Marcus told me, I had a lot to learn. The work was dirty, sweaty and loud and I loved every minute of it. When the metal saw bit through the wood it made a screaming sound that I imagined was similar to the sound inside my soul.

Tulip who? Marcus asked.

The person on the Community Board who always talks about tulips.

Marcus opened his mouth and closed it again. I knew there was a reason we were friends, he said. *Yes*, I do wonder about the tulip lady, but I call her the "darling" lady. What is her deal? Why is she always apologizing?

I'm thinking she wants to clear her conscience, I said. I bet she did something very, very bad.

Exactly. She must have really burned this "darling" character. It's so intriguing. Marcus paused. What if two amateur sleuths try to find her?

No, I said sternly. Don't even think about it. Let the tulip lady come clean without fear of repercussion or judgment. The board is a safe space for her, let's not ruin it.

I think I'm done with the Community Board anyhow, said Marcus. My posts about the playscape crashed and burned.

They did not. Just give it some time. Those *Oprah* magazines are going like hotcakes. I pulled my safety goggles back into position. Now let's rip these boards, I said.

Today we were working on the magical tire tower, the coup de grâce of the playscape. It was a distinct nod to Lady Marjory's junk playgrounds of postwar London, but she'd built for kids who cowered in bomb shelters and sent their dads off to war and probably subsisted on dandelions and local squirrels. Murbridge kids weren't quite so hardy. Rather than a mountain of old tires in the middle of a field, Marcus's tower of faux tires would include a central core of heat-activated color and sound. As a kid climbed, the tower would change color and play samples of Marcus's greatest hits: Ella Fitzgerald, Beethoven's Ninth, Bob Marley, the Pixies, Cher. He'd already hired a digital sound artist and engineer to build the computerized parts. He and I would help Burt and the crew with the tower's frame, hence the need for me to become acquainted with the table saw.

I resumed cutting, but I noticed that Marcus hadn't moved a muscle. He was standing motionless, arms rigid at his sides, hands balled into fists, an unhealthy sheen to his eyes. We hadn't taken a break all morning, even when Burt and the crew showed up with donuts and iced chai.

Marcus, I asked now, what's going on?

Nothing, he said through gritted teeth. But you are not cutting straight lines. They're sloppy and inefficient. I've been quiet about it all morning, but your technique is atrocious.

Okay, let's step away from the highly dangerous power tool, I said and pulled off my work gloves. Time for a break. Maybe Burt and the boys left some donuts?

Doubtful. That's a donut-loving crew.

What about some *Law & Order* to calm down? I suggested.

You are obsessed with Detective Logan, Marcus replied, but his fists relaxed, his shoulders fell.

Only a minor obsession, I replied. One episode, then we'll get back to improving my table saw skills.

Deal, said Marcus. He looked at his watch. Is eleven a.m. too early for popcorn and martinis?

I shrugged. We'll call it an early lunch.

APPROXIMATELY FIVE HOURS later, we were on episode number four, martini number three, when I heard a loud banging.

Marcus, I said, pausing the show; we were mid-interrogation scene. I think someone's at the door.

Marcus disappeared to check. A few minutes later he returned with a medium-sized, red-faced, red-haired man wearing what looked like a Native American headdress from the dollar store: gleaming pleather, feathers in primary colors that drooped from their glued-on mounts, silver bells left over from a Christmas shop explosion.

He bowed. Hola, he said. I'm Jake Zdzynzky.

Marcus looked at me, raised one eyebrow and said: Jake, this is my friend and colleague, Darcy Clipper.

Jake tilted his head. The bells on his headdress tinkled. Clipper? he asked. Are you Stan and Jeanine's kid?

That's me, I said.

Best poker game in Murbridge, said Jake. Every week, I cleaned out that whole room. Shame when Stan shut it down. How are they doing?

They're great, I said. Fantastic. Living the good life in Arizona. Sun, lizards, macramé.

Huh, Jake grunted. I hear it's a dry heat down there.

We settled ourselves on the sectional in the living room. Jake removed his headdress, bells a-jingle, and placed it on a cushion.

I'm getting in touch, he said. You know, with my native ancestors. He pointed to the ceiling.

I didn't realize you were indigenous, Marcus said. Tell me, what tribe?

We're a diverse nation, Jake said solemnly. We're all one tribe. And I believe that's a racist question.

Marcus smiled.

I voted for Obama, Jake said. Both times.

How can I help you today? Marcus asked, still smiling.

It's a shame about the petition. Jake sat back, crossed an ankle over a knee and exhaled loudly. I mean, you can't blame your neighbors, really. You're making a lot of noise, dust and whatnot. Am I right, Mr. Dash? Or are you Mr. LaGrand?

Please. Call me Marcus.

Marcus, you've got a big build going on here.

As you know, the Select Board approved our permit months ago. We're proceeding according to the plans I submitted. Your efforts to overturn that permit strike me as inappropriate and very fucking shady.

I stifled a giggle. Jake blinked.

Well, I don't think we need to use profanity. Jake glanced in my direction. Especially not in the presence of a—

I coughed loudly and violently, hacking up a pretend bit of phlegm, and then pretended to deposit it into a tissue. I picked up my martini glass and sipped. Allergies, I said.

Jake turned back to Marcus. I've come here to make you an offer. A very generous offer. Remember when you and your partner bought this house? Remember the anonymous bidder?

Marcus nodded. I do.

That was me. Well, technically my investment vehicle, Zeus Capital LLC, but really it was me. And listen, I'm still a big fan of this space and especially your empty lot next door. A big big fan. My business partners and I have been eyeing that lot for years. We've kept the plan under wraps, but—here Jake lowered his voice and leaned forward and, despite myself, I leaned forward too—just imagine: an epic entertainment complex. Restaurant, spa, indoor pool, six-screen cinema showing family and, ahem, adult fare. It'll be amazing. Eventually, I'm even thinking *casino*. He raised his eyebrows. Given, you know, my heritage. The tax benefits! Jake whistled. Don't get me started.

A casino in Murbridge? I said. Are you insane?

Jake ignored me. I've been doing market research, he continued, eyes on Marcus. Some informal polling of the community. And I can tell you there's a lot of local interest in the project. A *lot*. It's a sure thing. A no-lose proposition. Nothing could derail us. We'll pack 'em in, shoulder to shoulder!

Marcus was slowly shaking his head. Oh Jake, I don't even know where to begin.

Jake shrugged. I don't expect you people to get it. But I do know that you and your family are having a rough time here in Murbridge. I'm getting the feeling you don't really fit in. This is an old town, old families, we like to do things a certain way. Know what I mean? So on behalf of Zeus Capital LLC, I'd like to offer you a very generous exit strategy.

Marcus remained stony-faced, silent for five seconds. Ten. Twelve.

The tension in the room became intense, unbearable. I was just about to yell something nonsensical or begin tickling Jake when, at last, Marcus spoke. Jake, he said, you have nothing I want. No offer would make me leave this town or abandon my plans for the playscape. Thank you for stopping by—here Marcus stood up—but I think it's time for you to go.

Jake placed the headdress back on his head—*jingle tinkle jingle*—and then stood up.

The petition isn't going away, he said as we walked him to the door. The people have spoken. They want a reevaluation of your permit and, as chair of the selectmen, I can only serve the people's will. Here Jake paused. And, Marcus, he said in a low voice. I think things will only get worse for you here. I suggest you consider my offer. I'll email you. Bueno?

Have a nice night, Marcus said and closed the door.

You were awesome! I cheered. Just like Brando in that *Godfather* scene where he talks all growly and doesn't smile.

The nerve, said Marcus. *Things will only get worse,* he repeated in a whiny Jake-ish voice. Was he threatening me?

It was hard to tell. The headdress was very distracting.

That man doesn't know who he's up against. Marcus paused. But seriously, Darcy, I'm worried. What if he's dangerous?

Dangerous? Jake? Only if you're close enough to get a whiff of his breath. Hella halitosis.

But Marcus did not laugh at my obviously amusing comment. His brow was furrowed, his eyes dark.

What if Jake is only the tip of the iceberg?

What iceberg?

The Murbridge-is-rotten iceberg.

You've lost me.

Maybe things *will* get worse for us. Maybe Jake really *does* speak for the people. Maybe I was wrong about this town.

And now I understood what Marcus was saying. Oh no no no, I said, shaking my head. Jake is not the tip of any iceberg. He's an outlier. A rogue asshole. He won the selectmen election because only three people showed up to vote. Jake just wants to go on Disney Cruises!

I don't care why Jake wants us out of Murbridge. Disney, money, mushrooms, sex, race, whatever. I want to belong here, I want my family to belong here. I want my sons to feel surrounded by love and acceptance. I want them to feel at home. Marcus stopped. His voice had a solemnity I hadn't heard before.

I know this town, I said. Murbridge is not rotten. Trust me.

For a moment longer than felt comfortable, Marcus gazed at me with narrowed eyes and an expression of deep skepticism. Okay, he said at last. I'll assume Jake's a rogue asshole with bad breath—for now. But I'm on high alert for more indicators of general rottenness. And then Marcus grinned.

Let's get back to Detective Logan, he said, picking up the remote control. We were mid-interrogation scene. The suspense is killing me.

Dear Mom and Daddy,

Thank you for the information on Jake Zdzynzky. Long story short—not that I owe you any information about my present life, but I am a kindhearted person—I've been working part-time on a private playground construction project. Jake is trying to shut it down because he claims it's an eyesore and unbecoming to a town like Murbridge. He's the eyesore, but I digress.

While the tidbits regarding Jake's halitosis and misogyny were certainly interesting and definitely accurate, you unfortunately failed to produce any information that's helpful. Would you say he has violent tendencies? Any history of psychosis? Leadership role in an underground militia? I fear that my sheltered upbringing has limited my ability to see the true evil intent lurking beneath Jake's goofy exterior.

And why exactly did you move to Arizona? Do you think Murbridge is rotten?

Please only respond if you have information that can be of use to me.

Sincerely,

Darcy

Darcy,

Thank you for your recent message. We hadn't heard from you in nearly two weeks and were beginning to worry. Daddy wants desperately to put this time behind us and so do I. But I have a few words for you first. You may not enjoy hearing this, but it's high time I spoke my mind. Darcy, we've tried to understand your concerns, but enough is enough. You're a grown woman and we cannot continue to hold your hand every step of the way. We may need to sell the house. There, I've said it. We know you're adamantly opposed to the idea, but Murbridge has changed since you've been gone. We've changed too. It's just not the right fit for us anymore.

While I'm speaking frankly, I will also say that your antagonism and blame have caused me and your father much pain. And when I say pain, I mean literal physical agony. Daddy's been getting those migraines again and I have the worst tension in my upper back. Pilar, my favorite masseuse, tells me it's like pushing on leather when she rubs me down. Leather, Darcy. Hard, unyielding cowhide. That's what you've done to me. But I have no doubt that if my back muscles can move beyond this, we all can move beyond this.

Regarding your question, Jake Zdzynzky, as I believe I already told you, is a flawed human being, as we all are. He does have a penchant for get-rich-quick schemes. Hence the cheating at poker. He also owned a Blockbuster franchise way back when, poor guy. And invested with some man in New York who conned a lot of very rich people. Then he took over the family business Gems-n-Things, which no one would mistake for Tiffany's. The distinction between the gems and the things is often difficult to determine. Jake has ridden a lot of waves, but I don't believe he'd ever resort to violence. Have you been watching too much *Law & Order* again, Darcy? Your last letter described an incredibly odd situation. Playscape? Evil intent? Underground militia? What the hell is going on over there?

Let me convey a note of caution: we're all trying to do the very best we can, Darcy. Even someone like Jake. While it's not your job to help him, perhaps you can try to understand him and approach the situation with the tiniest bit of empathy. Do you get what I'm saying, dear? You young people see the world in black and white, this or that, one extreme or the other. There's a lot of gray. There's a lot of muddle. I'd like to think that Jake has changed since those unfortunate poker nights. Anyone can change; it's one of the few reasons to remain hopeful in this crazy world. Think about that, Darcy.

Now I must get to bed. Your father is yelling at me to turn off the goddamn light. I hope to see you soon.

Love, Mom

PS: We moved to Arizona because after thirty-one years of listening to your father complain about humidity, I decided enough is enough. No, Darcy, Murbridge is not rotten.

Volunteers will be at Price Chopper, Trader Joe's and Costco today to collect signatures for SAVE MURBRIDGE, STOP THE BUILD petition. Our children deserve better! Honorably yours, Leader of the Selected Men, Jake Zdzynzky

•

Help me, please help. I'm being held against my will. Won't someone help me?

•

Reminder: our annual Mushroom Festival is only 6 weeks from today! We need volunteers for the FunGuy competition, bobbing for mushrooms and cleanup. You make the festival happen! Volunteer today! Contact Hildegard Hyman or Pat Pernicky.

•

NOTICE: a special Board of Selectmen meeting will be held Tuesday following the Mushroom Festival to discuss recent developments in zoning consideration. See attached agenda. Honorably, Jake Zdzynzky, Selected President

•

Darling, can you hear the rain? It's a lovely sound. Don't be afraid. I'll be with you soon.

•

Darling, remember the dark grass and bent tulip stems? Remember the foggy night and the cold grip of my hand? I tried but I could not warm you. Please forgive me, darling.

•

Help me, I urgently need help! I'm a prisoner in need of rescue. Please help!

OMAR, I THINK WE'VE GOT a situation.

I had my laptop open, my phone on speaker.

Is someone else spying on you? asked Omar.

No. This is a non-drone-related situation involving a person being held against her will.

Come again?

I'm concerned about the tulip lady.

Darcy, please back up.

The tulip lady. She posts on the Community Board all the time. You haven't seen her?

I don't spend as much time on that message board as you do.

This, I realized, was probably true of most Murbridge residents. So I told Omar about the charming and anonymous tulip lady, the mysterious messages and the recent cries for help.

Listen to this one, I said. *Help me, please help. I'm being held against my will. Won't someone help me?* I paused for dramatic effect and then said: Is that chilling or what?

Bone-tingling, Omar replied. And why do you think the cries for help are coming from the person you refer to as the tulip lady?

A hunch.

A hunch?

A very strong hunch.

Darcy, you need to stop watching *Law & Order*.

I'm totally over Detective Logan. And I'm not imaging this! I know it's the tulip lady asking for help. She appears just a few posts down with her usual messages to "darling."

Darling?

Yes, darling?

Pause. So let me get this straight, said Omar sternly, an anonymous someone addresses messages about tulips to an anonymous "darling" on the town Community Board and you think this person needs help?

Yes. Exactly. Please, can you make sure she's okay? There's got to be a way to track these messages. Cell towers, surveillance cameras, satellite signals, infrared heat maps.

You *have* been watching *Law & Order*.

Please don't condescend. This is serious.

Omar sighed. I'm sorry, I'm just tired. I was up all night with my dog. She's been really sick, poor baby.

Oh, I didn't know you had a dog, Omar. What kind? What's her name?

Her name is Lucinda and she's a top-of-the-line, full-bred mutt. I'm guessing pit bull, Maltese, poodle mix. I got her from a rescue in Springfield.

Memories of my pet-finding days came flooding back. The mutts were always my favorite. Scrappy, honest, the most earnest hand lickers. Knowing that Omar was a pet owner placed him in an entirely new light. Where before I'd valued his shoulders and drone expertise, I now valued his heart. And also his shoulders.

What does the vet say? I asked.

I'm headed there after work. They're still running tests. But thanks for the concern, Darcy. I'll let you know how it goes.

Please do.

Maybe you two can meet sometime.

You mean face-to-face? Nose to snout?

That's an odd way to put it, but yes, that was my meaning.

I paused. Omar's suggestion would move us out of the professional, perfunctory, drone-related sphere and into something new. Meeting a person's dog meant you were more than acquaintances; it meant you were friends. I immediately began to sweat.

Yeah, okay, maybe, I said, hoping to walk that fine line between polite and discouraging. And you'll check on the tulip lady for me, right?

Yes, said Omar. I'll see if I can track down a board moderator, someone who has access to people's real names and information.

Pat Pernicky is the moderator.

Of course it's Pat. Okay, I'll give her a call. And Darcy, whatever we find out, don't worry about the tulip lady. If she has internet access, she'd contact the police directly if she were in any real trouble—not post on a town message board.

I see your point.

Please don't turn into a conspiracy theorist, Omar continued. We've got enough of those already. I spend half my time tracking down UFO and Rudy Giuliani sightings.

Conspiracies? Ha! Don't worry about me, Officer. I'm sane, vain and in the game. If you need me, baby, I'll be riding the stability train.

I stopped speaking. Oh no, I thought, it was happening again, my verbal diarrhea. An image of Barnum and Clementine flashed before my eyes.

Sorry, what did you say? Omar asked.

Nothing to worry your pretty little head about, Officer Omar. And don't worry those shoulders either. Head and shoulders. Dandruff. I mean, don't worry. I mean—I have to go now.

I hung up, breathing heavily, my heart banging away as though I'd just run around the block, or halfway around the block.

Fred! I called to my absent fern, why am I still such a freak?

EXACTLY ONE WEEK later, Marcus and I drove to Pittsfield, a town located far enough from Murbridge that running into someone familiar was highly unlikely but near enough that we would make it back in time for Xanther's 3:15 lacrosse game.

Together, we stood outside a Starbucks.

We'll take it slow, said Marcus.

Promise me you won't leave, I said and grabbed his hand.

I promise. Just remember what we talked about. Remember your breathing. And the wheat field.

Okay. I inhaled and exhaled through my nose. I imagined a field of golden wheat blowing in the wind. I'd never seen such a field in real life nor did I have any positive connotations with farming, flour, Kansas or any other wheat-based concepts (although I sure did like pasta), but this was what Marcus had advised. Or rather, what Marcus's therapist and support group in Ann Arbor had advised. There were benefits to having a best friend with a history of nervous breakdowns.

After the disastrous Omar conversation, I'd confided in Marcus. My embarrassing social awkwardness, my gaiter wearing, my avoidance of eye contact, my weird urge to say inappropriate things—I laid it all out there for Marcus to examine, critique and ridicule.

But he did nothing of the sort. Marcus listened carefully and then said: I'm no shrink but your symptoms seem more situational than clinical. You were fine before the period of self-imposed isolation and canned food consumption, am I right?

I nodded.

Okay, then. You just need a basic refresher course. Marcus patted my hand. Don't worry. I know exactly what to do. You'll be back to normal levels of social awkwardness in no time.

Today was my first Starbucks. I closed my eyes.

I've got the wheat field, I told Marcus. The golden shafts are blowing. It's very peaceful.

Perfect. Marcus squeezed my hand. Okay, I think we're ready.

I opened my eyes and pulled open the door.

Inside, there were about a dozen people, a few sitting down, looking at their phones; a few more waiting around, looking at their phones; four people standing in line, looking at their phones. We took a place at the back of the line.

See? whispered Marcus. No one even noticed you. You're just a regular person. No one cares about you!

I imagined the wheat. Yes, I breathed. No one cares what I say or do. I scanned the room for problematic people—Mrs. Pevzner, Georgina Oliver, Omar—and felt my shoulders drop when I recognized no one. A Starbucks full of strangers who didn't care about me. *Jackpot.*

I closed my eyes as we waited: *wheat, wheat, wheat.*

Okay, I think I can do this, I said.

Just remember the words, whispered Marcus.

The line moved up again.

Do you want to practice first? whispered Marcus.

No, I'm ready.

We were two people away . . . one person. And then it was my turn.

The words, remember the words.

Good morning, I said. I'll have a double-shot Americano, twelve-ounce with milk, and a blueberry muffin, please.

Name? asked the Starbucks employee, a teenagery-looking gender-fluid person with a pierced nose and expertly applied black eyeliner.

Darcy, I answered with confidence, making direct eye contact that I hoped was not freakishly intense.

And mmm amp blab syllable you blab?

The teenager had asked me a question, but I had no idea what they were saying. My wheat field began to fade.

Excuse me? I said. I could feel Marcus tensing up beside me.

Mmmm you syllable blab syllable syllable mmm oh? Their mouth was moving, their kohl-rimmed eyes seemed kind, but they appeared to be playing a trick on me. Or perhaps my hearing had worsened over the last few months of speaking so loudly to Fred.

Relax, Marcus whispered into my ear. Remember, we practiced this. Unexpected follow-up questions. Just take it slow.

The teenager's face was frozen in a look of cheerful expectation with a distinct undertone of impatience. Behind me, bodies shifted, sighs were heaved.

Wheat, wheat, wheat.

Sorry, could you please repeat that one more time? I said. My hearing isn't so great.

The teenager blinked and then said very loudly: ALMOND. SOY. HEMP. OAT. SKIM. TWO PERCENT. OR WHOLE.

Oh! I could have cried with relief. Marcus and I *had* practiced this.

Whole is fine, I replied. Thank you.

I paid, I accepted my change, I moved along, I took my place to wait for the order. Relief flooded me: yes, I was just another anonymous loser hanging out in Starbucks.

You did it! Marcus said and hugged me.

Next time, I'll ask for something really complicated, I said. Like a triple grand Frappuccino rainbow caramel thing with extra whipped cream and lots of sprinkles. And I'll definitely ask for hemp milk.

That's my girl, said Marcus. I'm so proud.

NEIGHBORS: (trigger warning)—I'm shocked and saddened to report the discovery of <u>pornography</u> in the Little Free Library at 32 Lincoln Avenue, site of that enormous construction project. Last night, during an evening walk, my wife and I saw several magazines that caught our eye: Toes & Arches, Senior Love, Bear Love and Big Bad Babies alongside recent copies of Martha Stewart and Oprah. My wife grabbed the lot. (Books take so long to read—she prefers magazines.) But imagine our horror when we arrived home: some of the magazines contained photos of a highly sexual nature. It was disgusting stuff, truly abnormal and vile. Men pretending to be giant babies? Women having sex with stuffed teddy bears? Dirty toe cleavage? Gross. I could barely flip the pages without gagging. Let me be clear: I'm perfectly fine with consenting adults participating in such activities behind closed doors. If a young man wants to dress like a baby and run around with other babies, peace be with you. But the Little Free Libraries are open to all—including women and children—and should not contain graphic sexual material. It's clearly inappropriate and possibly illegal to circulate porn in a family neighborhood. I'm looking into possible litigation on the subject and will update the community as I know more. For now, I send this post as a warning. First, to my neighbors: look closely before grabbing a seemingly innocent piece of literature from a Little Free Library. Second, to the person who believed it AOK to stock our community book shares with porn: STOP immediately or suffer the consequences. Honorably, Jake Zdzynzky, concerned community member and President of the Selectmen

---

THE NEXT DAY, I ARRIVED early for work. Marcus was drinking coffee and biting his fingernails in the kitchen, the boys were upstairs with their morning screen time.

Marcus, stop biting! I said as I walked through the door.

Everyone assumes we're responsible, said Marcus, putting his hands in his lap. I built that frigging library in the first place.

And you didn't—?

Of course I didn't!

Sorry, I had to ask. You did say banned books.

Really, Darcy. I didn't mean actual pornography.

It's probably just some teenagers playing a prank. It'll blow over.

Marcus paused. Or it was Jake.

That's very conspiracy theory.

He said things will only get worse. This is what he meant. He's trying to turn the town against us. Pressure us to sell.

Oh Marcus, I don't know. That seems like a stretch.

No, said Marcus firmly, it was Jake. The problem is proving it.

On *Law & Order* they always look for surveillance cameras, I replied, trying to be helpful.

Who would conduct surveillance on a Little Free Library?

Maybe we should break into Jake's house and look for copies of *Arch & Toe*?

Look who's talking now, Darcy. That's breaking and entering. We could get into big trouble.

What does Dan think?

Oh, Dan's busy with this thing in Lithuania. Or is it Latvia? I can never keep my Baltics straight. I haven't told him. I'd never bother him about something like this. Marcus paused. But why do you care what *Dan* thinks? What about what *I* think?

Marcus, does Dan actually exist? I asked.

Of course he exists. He travels a lot, but I can assure you, he is in fact a flesh and blood man who gets jet-lagged and pissy on the regular. And who I wish was home more often.

Just then, Xanther entered the room. He was gangly and big-footed and I swear he'd grown another inch in the past week. Dad, Xanther said and tilted his head, pushing his chin toward Marcus.

Let me look, Marcus replied. He took hold of Xanther's chin, looking intently at each cheek.

Not bad, Marcus said. Only one, and he pointed to a tiny drop of red rising at the top of Xanther's neck.

Shit, Xanther replied and reached a hand to wipe away the spot. Okay, gotta run. Playing some D&D at Jonah's house. Bye, Dad, bye, Darcy, and he kissed Marcus on the cheek and loped out of the room.

Shaving, Marcus said. You should have seen him the first time. It was a bloodbath.

You're such a good dad, I said. Really, Marcus. I know you need more than parenting to justify your life, I get it, but your boys are—I stopped. They're just—I stopped again as a thickness rose in my throat, not social awkwardness, but a memory of those long months of IVF needles and drugs, waiting and disappointment. I blinked and waited for the memory to pass.

Marcus, would you say you have a parental instinct? I asked.

Marcus snorted. Me? What do you think? I just love the hell out of them and try my best. He smiled. Hey, why don't you come for Friday falafel night? Dan promised me he'd be home this weekend. You can put to rest any lingering doubts about his existence.

You mean you want me to eat dinner with you and your whole family?

That's exactly what we do with our falafel, said Marcus. It doesn't hold up well for tennis. I've tried.

I considered. Yes, I wanted to eat falafel with Marcus and his family, really I did, but I didn't feel ready. Or prepared. Or worthy. That was the crux of it—I didn't feel that I, socially awkward, unloved, underemployed, underfriended Darcy deserved an evening with a beautiful family like the one belonging to Marcus. Plus, Dan was an extremely intelligent, successful and wealthy man who, if the fridge photos were accurate, was also smoking hot and the idea of speaking coherently and articulately to Dan stressed me out. The nearly disastrous conversation with Omar remained fresh in my mind. True, I'd made progress with the Starbucks visit and Marcus's coaching, but I wasn't ready for full-on social interaction with a specimen like Dan. Or the kids. Especially the kids. Look what had happened with a bloody-faced Xanther. Every time I even looked at little Phin, something went squishy inside my chest.

I can't this week, I said.

Okay, said Marcus. But consider Friday night an open invitation. I hope you say yes soon.

I love falafel, I said. I will. Soon. And listen—this Little Free Library thing will blow over. It's a prank. No one cares! I paused. What did you do with the magazines?

They're upstairs in my sock drawer. I'm going to search YouTube on how to dust for fingerprints.

I've never seen men in giant baby suits, I said.

Leave it that way, Marcus replied. Trust me, you'll sleep better.

THE NEXT DAY, I took a morning supply run to Home Depot for some sandpaper, grout and Skittles. When I finally got to Marcus's place, I noticed a small group of people walking in circles holding what looked from a distance like giant flowers. Is today a Dutch national holiday? I wondered. But as I drew closer, I saw they were not flowers at all but signs. Big signs, printed with big ugly letters. STOP THE BUILD! IF THERE'S SMOKE, THERE'S FIRE! NO MORE PORN! PROTECT OUR CHILDREN! GO HOME!

There were only five people, but they were yelling very loudly and they did not stop to say hello as I walked past.

I went around to the back door. Marcus was sitting at the picnic table, drinking mint tea and reading some Rumi.

Marcus, do you know what's going on out there?

Marcus closed the book. Free speech, he said.

I really thought this would blow over.

Marcus shrugged. It's only five people. Shall we get to work?

THE NEXT DAY, there were a dozen people and their signs were bigger.

Marcus was inside, drinking coffee and reading *The Atlantic*. The free speech is getting louder, he said.

I don't even recognize anyone out there. I think they must be from out of town.

You still think this will blow over? Marcus asked and began sniffing. I'm getting a distinct whiff of rot. Sniff sniff.

Maybe you should call the police, I said.

That will only make things worse. Marcus paused. But wait—are you trying to arrange a visit with your Officer Omar?

I rolled my eyes.

You like a man in uniform, Darcy, admit it.

We're acquaintances, Marcus. More like professional colleagues. I'm trying to establish a pattern of harassing drone behavior. That's all. Oh, and he's also agreed to check on the tulip lady for me.

Wait—what's wrong with our darling tulip lady?

You didn't see the posts? I cracked open my laptop and brought up the Community Board. Look. I pointed to the screen. *Help me, please help me.*

Oh, that's not the tulip lady. There's no "darling."

I know it's her, I said. And I'm worried.

We bent our heads to the laptop, refreshing the Community Board posts, scanning for more "darling" references. And then we hopped over to People.com and then TMZ and then we decided to check out real estate in the Bahamas and then the Caribbean and then maybe a Pacific island or two. I was relieved to have distracted Marcus from the protestors. I still believed the public outrage would die down. A dozen protestors did not mean that Murbridge was rotten. A dozen protestors indicated only that a dozen grumpy people had nothing better to do on a Wednesday morning than walk around in a circle and yell silly slogans.

After an hour or two of comforting, pointless internet browsing, we heard a noise.

What the—? said Marcus, jumping up. That sounded like glass breaking.

Glass? I said, eyes still on the seven-bed, ten-bath villa currently going for $12.7 mil on St. Barts. Um, I don't think so.

I think it came from inside the house, said Marcus.

The boys were at camp, due home in time for dinner. Harriet had taken the week off for a trip to the Cape. Burt and the crew had already left for the day. There was alarm in Marcus's voice, but it seemed distant, not close enough to touch me.

I don't think so, Marcus, I said. No one's home. You're imagining it.

I am not imagining it, Marcus replied. We both paused, listening. Silence.

See, it's nothing, I said. Probably your neighbor just dropped a pitcher of margaritas and the glass broke. Hey, can we have some margaritas?

But Marcus wasn't listening to me. He cocked his head and then disappeared through the patio doors.

I stayed where I was, wondering about the tulip lady and was she really in trouble and was I becoming a conspiracy theorist? And who wants to live in a house with ten bathrooms? And did Omar think I was definitely a fool or could I remedy the situation? And wow, Omar's shoulders did look nice in his uniform. And maybe I was ready to meet his dog, and I bet his dog would love me. Basically, I was thinking about myself and not about Marcus or the noise that had, indeed, come from inside. Five minutes passed. Then ten.

Marcus? I called.

No reply.

Marcus? Are you making margaritas?

No reply.

Marcus? Salt on mine!

Silence.

Marcus?

I pushed myself up and wandered inside.

Where are you?

I found Marcus in the front living room. He was sitting on the couch with his head in his hands. The picture window was cracked, jagged, with dusky air and mosquitoes floating into the room. Broken glass from the window littered the floor and in the middle of it all was a brick wrapped with a scrap of paper.

What the hell? I said.

Marcus lifted his head. This is not free speech.

I tiptoed through the glass, picked up the brick and unwrapped the paper.

Go home faggs, I read slowly. But look—I pointed to Marcus. They misspelled *fags*—they put two *g*'s.

Marcus smiled grimly. They're homophobic and they're bad spellers. What is *wrong* with people?

I don't know, I said and the words felt pathetic and small. Some people are just so—so—so—

Crappy? Marcus finished my thought. Ignorant? Angry? Hurtful? he continued, his voice rising. Xenophobic? Homophobic? Racist? Full of hate? Crazy, lazy, stupid, resentful, *afraid*? He paused. Some people are all these things. My brother is homophobic, to cite one example. Dan's mother is racist—she loves her grandsons, but she can't stand me. He inhaled deeply and shook his head.

I looked outside, scanning for the protestors, but the street was empty now.

Marcus, I asked, what should we do?

We surveyed the broken window, the shattered glass, the streak of dirt where the brick had skidded across the carpet.

Well, he said. Let's clean up before the boys get home. And then we'll call Officer Omar. And then we'll finish plans for the tower and the paintball course and show Jake and all these fuckers that Dan and I are not going anywhere. We are *already* home.

CONSIDER THE CHINYINGI footbridge, *National Geographic,* October 1997. The Zambezi River stretches sixteen hundred miles across southern Africa, from the central Zambian wetlands to the Indian Ocean. It's wide and wild and very difficult to cross. One night in 1971, a Roman Catholic priest, a nice old nun and three Zambian apostates tried to cross from the town of Chinyingi to the Zambezi's western bank. It was a notoriously perilous stretch due to the strong current and unpredictable winds. That night, the current surged, the priest navigated poorly and the boat sank. All five perished. News of the tragedy reached a neighboring mission run by a man named Brother Crispin. The deaths moved him. Crispin was a priest, not an engineer, but he began collecting cable and pipes from nearby copper mines. He began sketching and calculating and scheming. Over the course of the next five years, Brother Crispin designed and helped build a seven-hundred-foot-long bridge across the Zambezi River at exactly the spot where that fateful boat had overturned. The bridge still operates today, a slender reed of cables and rope, just wide enough for single-file passage over the churning, dark water below. How did Brother Crispin manage the feat? Many had tried to bridge the river; all had failed. Why did the death of his colleagues affect him so deeply? Was it a shudder of recognition—*there but for the grace of God go I*? Was it regret? Anguish? Guilt? I wonder about Brother Crispin. I wonder about the circumstances that led him to step outside himself and build something grand and enduring, a monument to an emotion that to this day remains hidden from view. A creative solution to a problem that no one but the creator would ever fully understand.

Are any other parents concerned about this Baby Yoda character? Is he a drug lord? Or gang leader? My kids keep mentioning him, but they only laugh when I ask for an explanation.

•

Help needed: I've looked in every Little Free Library in town for porn but no luck. Where exactly did someone find those Bad Baby magazines?

•

ALERT: all the avocados at Price Chopper are rock hard. Don't bother.

•

Neighbors, I took the most wonderful nap yesterday. Have you napped recently? I cannot recommend it highly enough.

•

Darling, do you remember the early summer rains? Do you remember the sound on the roof? I watched you fall asleep, I blessed that rain for how it soothed you.

•

Darling, I'll be with you soon.

THAT SATURDAY, I MADE MY weekly chocolate delivery. Fanny was snoozing in her wheelchair on the lawn when I approached on tiptoe. Just as I lowered myself into my chair, she sat bolt upright and gripped my arm.

Darcy, Fanny said, I must get home. I *must*. Today. Now. She was more agitated than I'd ever seen her. Are you here to take me home?

Fanny looked one way, then the other. A nun loitered near the duck fountain. Fanny narrowed her eyes. That one, she said, cocking her head toward the fountain. She'll go inside in exactly seven minutes to drink her afternoon tea and then fall asleep in a chair. That's our chance! Bring your car around. I can move pretty fast when I need to.

Fanny, remember, I walked here. And besides, *this* is your home.

Are you still chicken, Darcy? *Bok bok bok*? Fanny began waving her elbows like a chicken, clucking and generally mocking me in a way that I found inappropriate for her age.

Fanny. Please.

She lowered her elbows. I'm sorry, Darcy. I can see I struck a nerve. But you're taking too long, dear. I'm running out of time. And there's no one else but you. I've searched and searched for someone, anyone, to help me escape. Please, darling. I'm begging you. Darling, please.

Darling? I said. Fanny, do you post on the Community Board about tulips?

Fanny inhaled sharply. *Shhhh*, she whispered. Don't tell the nuns. We're not supposed to use the computer after three p.m., but I sneak in while the sisters are eating their dinner. Oh, the people in this town are so bonkers! It's wonderful entertainment, dear. I hope you log in from time to time.

Oh, I do, I answered. But why do you always talk about tulips?

I love tulips, Fanny answered. So did Barnaby. Sometimes I pretend I'm writing to him, sending my messages out into the universe. I know it's silly

No, it's not silly. I paused. And so you're the prisoner who needs to escape?

Fanny nodded. Yes, dear. I thought drama might provoke some kindhearted neighbor to respond. Because you clearly won't help me. That last she said in a dark, accusatory voice. I felt a guilty pang strike my meek and cowardly heart.

I'm sorry, Fanny. What if I take some photos of your old house? Would that help?

No. I need to be there. Put my hands in the dirt, my feet on the ground. Photos won't work.

What if I bring you some dirt? Tell me the address. I'm sure the new owners won't mind if I scoop a handful or two.

Fanny shook her head. No, it's not the same.

Well, I'm glad it was you who left those messages, I said, trying to hurry the conversation past my failings. I was so worried. I even asked the police to investigate.

Police? Fanny sat up straight. Her voice had the sharp edge of alarm. What did you tell the police?

I just told my friend Omar that I was worried about the tulip lady.

Did you tell him it was me?

No, I didn't know it was you.

Oh Darcy. I wish you hadn't said anything. I could be in very serious trouble.

I'm sure the nuns will forgive you.

I'm not talking about the nuns, dear. I'm talking about the authorities.

I placed a hand gently on Fanny's shoulder. Posting to the Community Board is not a serious offense. I'll vouch for your good character.

Fanny looked at me sideways. Obviously it's not the posting itself that concerns me.

Oh. I removed my hand. Then what is it?

I did something once. An act that many people would view as morally wrong.

Fanny, you're scaring me.

You're easily scared, dear. I think we've established that.

I groaned. Fanny, please explain. I can't help you if I don't understand what you're talking about.

Fanny closed her eyes for one second, two seconds, three. Then she opened them. A long time ago, she said, I committed a very serious crime. I did not consider it a criminal offense, but many would disagree. No one knows the truth, Darcy, and I would like to keep it that way. Please don't tell anyone about my posts to Barnaby, and especially not the police.

There were so many questions I wanted to ask, but Fanny's eyes were red; her hands, I noticed, were trembling.

I nodded.

You know, dear, she continued, maybe it is better if I stay here. Maybe you're right. Maybe this is the best I can hope for at my age. She patted my hand and gave me a comforting smile, the kind you might give a child.

Oh Fanny, I want to help you escape. I do.

Just keep bringing me chocolate, Fanny said. I'll be fine.

THAT MONDAY MORNING, Marcus was in a mood.

The petition is gaining steam, he said. Jake claims he's got over two hundred signatures. I'm sensing some serious rot in this town, Darcy. Serious. Omar told me there's nothing more he can do about the vandalism. He filed the police report and that's that. Unless the FBI decides to prosecute it as a hate crime, like that'll happen. But, said Marcus, I discovered one very interesting tidbit of information.

Can I please drink my coffee before you tell me? I had a rough weekend. My brain needs to boot up.

Fine.

I sipped while Marcus emptied out the fridge, scrubbed the shelves, refilled the fridge, made paninis for the boys, bleached the sink, fixed a broken ukulele string, mopped the floor, sewed a nose back on a stuffed hedgehog and ran a load of laundry. It was like watching an Energizer Bunny or an episode of *Breaking Bad.*

Are you ready yet? Marcus asked, a dish towel slung over one shoulder.

I feel more exhausted now after watching you but sure—I drained the rest of my coffee. I'm ready. Go.

Okay, so Jake is planning a "Stop the Build" petition table at the Mushroom Festival. He's handing out fidget spinners to anyone who signs the damn thing.

That seems like a conflict of interest, I said. The Mushroom Monarch is a purely bipartisan position. Why is he bringing politics into the sanctity of the Mushroom Fest?

I don't think the guy much cares about separation of powers, Darce. But the significance here is the bribe.

A fidget spinner?

Not a very valuable bribe, true, but in exchange for signing a random piece of paper? I think a fidget spinner would be very persuasive. Those things are fun.

So we're going to sabotage Jake's fidget spinners?

No. What I'm saying is that maybe Murbridge isn't rotten after all. Maybe Murbridge is just easily bought.

And wait—which one are we hoping for? I think I need more caffeine for this conversation, I added, holding out my cup.

Marcus made me another espresso from his shiny Italian machine. We are hoping for easily bought, he continued. Ideally every
person in this town acts on principle, but that's a lot to ask. I think
accidentally doing the wrong thing is something we can fix. Do you
see where I'm going with this?

I nodded. Because if people can be swayed one way by a fidget
spinner, they can be swayed another way by something equally friv-
olous like a nifty travel mug or a hug. Or facts! The truth is often very
persuasive.

So, Marcus continued, I have a favor to ask. I want you to volunteer for the Mushroom Festival. Talk up our mission to the other
volunteers. Togetherness, acceptance, resilience, children. Explain
what we're all about. They'll listen to you—you're a nice girl from
Murbridge. And while you're at it, sniff around. Eavesdrop. What are
people saying about the playscape? Is Murbridge rotten or are people merely eager for fidget spinners? Feel the tenor of the room and
report back.

It's outdoors at Fink Park, I said. The tenor of thirty acres will be
tough to gauge.

I think you understand what I'm asking here.

But, Marcus, I hate the Mushroom Festival.

No. How can you say that? This is your town!

Yes, and every year as a child I'd march on down to the Mushroom
Festival and eat too much cotton candy and not win any prizes in the
ring toss and end up a sugary puddle of despair.

Darcy, please. We only have a week before the special selectmen
meeting. I'm officially worried. We could lose our building permit. I
need to be prepared for that meeting. I need to know what we're up
against.

But I don't want to go! I wailed. The ring toss still haunts me. And
all the people! I'll feel overwhelmed.

Marcus didn't say anything more. His lips became a thin, hard line and his eyes went dark and impossible to read. I remembered that day in Starbucks, Marcus holding my hand, cheering me on. And then lots of Marcus images flashed through my mind like a movie montage with soft focus and tinkly music. In each of the images, Marcus was smiling or he was making me smile; Marcus was helping me or I was helping him.

And so I said: I'm sorry for whining. You are a true and amazing friend. Of course I'll help.

Marcus grinned. If you can face down one Starbucks barista, you can handle a tent full of ring tossers. I think this will be good for you, Darcy Clipper. Give participation prizes! Everyone's a winner.

You're right, I said. Everyone *is* a winner. Just stepping up to that counter takes guts. But—I stopped. I hadn't told Marcus about my upcoming thirtieth birthday. I didn't want to think about it or talk about it or worry about it. Ever since arriving in Murbridge, I had willed myself to forget about my birthday. And with this brilliant technique, I would remain in my twenties forever and ever.

There's one other thing, I said quietly. The day of the Mushroom Festival is also my birthday.

What? Marcus yelled. You'll have to speak up!

The day of the Mushroom Festival is my *birthday*, I said very loudly. I'm turning thirty.

Thirty? No. Really?

Yes.

I don't believe it. You seem much older.

Gee, thanks, Marcus. That's exactly what I want to hear right now.

No, you don't look over thirty. You just seem so—so mature and traumatized. Usually people in their twenties haven't lived enough to have real issues. But you—you're way ahead of the curve.

Um, thanks, I guess.

Marcus pursed his lips. He tilted his head. Okay, he said, so here's what I think. I think that staring down your painful past at the Mushroom Festival while also ensuring the future success of your current endeavor is the perfect way to celebrate a milestone birthday.

By *my* current endeavor you mean *your* current endeavor.

Marcus looked wounded. Darcy, this playscape is ours. We're in this together. And after the Mushroom Festival, we'll celebrate. We'll go to Luza's and eat ceviche and drink pisco sours until the cows come home. Or at least until Harriet needs a break from the boys.

I do think participation prizes are a good idea.

The best idea, Marcus said, nodding.

I examined a cuticle and bit. Okay, I said. I'll volunteer.

CONSIDER MARCO POLO—AND I don't mean the annoying game played in public pools by splash-happy children, but the person, the man. *National Geographic*, September 1988. In the year 1271, an adolescent Marco Polo traveled with his father, Niccolò, and his uncle Maffeo from Venice along the Silk Road through Asia. Eventually the Polos ended up in Cathay, where they met Kublai Khan, the famed Mongol leader. Khan was so impressed with young Marco's smarts and sword skills that he hired him on the spot to serve as a foreign emissary. All told, the Polos were gone for twenty-four years. Here are some things Marco saw: paper money, a centralized postal service, the royal palace at Xanadu, the metropolis of Quinsai, oases in the Takla Makan Desert, porcelain, black powder that created the most astonishing explosions, a royal Persian wedding ceremony with thousands of guests, real live crocodiles and a mythical horned beast later identified as a rhinoceros. Imagine being so far from home. Imagine how exotic and strange the world must have seemed. Food and smells and people and language and dress and buildings that Marco had never encountered before, never even imagined might exist. It must have been disorienting. It must have been exhilarating and exhausting. Twenty-four years of this! I think my senses would have shut down long before Marco's did. The human capacity for wonder is immense, but it's not infinite. At least not for the human called Darcy Clipper. After one year, maybe two, I would have said farewell to the rhinos, shot off one last round of fireworks and then turned around and made my way home.

Final volunteer meeting for the Mushroom Festival! Thursday, 6:00 pm at Murbridge High School. Nibbles will be served.

•

Can anyone identify a human bone? I think my dog brought home an adult femur. Or maybe it's just a very good Halloween decoration. Any experts out there?

•

Reminder: SPECIAL Selectmen Town Meeting next Tuesday to hear public comments on the SAVE MURBRIDGE, STOP THE BUILD petition. All town residents strongly encouraged to attend. Honorably, Jake Zdzynzky, President, SMB

•

ISO: highly responsible adult or very mature teen to babysit 5:30–7:30 next Tuesday. We'd love to attend the town meeting but our manny, Andy, has taken an unexpected and hopefully brief sabbatical. Our twins, Jett and Viggo (45 months), need a responsible babysitter, preferably one with excellent hand-eye coordination and reflex response. Some gluten-free cooking required. Must know CPR. Thanks! BestBoyMommy22

•

Darling, I feel your disquiet. I'm sorry I left you all alone. Don't cry, I'll see you again. I'll come for you. Soon, darling. Soon.

THE VOLUNTEER MEETING was predictably long, boring, sparsely attended and held inside a windowless, airless classroom at Murbridge High. At least there were snacks. Hildegard Hyman thanked us all profusely for volunteering, handed out juice boxes and packets of Goldfish and then assigned roles. Luckily, there was zero competition for ring toss assistant. Not so for the roller coaster—volunteers had to thumb wrestle for that coveted post. Pat Pernicky sat in the corner, typing furiously on a laptop the approximate size of a napkin.

I'd brought along my old-school paper notebook, just in case I might need to note something, and did not wear my neck gaiter, which seemed a small but significant victory in my socialization skills. True, I didn't talk to anyone and I sat in the back row and I wrote *Linda* on my name tag, but still. Baby steps.

During the meeting, I observed the rapid-fire organization and rapport between Hildegard Hyman and Pat Pernicky, the two women who'd been in charge of nearly every aspect of Murbridge civilian life for as long as I could remember. They were ageless: hair always the same color of grayish brown, shoes always sensible, cardigans always at the ready. Hildegard was the front woman, no-nonsense practicality and carefully doled-out charm. Pat was strictly behind the scenes, the Alfred to Hildegard's Bruce Wayne, her eyes dark and watchful, full of obscure data and town secrets. How did they manage such seamless competence? Did they get paid? Did they have real jobs? Did they have families? Were they a couple? Were they sisters?

For the first time I found myself looking at these two women as living, breathing human beings, not just permanent fixtures in my childhood memories of every town fair, every parade, every library book sale and holiday performance of *A Christmas Carol*. Hildegard and Pat were inscrutable, but they had integrity. They were the opposite of rotten. Hildegard and Pat would never help Jake pressure Marcus and Dan to sell their house. Would they?

In my notebook, I wrote:

· Ring toss—10 am start
· Darius Studepackle, supervisor
· Playscape petition—next to men's room
· Hildegard & Pat—not rotten?

After Hildegard's presentation, the volunteers fanned out into little groups to drink their juice and eat their Goldfish. I watched Jake Zdzynzky corral three teenagers to work the SAVE MURBRIDGE petition table. The fidget spinners were silver with *Happy New Year! from Zdzynzky Gems-n-Things* printed on the side.

It's leftover stock, I heard him say. Just put your finger over the *Happy New Year* part when you hand them out. One per signature, while supplies last, and they won't last long! Then Jake's voice lowered to a stage whisper: Don't tell your parents, but I might be able to throw in some *beer*.

As the teenagers giggled, Jake scanned the room and, seeing me, sauntered in my direction.

Oh, hi there, Linda? he said, straining to read my name tag. You bear a striking resemblance to Darcy Clipper.

Linda's my, um, middle name, I said.

Well, *Darcy,* it's nice to see you finally giving back to the community. You're a first-time volunteer, am I right?

Yep, I answered. First timer.

Too bad your friend didn't decide to join us. That new fellow—what's his name again? Jake put his hand to his chin as though struggling to remember Marcus's name, although I knew he knew it. And he knew that I knew he knew it.

Still, I played along. I'd promised Marcus I'd take the tenor of the room. Here, standing right in front of me, was the fattest tenor in the whole building.

His name is Marcus, I said. Marcus Dash-LaGrand.

Yes! cried Jake. *Marcus.* Well, please tell Marcus that I'm feeling optimistic about the petition and our efforts to save Murbridge. *Extremely* optimistic.

Okay. I yawned dramatically. And why's that?

Because this year's attendance will be through the roof! It'll be the best Mushroom Fest ever. And more people means more voices voicing their opposition to your friend's scheme.

It's a playground, not a fraudulent investment vehicle, I said. I know you've had trouble with those in the past. I said a silent thank-you to my mom for her inside information.

Jake remained nonplussed. True, I've made some missteps in the past, he said. But this time is different. This is my chance, my last chance, to really—really—really—really—

Jake was looking beyond me, probably at huge dollar signs dancing on the classroom walls of Murbridge High, when Pat Pernicky snapped him out of his reverie.

Really what, Jake? she called from across the room. Your voice sure does travel. And the suspense is killing me.

Thanks for the question, Pat! Jake called back. This is my chance to *really* make my mark on Murbridge. The Mushroom Fest is just the beginning.

Hildegard Hyman looked up from the spreadsheet she was compiling. She'd been yelling at people all night, but now she said calmly: Sounds great, Jake. You're the king. Oh, and by the way, don't give beer to the volunteers. They're obviously underage and you could get arrested.

Jake exhaled loudly. Yes, Hildegard, sure, okay. We were just having some fun. I meant root beer, obviously. Don't get your panties in a twist.

Once he'd turned away, Hildegard shook her head. An unmistakable expression of frustration-dislike-aggravation-disgust passed across her face.

Bingo, I thought. For a moment, Hildegard and I locked eyes. She didn't blink and neither did I. I felt an understanding pass between us, the understanding that Jake Zdzynzky was full of shit. In my notebook, I crossed out the question mark and underlined the *not*: Hildegard & Pat, <u>not</u> rotten.

THE NEXT DAY I overslept and rushed to Marcus's house, un-showered with a major case of bedhead. But when I arrived, the site was quiet. The backhoe, unmanned. The pool, a silent empty hole in the ground.

Marcus was in the kitchen, wearing a *Kiss the Chef* apron and measuring cups of sugar into a silver bowl. The aroma was glorious.

Sorry I'm late, I began, I thought I only pressed snooze once but then—

Marcus waved his hand. Forget it, he said. Nice hair. Want a cookie?

I sniffed. Snickerdoodles?

Marcus nodded. Cooling. I'm already on batch number four.

You are the best boss ever, I said. But, um, where is everybody?

Marcus ate some cookie dough from the bowl. Around, he said, through the mouthful.

It was then I sensed it. Beneath the buttery smell and floury air lay the unmistakable scent of trouble.

Marcus, are you stress baking? I asked.

What? No, of course not. He ate another glob of dough.

Just then Ludovic appeared in the doorway. Yo, Daddio, he said. Today Lud had purple hair and appeared to be holding a ukulele, or maybe it was just a very small guitar.

Ludovic, you know I'm not on board with the *yo* greeting, Marcus replied. Speak like a person.

Sorry, Dad.

Have you practiced today?

Lud nodded.

Are you ready for the concert?

You bet. I'm really psyched.

Marcus smiled, a rare full-on dazzling Marcus smile that he reserved only for his boys and for perfectly straight cuts on the table saw. Have I mentioned that your rendition of "Smells Like Teen Spirit" is truly awe-inspiring? Marcus said.

Yeah. Lud grinned. You've mentioned that.

And that your arrangement would win a ukulele Grammy, if such an award were ever handed out to deserving preteens?

Lud's grin got wider, his cheeks turned pink. *Dad.*

Darcy, seriously, Marcus said, turning to me. This kid is a genius. You wouldn't believe the sounds he makes on a lowly ukulele. It'll blow your mind.

Lud, I'd love to hear you play someday, I said.

You should come to the concert tonight, said Lud. Dad, did you tell her?

But before I could reply, Marcus answered for me: Darcy can't make it, he said without looking at me. Now go help your brother get dressed, and he shooed Ludovic out of the room.

Marcus, I'm free tonight. I can come to the concert, I said, but he pretended not to hear me.

There was a quick, loud rap on the patio door and Burt walked into the kitchen. He was wearing black yoga pants, a purple tank top, his man bun unleashed and flowing free. I noticed a new tattoo on his left shoulder: *MOM*, within a flowery heart.

Marcus, what's the deal with the pool? said Burt. Brendan told me you canceled the crew. You want to suspend excavation?

Um, yeah. Dan hasn't been too keen on the whole pool idea, as you know, so I've decided to take a step back. Reevaluate. Marcus began measuring flour into the bowl.

But we're halfway there, said Burt. You've got a giant hole in your backyard. Two weeks ago you told me full speed ahead. I believe the words were *I'll literally die if I don't have a body of water to throw myself into.*

Burt did a remarkably astute impression of Marcus, but Marcus didn't even break a smile. Burt stared levelly at him. This was the glare of a man who knew his time was valuable and did not enjoy wasting it.

I think we should press pause for a week, Marcus said. Or two or three. Marcus cleared his throat. Pause the whole site, actually. Dan and I are rethinking our commitment to Murbridge.

What? Burt and I said in unison.

What happened to full speed ahead? Burt asked.

And *we'll show those fuckers we're home*? I asked.

Well, I've decided—we've decided—to reconsider.

Burt exhaled long and low. Okay, then. But I suggest you review our contract. There's a termination clause and it's painful. He turned back to the patio. The screen door banged shut behind him.

Marcus started the stand mixer and scraped down the bowl as it whirled.

Marcus, I called over the noise. What the hell is going on? Were you planning to talk to me about this?

He pretended not to hear me for another minute and then he shut the mixer off.

Darcy, he said as he began dropping cookie dough onto a sheet. Dan and I decided, together, that we need to rethink, you know, the whole playscape scenario. And maybe we'd, um, wait until the protest situation, um, died down. He turned to me with eyebrows raised, a distinct sheen of sweat across his forehead.

Marcus, you're an incredibly bad liar, I said.

Why would I lie?

I have no idea. But there haven't been protestors for two weeks at least. And your left eye is twitching.

Marcus's hand shot up to massage his left eyebrow. Shit, he said and sighed. Listen, something happened, but I can't tell you.

Just then, Phin entered the room. He wore a giant fur hat but otherwise was naked.

Daddy, you can tell her, he said.

Phin, go put some clothes on.

Don't change the subject, said Phin. You can trust her. Am I right, Darcy?

Marcus, what is your naked child talking about?

Phin, *clothes*.

But Daddy, you need some help. I'm just a kid. Phin shrugged and left the kitchen.

Darcy, Phin is a lunatic. Don't believe a word he says. Besides, it doesn't matter. Jake Zdzynzky can build his indoor lalapalooza or whatever. It's okay. We're going to sell him the house and the lot and leave Murbridge. Sometimes the bad guy wins. Marcus turned his attention back to the cookie sheet.

What? No! I cried. You can't leave. Jake can't win. The volunteer meeting last night was great. I felt the tenor and I think our building permit is safe. Jake can't steamroll this through. Hildegard and Pat are absolutely not rotten.

The permit is irrelevant.

Why? Why won't you tell me what's going on?

You wouldn't understand, Marcus said, not looking at me.

Try me.

No.

But why? Let me tell you about Hildegard.

Go home, Darcy.

Maybe if you just—

Darcy, events in my life have now traveled far outside your frame of reference. I don't feel comfortable discussing these issues with you. I know you mean well, I do, but that's just not enough. Please respect my wishes and go home. In the immortal words of the Irish diva herself, Sinéad O'Connor, this is the last day of our acquaintance.

Ouch, I said. That hurts.

Marcus did not reply. He turned his back on me and switched on the mixer. The sound of motorized mashing filled the room.

I left the kitchen, left the house and trudged home with my head down. As I walked, I reviewed the current state of affairs. Today was the 185th day of my self-imposed isolation and canned food consumption, only I was no longer isolated and my diet consisted of way more than canned food. So much more that my shorts felt a little tight.

How could Marcus dismiss me so cruelly? Why wouldn't he trust me? Why was he abandoning Murbridge? What the hell was going on?

Night was beginning to fall. In Fink Park, a dad yelled at his kid to hurry up. A groaning old Mazda roared past me, spewing out exhaust. On the sidewalk, I passed two teenage girls, both with their necks bowed to their phones, their thumbs scrolling scrolling scrolling.

Outside my house, I stopped and looked at the sky. Light from the Dykstras' back patio half blinded me so I only saw one lonely star, trying valiantly to make itself shine. I had existed on this planet for twenty-nine long years and 364 long days and what did I have to show for it? What had I done with all that time? All those months, weeks, days, minutes?

I considered Pablo Neruda from my favorite *National Geographic*, the man who loved love and believed in our common destiny. What a freak. Common destiny? What a joke! Not a single relationship was worth a damn, I thought, watching that lonely star. No one, and I mean no one, had a happy marriage. Or a happy friendship. Or parentship. Or childship. Parents abandoned kids. Kids disappointed parents. Spouses found someone better. Friends could care less.

And sometimes the bad guy won.

Dear Ms. Hyman, my sincere apologies but I'm no longer able to volunteer at the Mushroom Festival tomorrow. I am so sorry, but something has come up.

Sincerely yours, Darcy Clipper

Darcy, I received your message but regrettably it's too late to quit. See you at 9 am at the volunteer tent! Best, Hildegard

---

Dear Hildegard, maybe I wasn't clear in my email. I can't volunteer so I won't see you at 9 am at the volunteer tent. In fact, I plan to spend the day of the Mushroom Festival in bed. I don't feel well today and I'm guessing I won't improve by tomorrow.

Thank you for your understanding, Darcy.

Darcy, maybe I wasn't clear in my email. Every year, it's a shitshow trying to put on the Mushroom Festival with volunteer labor. I call in every favor, guilt-trip every family member, colleague, neighbor and acquaintance. I believe you've lived in Murbridge your entire life and, as I understand it, have never once volunteered for our annual festival. Is that right? You owe it to the town and to yourself to show up tomorrow, Darcy, so man up. Take some vitamin C, shotgun a Red Bull, suck on some CBD, whatever floats your boat. It takes a village to make a Mushroom Fest. With gratitude, Hildegard

---

Hildegard, thanks for the pep talk. I imagine your job is not an easy one. People are flaky—believe me, I know. But my excuse is for real—it's my 30th birthday tomorrow. I forgot when I signed up to volunteer, but now I've remembered and I simply can't face the day in any position other than the horizontal.

Yours, Darcy

Hi Darcy, I'm so glad you remembered it's your birthday! That's an easy thing to let slip. Happy birthday to you! Make sure you take these opportunities to celebrate yourself—don't be shy. Self-care is important. Now that I know about your big day, I'll be sure to make a special announcement over the loudspeaker and treat you to a free sno-cone. See you tomorrow! With best birthday wishes, Hildegard

---

Okay, Hildegard. I give up.

And make it grape, please.

ON THE DAY OF THE 57th Annual Murbridge Town Mushroom Festival, aka my thirtieth birthday, I woke early. Blue sky, sunshine. No chance of a rain delay. No chance festival attendance would be sparse. Today promised a rollicking, parking-lot-is-full, watch-your-handbag kind of day.

I pulled my laptop into bed and opened my email. Five new messages. One from my dentist wishing me happy birthday, another birthday greeting from a spa in Pensacola where I'd once had a mediocre massage and a creepy third from my grandmother's old AOL account, which, despite her death five years ago, still auto-sent birthday emails to all her grandkids.

And then a message from my parents:

Darcy, happy happy birthday to our dear girl! You've brought such joy to our lives ever since the day you first popped from my vagina. I was woozy from all the drugs and immediately thought

I'd given birth to a tiny Burt Reynolds. But then you started to cry and you were just the spitting image of your father. Have I told you that story before? I probably have, but it never gets old. We love you, Bunny, and wish we were all together on this special day. Daddy Venmo'ed you $100, so take yourself out, have a steak and martini on us. We'll see you in a few months and can celebrate in person then.

Love and extra-special kisses,
Mom and Daddy

And then, last of my new emails, was this:

Hi Darcy,

Happy birthday!
How are you? I'm guessing you're surprised to hear from me after all this time, but I'd really like to talk. I feel horrible for what I did. Remember our game with the coconut oil? I miss that game. I miss you. I want us to be married again and live in our condo and play bingo with our friends. Bianca isn't the person I thought she was.
Please reply.

Yours,

Skip

I stared at the screen. All these months I'd been waiting for Skip Larson to pop into my in-box and now, at last, here he was. And yet, the strangest sensation came over me. My heart beat calmly, my eyes remained dry, my palms did not sweat. I felt, in a word, unmoved.

I recalled the one and only time I'd seen Bianca in the flesh: her lavender fingernails on the steering wheel of the Prius that drove away with my life. What sort of person had Skip believed her to be?

What sort of person was she in fact? Did she snore like a freight train? Did she have an extra nipple? Did she keep all her fingernail clippings in a jar by the bed?

Oh Skip.

I didn't know what to say. I thought of our condo and bingo nights. Our couples membership at the Y, Valentine's Day gifts, fluffy towels and a double sink, my nine-to-five at the insurance agency, corporate events, holiday parties. The accoutrements of a normal, successful adult life. Was this what I wanted?

I began to write a reply.

Draft email files

Dear Skip,

Thanks for your note and birthday wishes. Yes, I was very surprised to hear from you. Surprised and happy that

---

Dear Skip,

It was with interest that I read your recent email. At the present moment, our relationship status remains unclear due to the unfortunate events of

---

Dear Skip,

Your infidelity was low-down and dirty. Just thinking about you and Bianca makes me so mad I could

---

Dear Skip,

So what's the deal with Bianca? Please be specific.

I spent nearly two hours writing, deleting, rewriting, re-deleting. *Clear your head, Darcy. Get ahold of yourself.* I slapped my palms against my face and asked: What would Hildegard Hyman say?

Finally, I wrote the following:

Dear Skip,

Thank you for your message. I was surprised to hear from you. My feelings for you are confused. On the one hand, I loved you. Maybe I still love you. On the other hand, you left me for another woman. You skipped out, Skip, and broke our marriage vows and crushed my heart into a billion pieces. You gave no indication you were unhappy with our relationship, apart from an increased use of the word no in our email and text correspondence. I don't believe that suffices as adequate warning that you intended to disrupt our life together. On the one hand, I'm angry at you for causing me so much turmoil. But on the other hand, I'm grateful to you for pushing me out into the world. Without you, I've discovered new skills, made new friends and become involved with a project that's bigger than me and my problems. I'm building something, and it's not just for me, it's for everyone. Have you ever felt that way? I guess what I'm trying to say is that not everything is black or white. There's a lot of muddle in the middle and our situation is complicated. I need time to consider.

Regards,

Darcy

I read the email a second, third and fourth time. Then, I pressed send.

I ARRIVED AT the Mushroom Festival too late to take advantage of the free snacks at the volunteer tent so I headed straight to the ring toss booth. As I walked through the fairground, memories of the ring toss danced before my eyes: the neat grid of empty glass Coke bottles, the containers full of red rubber rings. The maddening, slippery sheen of the bottlenecks. The heartless sign that commanded, with far too many exclamation points, NO LEANING!!! Nostalgia or regret or deep-seated rage, it was hard to define the emotion precisely, washed over me.

And then I heard a once-familiar voice. *Darcy?* Darcy Clipper, is that you? I turned and there, standing before me, was the girl voted Most Attractive and Sweetest Smile and Most Likely to Marry Elon Musk. The girl I'd hated most in high school, junior high and elementary school. We'd been together at Murbridge-area public schools for twelve long, long years. Georgina Oliver was her name. Emotional manipulation was her game.

Oh, hi, Georgina, I said. Yep, it's me, Darcy. She seemed to be alone, although perhaps Elon had wandered off to find some soft serve. Or maybe he was too busy beaming himself to another planet or practicing tantric sex in Bali to appear at the Mushroom Fest.

I can't believe it's you! Georgina squealed and hugged me, as though we had once been friends. Aren't you in Boston now? But you just couldn't stay away from the Mushroom Festival! Georgina snickered. She still looked the same: blond bob, straight-arrow nose, a teeny-tiny waist, 110 pounds of pure evil.

I do love mushrooms, I answered.

We like to sneak in early, she said. Before the best ice cream flavors sell out. Where's your husband? Georgina strained her neck to look behind me. And your parents? Are they still alive?

Yep. Still kicking it. They're down in Arizona. Trying out a retirement community. And my husband, well, he's also still alive.

Georgina's eyebrow shot up, her lips parted. Like a bird dog, she could sense when an animal was bleeding. I opened my mouth to say it, to just spill the truth right then and there, but before I could speak I heard a scream: Mommy! The child sounded like one of those velociraptors in *Jurassic Park*. High-pitched, single-minded, deadly.

Georgina's head whipped around. Oh Jesus, Brad, couldn't you just keep her for ten goddamn minutes?

Brad Metcalf, Georgina's high school boyfriend, was limping toward us, dragging a shrieking, crying red-faced child of indeterminate age. The child seemed small enough for two but loud enough for ten.

You remember Brad? she said with a grimace. Then, leaning toward me, she whispered: Still dumb as a stump. Did you know he failed senior year PE and couldn't go to college?

I shook my head. I didn't know that, I said.

I got knocked up at prom. Kid you not, Georgina continued in a whisper. So of course we got married and blah blah blah. She leaned back and called to Brad: Where's Kevin? And Kaitlyn and Kourtney?

Brad shrugged. Around, he said.

Did you tell them not to talk to strangers?

Uh. Yeah?

Oh my God, Brad. They are at peak age for molesters. I told you to talk to them. Do I have to do *everything*?

Brad shrugged again. The child continued to call Mommy, Mommy, Mommy and now stretched out her arms toward Georgina.

So good to see you, Darcy, she said, smiling brightly. You look great, by the way. You've lost all that baby weight. And the acne cleared up! Sorry I didn't get a chance to meet your husband. Have fun today! She winked. And then she turned to Brad.

Give her to me, Georgina snarled. She popped out her right hip, grabbed the child and stuck a lollipop in the kid's mouth. The child immediately stopped crying and began slurping noisily.

See how hard that was? Georgina said to Brad. Just give her *candy*.

Watching Georgina, Brad and their sugared-up kid walk away, I felt a wave of self-confidence wash over me, greater than my Starbucks victory, greater even than the feeling I got when planing a two-by-four with the table saw. The birthday gods had looked down upon me and smiled. *To Darcy we bequeath the most gratifying of gifts: the recognition that a once-loathed individual now lives a life way worse than yours.* I felt a tinge of sympathy for Georgina. No more likelihood of success, no more prettiest smile, no more Elon Musk. The old adage was true: don't peak too early. Which led inevitably to the related realization that *my* peak years still remained ahead.

Wow, I thought with foolish optimism, maybe today will be my best birthday ever.

I wound my way through the hot tub tents and animal sheds; across to the food pavilion, where the line for deep-fried butter was already starting to form; over the hill to the southeast corner, where the carnival games were situated.

And there, past balloon darts, basketball swish, water gun fun and dunk a granny, sat the red-and-white-striped awning of the ring toss. The booth was empty. No players, no staff.

Huh, I said aloud. Guess I dodged a—

From behind me came another voice, this one unfamiliar and rangy with the ravages of adolescent hormones.

Hey, are you my assistant?

I turned and there stood an acne-riddled man-child of approximately five feet in height, sporting one sparse mustache and an unfortunate tattoo of a rat on his neck. I could smell his BO from six feet away. He wore an orange vest and a name tag that said: *Darius, SUPERVISOR.*

Hey, I'm your supervisor. But don't worry, I won't sexually harass you. He snickered. Hashtag MeToo.

Nice to meet you, Darius. I'm here to hand out prizes to each and every kid regardless of their ring toss acumen.

Darius yawned. Whatever. I need a nap. I'll be under the Orange Julius stand. Have fun.

The Mushroom Festival games began officially at 10:00 a.m. My first child arrived at 10:02. She was short, pudgy, of middle school age, I guessed, although kids these days are just so big. She tossed once, twice, three times. Each ring glanced off a bottle and fell to the ground.

Almost! I said. That was so great! Pick a prize. The orange monkey is calling your name.

The girl looked confused. But I didn't win.

You're a winner in my book, I said. What'll it be?

The girl smiled. Well, um. She bit her lip. I choose . . . THAT! Her finger landed on a stuffed unicorn that seemed roughly the same size as the girl herself.

Are you sure? I said. Might be tough to carry that one.

I'm sure, the girl replied. And so I pulled down the unicorn and off skipped my first satisfied customer, dragging a mythical beast behind her.

As though drawn by the sound of a whistle audible only to preteen girls, they arrived. Masses of them, in their spangly T-shirts and flip-flops, glittery lip gloss and purple hair streaks, some dragging parents, others giggling in little groups, all of them ready to try the ring toss and take home a prize, winner or not.

I hummed as I arranged the bottles. Hummed as I sorted the rings. Step right up! I called. Who wants to toss a ring and take home a stuffie?

For two joyful hours I cheered on ring tossers regardless of accuracy and handed out prizes regardless of result. I basked in the gratitude of these youthful losers and rejoiced at my dwindling supply of stuffed animals.

Until Darius returned from his nap.

Wow, that Orange Julius beats a Valium any day of the week, Darius said, yawning and stretching his arms overhead.

I waved good-bye to the last loser child, a six-foot-tall boy with chocolate on his face.

Hey, I heard some kids talking about free prizes? Darius asked, rubbing his eyes. What's that about?

I ignored him. A girl in purple overalls had stepped up. You can do it! I called. Go, purple girl, go!

She missed, then missed again, then missed on her third and final ring, this one a wild toss that hit Darius on the shoulder.

Oops, she said. Sorry!

He's fine! I called. Now, what'll it be? Bart Simpson? Weird green monster with one eye? A sloth?

But she—Darius began.

I held up a finger.

But you can't—

I wagged the finger and returned my attention to the girl.

She considered her options, she strained her neck to get a better view of the back-row stuffies and then she pointed to a small purple mouse. Great choice! I said. It matches your outfit. The girl beamed, hugged the mouse and disappeared into the crowd.

I turned back to Darius. His face had turned a startling shade of red.

You—you can't just *give away* the prizes, he stuttered. People have to—have to *earn* them.

She did earn it. She came, she threw, she participated. Who says she can't have a prize? I noticed that Darius's ears were also red.

Who *says*? he replied, his voice rising. The carnival rules *say*. The laws of the universe *say*. Everybody knows how it works. *Everybody.* You have to *win* the ring toss *before* you get a prize. Are you, like, mentally deranged or something?

Not particularly.

You're fired.

Fired? You can't fire me. I'm a volunteer.

You're still fired. Just go away, Darius said and then, to himself, Mom is going to kill me.

I left the ring toss feeling mysteriously and deeply ashamed. I had never before been fired from a job, volunteer or otherwise. Mr. Castro didn't count because I'd left first. The auspicious start to my thirtieth birthday was taking a distinct downward turn.

I wandered the festival in search of something to cheer me up, preferably something that was gross and fried. And then I caught sight of the unmistakable crown of the Mushroom Monarch: a circle of cremini look-alikes rendered in aging papier-mâché. Below the crown was the Mushroom Monarch himself, Jake Zdzynzky.

Although I no longer felt beholden to Marcus's agenda, I remembered Jake's bravado at the volunteer meeting. What exactly was he planning? I stopped and crouched. Jake was holding forth to a rapt circle of men and one woman. Hildegard.

Guys, guys, Jake was saying, how many of these zoning restrictions can we look at? Noise? Fence height? What else could we use?

One of the white guys, this one with an overbite, replied, *Children.* We can definitely use children.

Jake was nodding. And this is why the Little Free Library incident gives me pause, he said. The Dash-LaGrands built that library. Isn't it reasonable to assume they stocked it too? What does that say about their judgment? And *values*? To each their own, but where there's smoke—he shrugged and threw up his hands—know what I mean?

Hildegard opened her mouth and blew her bangs upward in a very dramatic gesture of outrage. That Hildegard really knew how to focus a room.

Jake, there's no smoke, she said. Some teenagers probably left those magazines as a joke. Get over yourself.

Jake harrumphed and shifted his weight and blinked very fast. The others waited for his reply. *Hildegard,* he said finally, we must stand firm to maintain the family values of this town. Porn? Ziplines? What's next?

The other men began nodding.

We must stand firm, Jake said again, louder this time. I will do whatever it takes to STOP THE BUILD!

Hildegard rolled her eyes. I'm late for the chowder tasting, she said and walked away.

The circle tightened, the voices dropped to a murmur so faint even I, master eavesdropper that I was, couldn't make out the words.

I left the Mushroom Monarch and his minions and made my way into the thick of the festival. Jake's words played on repeat in my head: *whatever it takes, whatever it takes.* How far would Jake go? I wondered. Bribery? Blackmail? *Murder?* Was Jake Zdzynzky actually dangerous? What had he done to scare Marcus into leaving Murbridge?

It was then I saw a line stretching around a hamburger stand, past the bumper cars and Twirly-Cups. I followed, thinking: Holy cow, this must be the best fair food ever. But I rounded the corner to find only a table and a banner emblazoned with the words: SAVE MURBRIDGE, STOP THE BUILD! Three teenagers from the volunteer meeting were handing out fidget spinners.

Come sign the petition! one of the girls called into the crowd. Get yourself a free fidget spinner *and* a chance to win ten thousand dollars!

I stopped.

Ten thousand big ones to sign Jake's petition? Was she joking?

Hey, I asked the girl, are you joking?

Nope, she said. Mr. Zdzynzky is sponsoring a raffle. It's, like, for charity. She smiled.

What charity? I asked.

She smiled again, broader this time. Oh, it's for kids. We're saving little kids and, um, maybe you can win ten thousand dollars! Fidget spinner?

No, thank you, I said. When will the drawing be? How will you notify the winner?

I think it's—well, I don't know if— She hesitated. He's paying me, like, twenty dollars an hour to stand here, so. The girl shrugged and then resumed calling into the crowd.

Of course she couldn't answer. Because Jake would never in a million years give away ten thousand dollars, And hello? There was no raffle infrastructure in place here. No spreadsheets, no primary contact information or alternate phone number, no numbered tickets with stubs kept in a secure location. Jake was lying; the raffle was one big fat lie.

I became immediately enraged with the injustice of it all, the taking advantage of one's position, the unscrupulous appeal to the public's baser instincts. Sure, Jake had been elected chair of the Select Board, but that didn't mean he could do whatever he wanted. Checks and balances, I remembered vaguely from my high school civics class. Absolute power corrupts absolutely. Did Nietzsche say that? Or was it Oprah?

And what about the people waiting in line? Didn't they know they were being played? Didn't they realize they would never win the prize? They'd end up with their shitty old playground, bored kids, a gaudy amusement park/casino in old historic Murbridge and Jake Zdzynzky laughing at them all the way to the bank.

Don't do it! I yelled at the people on line. Don't be patsies! Think for yourselves!

One woman looked at me and shrugged. She was eating an elephant ear. I need the money, she said. Worth the wait.

But you'll never win. Don't you get it? There's no prize money. You'll sign the petition and it'll all be for nothing.

She shrugged again. You're just mad because the line is so long.

I turned away from the whole sorry spectacle. I had no good comeback. I had no logical argument. I couldn't convince anyone of anything. I couldn't even convince Marcus that he should stay in Murbridge so that I wouldn't lose my best and truest friend.

I was ready to leave the festival. Forget eating new and interesting fried food and making new mushroom memories. I just wanted out. I turned toward the exit, head down, fighting against the crowds until—*blammo*—I collided with a sweet-smelling pillar of muscle and well-worn khaki. I sniffed. I recognized that smell from somewhere.

Excuse me, I said. I'm trying to get out of here.

Sorry—um, *Darcy*? The man laughed. Is that you?

I raised my head. Dark curls, flashing brown eyes, one dimple low and to the left, a slightly smushed nose broken during infancy when an older brother sat on his face. Behold, it was Todd Pevzner, my high school boyfriend, the first man to break my heart, the man to whom I would have lost my virginity but for an unfortunate parking brake incident, the details of which I vowed never to disclose in any forum. He was smiling his bewitching, slightly crooked smile, the one that had always made me swoon.

Todd? I said, trying to summon a fetching smile of my own. How *are* you?

Oh, I'm just great. It's so nice to be home. But you know that already! He slapped my shoulder and for a moment I thought maybe he was flirting with me. But then I saw behind him a woman. And five—it took me a moment to count—children.

Hey, meet Courtney, my wife, and these are our kids. One, two, three, four and five. (In reality, he said names, but I forgot them immediately.)

Courtney stepped forward, a baby strapped to her chest, Birkenstocks strapped to her feet, and held out a hand. Oh, it's so nice to finally meet you, Darcy. I've heard so many wonderful things about you and your parents. She grasped my hand firmly and her smile was genuine, kind, lovely.

Oh, hi, I said. Your grip is very strong.

And then, appearing behind Courtney, was the blondie baker herself, Mrs. Pevzner.

Darcy! You're alive! she said. Oh, we were so worried about you. All winter long, locked up in that house, all alone after your husband's torrid affair. I felt so sorry for you, Darcy. It's so good to finally see you out and about.

Thank you, Mrs. Pevzner. Yes, it's good to be out. And about. And to see you all, especially you, Todd. And Courtney. And all these small children. Wow, it's been a long time. Long, loooong time. Todd, what a nice smile. And Courtney, what a nice handshake! And what a nice-looking baby! And nice Birkenstocks! And all these super-duper kids. Wow. Wowza wow.

I heard myself speaking and realized I had once again lost the partition that normally exists between one's brain and one's mouth. All the help from Marcus, my face-to-face barista practice and yet here I was, quietly melting into a puddle of anxiety and shame. I blinked very rapidly and bit the inside of my mouth. What would Hildegard Hyman say?

I really have to be going, I said. I just finished volunteering at the ring toss and, boy, am I tired. I tried to smile in the manner of a normal, polite, sane person. I tried very hard.

Of course, Darcy, said Mrs. Pevzner and came in for a hug. I awkwardly embraced her, trying not to inhale or touch her skin in any way.

It was lovely to see you, she said. Please give my best to your parents. Mrs. Pevzner then took the hands of grandchildren three and four and turned into the crowd. Courtney waved a little wave and followed, kids one and two trailing behind. Only Todd remained.

Well, Darcy, he said. It's really something to see you. After all these years. He grimaced. Crazy how fast time flies, huh? Can you believe how *young* we were?

I nodded. Young. Yeah. We sure were.

Without warning, Todd opened his arms and swooped in. He hugged me so tightly, I couldn't tell if he was trying to suffocate me or feel me up. I allowed the hug for three seconds, five, and then began to back away. Um, Todd? I said. I really should be—

And then, just as suddenly, Todd released me.

Darcy, you've got all my mom's Tupperware, he said. And that's not cool. Not. Cool. Give it back, okay? No questions asked. My mom just wants her fucking Tupperware back.

And then, shaking his head, Todd followed his wife and kids.

I stood for a moment letting the crowd surge and swirl around me. Should I cry? Should I laugh? I was thirty years old and yet my life felt as strange and humbling as it had that night with Todd in the car, the parking brake between us, embarrassment and shame, hunger and joy, silly and sober, all jumbled together. Is it possible to grow older but not wiser? I wondered. Change is inevitable, but what about growth? Is it possible that life is not one long forward trajectory but a series of weird wide loops that always put you right back in the place you started?

Hello, Murbridge! Hellllooo!

A painfully loud voice rang out from above. For one intense and nutty moment, I thought it was God speaking to me. Then I realized it was just Hildegard Hyman on the loudspeaker.

I hope you're having a fantastically FunGuy day! Hildegard called with only a minimum of feedback and sarcasm.

Good-natured cheers erupted all around me.

Don't forget, the Mushroom Monarch will crown our new Fun-Guy just one hour from now. So head on down to the FunGuy tent to cheer on your favorite mushroom jokester! Hildegard paused. *Static. Static. Static.* And then a high feedback whine that made everyone in the state of Massachusetts wince.

The whine subsided and Hildegard returned: I'd also like to take this opportunity to wish a special happy birthday to a native of our town, a prodigal daughter, if you will. Darcy Clipper, wherever you are, I hope you're having the best birthday ever. I know birthdays can sometimes feel heavy. The passage of time, self-reflection and critique. But remember, Darcy, you've done a lot with your life. You've loved, you've lost, you've experienced pain and hope, some good stuff, some bad. Don't get discouraged, Darcy. Just keep on trucking. We're all with you on this journey. Hildegard paused. And now, you Murbridge hooligans, get on down to the baking tent and cast your vote for the best peach pie!

For a flash I considered finding Hildegard to cash in on my free birthday sno-cone, but I wasn't hungry. In fact, I felt nauseous. *Trucking*? Is that really the verb that best describes the act of moving through your days, trying to find meaning and connection with the world around you? Trucking suggests the act of sitting on a high stool, eating junk food, farting in an enclosed space and blowing your horn at people who get in your way. Maybe that's all there was. Maybe Neruda had it wrong with his clumsy dance and sorrowful song, his common destiny and showing the world who you really are. You hit thirty and trucking is the best you can hope for.

Once again, I put my head down and fought against the crowds until at last I reached the exit of Fink Park. At the gate stood a mammoth sign pronouncing: STOP THE BUILD! SIGN THE PETITION! WIN $10,000! And beside the sign stood a mammoth line of people waiting patiently to enter the Mushroom Fest. Women and men, boys and girls, all colors, all ages, all kinds of sun hats and goofy sunglasses. Probably they'd all sign the petition, dream of winning $10,000 and then truck on home to yell at the TV and practice their ring toss skills, hoping in vain to win a stuffie next year. As I passed by, a little girl in pigtails stuck her tongue out at me. I gave her the finger.

Why the hell did I come back here? I thought. Murbridge. Fucking Murbridge with its killer bees and spying neighbors, helicopter parents and obsessive soup makers, too many cats, too little kindness. What had I been looking for, all those months ago after

Mr. Castro kicked me to the curb? I'd been looking for peace, acceptance, the profound knowing of a place and the place knowing me. I'd been chasing the deep and whole contentment I'd felt each and every afternoon after grade school. Back then, I'd sit on the couch with a Fluffernutter, a *Price Is Right* rerun, the macramé blanket some great-aunt had knitted, wrapped up safe and tight. The pungent aroma of Mom's surprise casserole drifting in from the kitchen, Daddy striding through the door with his engineer name tag still attached to his blue short-sleeve button up. I'd been looking for that feeling of belonging, of existing within an envelope of acceptance and love. But that envelope had been licked shut, stamped and sent third-class to another planet, another dimension. That envelope was gone.

Thinking these sad thoughts, shedding a few pitiful tears in the process, I wandered far from the Mushroom Festival, over underused, overgrown sidewalks, down dark alleys, past homes and businesses, empty lots and cemeteries. Barely aware of my surroundings, I walked. I walked and I walked until I reached the Western Massachusetts Wetland Bird Protection Zone, site of the founding of Murbridge itself. All those years ago, Gideon Tinker and his hapless band of desperate Pilgrims, searching for a place to lay themselves down, to stop their wandering and seeking.

I paused on the viewing platform and looked out. The sun had dropped behind the western Berkshire hills and the marsh glowed orange in the reflected light. Birds were singing their little hearts out, their warbles lifting up up up to the sky as though in celebration of this amazing event, the nightly setting of the sun, and wasn't it gorgeous to be alive right here and now? I did not join their song. The first star appeared, mocking me with its twinkle and verve. As the sunset intensified so too did the birdsong until it seemed both had reached their crescendo, any more beauty was simply impossible, we would all die together right here and now from the magnificence of this sunset, the heaviness of my heart, the prospect of making it through the coming dark night.

At that moment, I saw deep within a tall willow, a flicker of red, yellow, blue. The colors hopped and shifted. The colors jumped and settled down. Was this a trick of the light? Or was this a rainbow bird? The colors jumped again, this time in a beckoning sort of way. Yes, a rainbow bird!

I scrambled off the platform and into the squelchy mess of the marsh. My sneakers immediately filled with water, but I didn't care. I wanted to reach that fowl. A once-in-a-lifetime event bird was happening twice in my life. Twice in one year! And on my birthday! Maybe luck had not deserted me after all.

Squelch, squirt, squelch. I waded in the direction of where I thought I'd seen the bird, but in the waning light and without the elevated view of the platform, I soon lost my way. Was it this direction? Or that one? Had I turned myself around? I thought of those Pilgrims again. Those nasty, horrible, selfish Pilgrims. Goddamn them. Why hadn't they just stayed in England where they belonged? Why had they come here to pillage and plunder, cut and build? They should have died on the journey west or died here in the marsh. We all would have been better off.

My foot snagged on a root buried in the mud and *splat,* down I went, face-first. *Ouch.* I pushed myself up, wiping mud from my eyes, swatting a mosquito or three, and realized that my ankle hurt. A lot.

Oh no.

I pulled my phone from my pocket but—the screen was blank. Could it be? Had I forgotten to charge my cell phone?

Classic, Darcy, I muttered. You are out of juice.

I began to yell. Help! Help me! Please help!

Where was I? How would I get home? Who would save me? Maybe I would be the one to die in the marsh. Of dehydration and mosquito bites. I swatted a gigantic bloodsucker on my knee, another on my neck and at that moment I caught sight of an interesting phenomenon. Beside me, rising up from a moss-covered log, grew a single mushroom with a long white stem and a jaunty brown cap.

Could it be? Was it possible?

The famed Murbridge mushroom, the elusive edible that generations of adolescents had sought in this very same marsh. Here it was, presenting itself to me at my most desperate hour. True, a hallucinogenic was probably the last thing I needed at this particular moment, but what the hell. You can't always play it safe. Today was my thirtieth birthday and, so far, it had not been a winner.

I plucked the mushroom and took a bite. Not bad. I chewed and swallowed.

A Murbridge-sized thank-you to all the volunteers, participants and attendees who made this year's Mushroom Festival the best and biggest yet! We hosted an astounding 9,602 people, awarded the FunGuy title to Ms. Soraya Strong from nearby Pittsfield and made it through 300 gallons of ice cream! Yay for Murbridge and the small-town way of life! The Select Board thanks each and every one of you. See you next year!

•

Missing: has anyone seen this woman? (photo attached) Darcy Clipper was last seen yesterday, noon-ish, at the ring toss table. Her friends and family are desperately worried. Please contact Marcus Dash-LaGrand with any information.

•

REMINDER: special Selectmen Meeting happening TUESDAY to hear public comments on Building Permit no. 7729 aka "Stop the Build" project. Please make every effort to attend. Your Leader and Mushroom Monarch, Jake Zdzynzky

•

My daughter came home from the Mushroom Festival with 22 stuffed animals. She said she won them, but I seriously doubt it. We can't fit them all in her room. Any takers?

•

Hey did anyone lose a turkey? My dog Delilah got ahold of what looks like a huge turkey bone and she won't let it go. She's going to town on this thing. Sorry in advance to anyone who might once have owned a turkey.

DARCY. DARCY. DAARCY. DAAAARCY.

Someone was saying my name, over and over again, in a singsong little voice. Maybe a goblin? A wood sprite? The tooth fairy?

Darcy. Darcy!

Now someone was squirting water into my face.

What the—

I opened my eyes. I was lying on my stomach, my head in dirt. Phin crouched beside me with a green water gun pointed directly at my forehead. He wore a cowboy hat, a Spider-Man costume and pink rubber boots.

He stopped squirting. Darcy, are you drunk? Phin asked.

No, I—I don't think so. I tried to sit up but found the act too demanding so I laid my head back down.

Then why are you lying in the mud?

Oh. Am I in mud?

Yes, you're outside our house by the big pool hole where Daddy told us not to go. You're getting in trouble. The last word he drew out into two long syllables: *truuu-buullll.*

Where's your daddy?

He's on the phone inside. Talking to the police.

Police?

They think you've been bludgeoned. They're going to call your mom.

Now I sat up. I wiped my hands on my pants, wiped my face with my hands. Shook my head and felt a teeny-tiny bit of fogginess beginning to clear. Don't call my mom, I said. I'm not bludgeoned. I think I better talk to your daddy.

Just then there was a shriek from the direction of the house. Shoo, shoo! Get away from there. Go!

Marcus was the one shrieking and the apparent subject of the shooing was an enormous German shepherd. The dog was digging very intently on the other side of the abandoned pool excavation. The dog ignored Marcus.

Get away from there! Marcus came running across the lawn toward the dog, swatting at the air with what appeared to be a rubber spatula. He stopped short when he saw me and Phin.

Darcy? Is that you? Oh my God, it's you! We've been so worried! Marcus covered his mouth with his hands, dropped the spatula and ran toward me.

Marcus, be careful! Your shorts will get all dirty, I said as he kneeled in the mud to hug me.

But he ignored me. I felt his heart beating through his chest, his arms around my back. He released me from the hug and grabbed my shoulders. Where have you been? We've looked everywhere. You've been missing since yesterday.

I whistled. That was some mushroom, I said. I had a flash of memory, images of the past twelve hours flying past like a tripped-out Instagram feed. Here I was, running through Fink Park in the dark, singing ABBA songs from the top of the deserted FunGuy competition stage, having a deep and satisfying conversation with a hydrangea bush, finding a person, talking to that person. There were binoculars and these big goggles that looked like spider eyes. Had I been talking to a gigantic spider? But there was also a deep and familiar calm. And then the spider eyes became regular eyes, and the one person became the Birdwatcher. And the Birdwatcher became many birdwatchers, a group of them, all with binoculars and headlamps and lots and lots of pockets. A multiheaded, multi-pocketed posse of quiet and calm. The Birdwatcher had found me, tripping and probably about to run into traffic or jump off a cliff, and understood that I needed guidance. He had kept me safe and brought me here to Marcus and Dan's house.

In the final image, the Birdwatcher said: Stay safe, Darcy. Next year, you should join us for our annual nocturnal birding hike.

Thank you, kind Birdwatcher, I whispered now and closed my eyes.

When I opened them, Marcus and Phin were both looking at me with grave, alarmed faces.

Are you still tripping? Marcus asked. Who are you talking to? Do you need to vomit?

It's okay, Darcy, Phin said, patting my hand, sometimes I throw up too.

I'm fine, I said. I just needed a few minutes to integrate the experience. Whoo! I shook my head. So, here's what happened.

I explained to Marcus, and to an incredibly attentive Phin, about my ignominious exit from the ring toss, meeting Todd's family, my self-pity and embarrassment, my sighting of the rainbow bird, my tumble and hurt ankle, the dead cell phone, the mushroom, the park cavorting, the Birdwatcher and his posse.

Phin, do not eat mushrooms you find in nature, I said. Unless it's your thirtieth birthday and you've had an exceptionally bad day.

Let's get you inside and hydrated, Marcus said quickly. Shrooms really suck the water right out of you.

As Marcus helped me up, the German shepherd yelped once, twice, and then resumed digging with even greater ferocity.

Hey Marcus, I said, I think that dog found something.

And then Phin gasped. Giant eyeballs! he cried, pointing toward the upturned earth. Look!

We looked and there, among the churned-up dirt from the dog and the dig, were scattered large white globes with feathery fringe.

Wow, those are giant eyeballs, I said and blinked. Good spot, Phin.

Those are tulip bulbs, Marcus said firmly. *Not* eyeballs. Although they do look like giant eyeballs, I can see your comparison. Well done, Phin, that's very creative imagining.

Tulip bulbs? I repeated. Tulip lady? I experienced a hazy coming together of *x* and *y*, one, two and three. That picture and this story. A person I should have helped. A question I should have asked.

I think I'm still hallucinating, I said to Marcus. Because it looks like that dog has a necktie in its mouth.

Oh for Pete's sake, said Marcus. Phin, can you run inside and grab the steak in the fridge, the big one? We've got to give this dog something else to chew on.

Sweet, dutiful Phin ran inside.

Here, doggie, doggie, said Marcus, walking slowly toward the German shepherd.

But Marcus, why does the dog have a necktie? I asked. It was a red one, damp and dirty as though it had been underground for some time. Dogs don't wear neckties, I said. Do dogs wear neckties?

Marcus did not answer. He kept walking slowly toward the dog with his hand held out, murmuring in a soft comforting voice. Phin returned with the steak, a very nice-looking rib eye, and the German shepherd released the necktie, yelped with happiness and pounced.

What is going on? I asked. Who is this dog? Did I find him? Did he find me? Whose necktie is that? What is a necktie doing in your pool?

Marcus turned back toward me. Darcy, he said. I feel terrible. You're right, I should have trusted you.

Phin piped up: Daddy, are you *finally* going to tell her?

Marcus nodded. Let's go inside. He picked up the rancid necktie and we left the German shepherd to its steak dinner.

I sat on a tall stool at the kitchen island as Marcus poured me a glass of water. Drink as we talk, he said.

I nodded and began to sip.

Darcy, Marcus continued, his voice grave. Phin found something out by the pool excavation. That's why I asked Burt to stop. It's sensitive. And you have to promise me that you won't tell a soul.

Not a single person?

No one.

Not even Fred?

Nope.

Or my mom?

Absolutely not your mom. *Promise.*

Okay, okay, I promise.

Come with me.

Marcus led me upstairs, past the boys' rooms, past the game room, past the cinema room and crafts room, to the third floor, where he and Dan had installed the master suite. I'd only been up here once before and on that day I'd decided I would be quite content to spend a zombie apocalypse holed up in Marcus and Dan's king-sized master bedroom with en suite shower, whirlpool tub and sauna.

Marcus, I said now, I need full-body hydration. Can I please take a bath in the whirlpool?

You do need a bath, said Marcus, sniffing and making a face, but I think you should sit down for this.

I sat cross-legged on the floor as Marcus rummaged through a top drawer of the built-ins.

Marcus, you already told me about your sock habit, I reminded him. Two hundred and forty-nine pairs is *too many socks,* but we all have our weaknesses. It's okay!

Marcus turned to face me. In his hands, he held a human skull.

I screamed.

Phin found it, said Marcus. By the pool excavation.

I closed my eyes and opened them again.

It's no hallucination, said Marcus.

Is that a real person's skull?

I think so. Look— He scraped a fingernail across the bone. That ain't plastic.

But who—how—*who*?

I have no idea, Marcus replied. Strange as it may seem, there was no name tag attached to the half-decayed skull buried in my back-yard.

There was the sound of small but determined steps on the stairs and Phin crashed into the room, breathing heavily. I heard Darcy scream! he said. Did you show her? He'd exchanged the cowboy hat for a turban, the water gun for a plastic sword, the Spider-Man cos-tume for Wonder Woman, but he still wore the rubber boots.

Phin caught sight of the skull and did a little jig. Daddy, let me tell her. I want to tell.

Marcus nodded at Phin.

So, Darcy, I really wanted to dig and so I started digging with a spoon and then I decided to use the yellow shovel and then . . .

Phin proceeded to tell me the long and twisted tale of his discovery: how he'd really wanted to play in the dirt, even though Marcus had forbidden the boys from entering the excavation area, and so he snuck around the back of the yard and found a perfect spot—big mounds of dirt and no direct line of sight to the patio. And in this wondrous, dirty, secret place, Phin dug happily for a long time and first he found a rock that looked like a fire engine, and then he found an old key, and then he found a twisty branch and then he found the skull. Phin played with these items for a long time and then heard Marcus calling for him and was seized by guilt for disobeying his father's direct order. So, as a peace offering, he brought his discoveries to Marcus.

Daddy screamed too when he first saw the skull, Phin said. Louder than you even.

I bet. Your daddy has some lungs. I turned to Marcus. So, what did the police say?

There was a beat and then Marcus pointed at Phin: Time to get ready for our day, kiddo. Could you go downstairs and please wake up your brothers? And do it nicely. No screaming.

Can I tickle? Phin asked.

Absolutely, Marcus replied. Tickles always work.

Phin wiggled his fingers and bounced out of the room.

Marcus looked at me. I'm not calling the police, he said.

What? Why?

Why? You're really asking me why? What do you think will happen once people find out about a dead body in our backyard? I'll tell you what will happen. Our lives here in Murbridge will be over. After the Little Free Library incident? And Jake's campaign against the playscape? If we get a brick in the window over some dirty magazines, what will they do with an actual body? The boys will be teased mercilessly, Dan and I will be ostracized, plus this place will never sell, we'll be forced to live in a haunted house.

But this isn't your fault. You're not responsible for an old skull in your backyard.

It doesn't matter.

Of course it matters!

What is it that Jake always says? Where there's smoke . . . ? Murbridge is rotten, Darcy. People support Jake and his petition—I bet half the town has signed it by now. In two days, the Board of Selectmen will withdraw my permit for the playscape. Dan and I don't belong here. I don't want my kids growing up here. We're leaving.

Oh Marcus. Please don't move, I said. The skull doesn't blame you.

We both looked at the skull. It looked back at us with huge eyes and a rather cheery expression, despite the dirt-encrusted teeth.

What are you going to do with this guy? I asked. Or gal. I hoped Marcus would tell me this was all a big joke. There was no human skull, we'd go back to building the playscape, he'd stay in Murbridge with his beautiful family forever and I'd join them for each and every Friday falafel night.

But Marcus was not joking. I'll rebury it, he replied evenly. Just put it back where Phin found it. We'll leave and forget this ever happened.

If you're going to do that, then you might as well just stay, I said. I won't tell anyone.

Marcus looked at me. Darcy, I can't ask Phin to keep a secret like this. It's not fair. He's too young to understand. If we're someplace else, he'll forget or it just won't matter. But if we stay here? It's bound to come out.

Marcus, let me call Officer Omar, I said. Please. He'll handle it discreetly.

You are not calling anyone, said Marcus. His eyes had an unhealthy sheen. This was the Marcus who took a golf club to the Hilton ballroom, who scared the Darien ladies with his intensity, who suffered a nervous breakdown in graduate school. Marcus wanted everything to be perfect. He wouldn't allow anyone to alter his vision. His vision of life in Murbridge, of his public playscape full of happy children, was falling apart. He wanted to hold on to the last little pieces of it. Himself, Dan, the kids. His family, the people he loved most. And who could blame him?

Marcus, I understand you're upset, but I think—

I've made my decision.

But what if—

I'm sorry, Darcy, said Marcus with finality. I hope you'll come visit us in our next home.

CONSIDER THE TOWN of Djenné, *National Geographic,* September 1988. Located in central Mali, Djenné dates back to 300 BCE when it flourished alongside Timbuktu as a stop on the trans-Saharan trade routes for gold, salt and slaves. Today the town still exists, smaller in size and importance but famed for its traditional construction technique and astonishing architecture. Buildings are made of sun-dried earth bricks, finished with plaster made of mud and rice husks and plumbed with ceramic pipes that direct water away from the structure. Despite these precautions, every year the bricks begin to disintegrate during the rainy season. Every year, town residents must replaster the walls and shore up the bricks to survive the rains. The town looks like nothing you've ever seen before. Like it's made of organic Lego or built by gigantic ants. For the people of Djenné, *architecture* is a verb as well as a noun. Architecture involves maintenance and community, it involves taking stock of what needs to be done to ensure the town's continued survival despite the natural forces that work to destroy it. During the summer, the whole town comes together to plaster the walls of the central mosque, Djenné's crown jewel. The event is part festival, part religious communion, part work party. Everyone plays a role. Men balance on poles protruding from the sides of the mosque as they slap on plaster while the women pass up buckets of water and the children keep the supplies coming. The whole enterprise shakes precariously, men on poles, women balancing buckets, children running here and there, but it's been done this way for centuries. This is their town and they will work together to keep it whole.

BACK HOME, I took a shower and then sat on my bed and stared at my phone as it charged. I was no longer hallucinating or dehydrated. I was clear-headed, sharp-eyed.

I called Officer Omar.

Hey Darcy, what's the latest drone report?

No drone tonight, I answered. I have a hypothetical situation I'd like to run by you.

Okay. Shoot.

Let's say, hypothetically, that a person living in a small Massachusetts town, much like our own Murbridge, inadvertently discovers human remains buried in their backyard. What would be the appropriate course of action, hypothetically speaking?

Wow. That's an interesting scenario. Everything okay, Darcy?

I'm fine. Just, you know, um—research for a murder mystery I'm writing.

I didn't know you were a writer! Okay, well, let me think. Human remains are serious, of course. You should call the police immediately. Officers could then determine if the remains are actually human. You'd be surprised how many people call in about dead deer or moldy old logs. Lots of active imaginations out there. If it *is* a body, then forensic experts will test how old the bones are, whether a criminal investigation is warranted, all that jazz. You know, over in the U.K., they're always finding backyard burials. Old Celtic guys surrounded by pots and goats and all these offerings to the pagan gods. Awesome stuff. Just awesome.

Okay, that's some interesting history, Omar, but allow me to return to our hypothetical situation in small-town Massachusetts. Let's suppose the person does not call the police, but just reburies the bones in the backyard and goes about their business. No harm, no foul?

No. That's the wrong thing to do.

Wrong as in inadvisable but understandable?

No, wrong as in illegal. Destruction of evidence. Obstructing a murder investigation. I'd have to check my police academy manual for other offenses, but no *way* should you rebury. That would be a huge mistake. Huge. Serious repercussions, possible criminal charges. And nightmares for the rest of your life. I mean, hello, *ghosts*?

I hesitated. But what if said person who hypothetically finds a mysterious body also solves the mystery, tells you who it is and what happened?

Well, in that scenario the person would probably get a medal from the town. Or at least a hearty thank-you from the local police force. That would make my job a heck of a lot easier.

Mmmmm, I said. Interesting.

Is there anything else I can help you with, Darcy?

No, Omar. Thank you. This has been very informational.

If you need me, let me know. It's always nice to hear from you.

I hung up the phone and considered my situation. Was I aiding and abetting Marcus? What if that body was Daddy or Mom? What if there were others down there, ancient others? Every lived life deserves respect and reverence. No one deserves to wind up in a sock drawer. And what if the deep-down suspicion that tickled at the edges of my mind, which might be mushroom residue or might actually be a solution to this riddle—what if my suspicion was right?

I pushed redial.

Darcy, Omar answered on the first ring. Tell me.

TO REACH THE Marian Sisters Home for Elderly Women by car, you drive west through town, take a right on Prospect Street, go up the hill, turn left onto an unmarked twisty, narrow road with root-cracked pavement, bump along for about fifteen minutes, take another right, bump along for another fifteen minutes and then, hidden behind a stand of tall pines and thick hedgerow, you'll find it.

I had always come on foot. But this time was different: Fanny and I would need to make a fast getaway.

Inside I found a welcome desk but no one to express the welcome. The place smelled like a hospital—disinfectant, vomit and hamburgers—but with a distinct undertone of incense. Catholics.

Hello? I called.

Nothing. Maybe breaking Fanny out of here would be easier than

I'd thought. I turned to exit out onto the lawn and nearly collided with a nun.

Oh! You scared me, I said.

I'm sorry but our visiting hours are from two p.m. to five p.m. on Wednesdays, Fridays and Saturdays, said the nun. Today is Monday.

Are you sure? I said. I could have sworn today was Friday. It has a Friday feel, don't you think?

I am most certain that today is Monday, she said. And Monday means no visitors.

I'm here to see Fanny Scott, I explained. It's kind of important.

Sorry, said the nun. No visitors.

What if she's my granny? I asked. Can I visit?

Not on Monday.

What if she won the lottery and I'm here to deliver the winnings?

Come back Wednesday.

Well, Sister, I'm here on urgent police business, I said in my best Detective Logan voice. To interview Fanny Scott with regards to a possible murder investigation.

The nun paused. She looked me up and down: yoga pants, T-shirt, hoodie, my ratty old Vans.

May I see some kind of identification? she asked.

Of course, I answered. But of course I had no identification on me. Who carries ID while wearing yoga pants? And to confirm that I was Darcy Clipper—unemployed lifelong Murbridge resident and decidedly nonpolice material—would not help my case. I gave a show of retrieving my ID. I reached into my hoodie pockets, trying to buy enough time to concoct some other plan, wondering if the nun knew jujitsu or carried a Taser. And then, deep within, a nugget of hope: Officer Omar's business card, the one he'd given me months ago. There were some benefits to never changing or laundering your clothes. I pulled out the card and handed it to the nun. She read it, flipped it over, looked at me.

And you are Officer Omar Abdullah? the nun asked.

I am.

You don't look like an Omar.

Family name, I said and shrugged.

She eyed me one last time and then handed back the card. Officer, she said, I believe Fanny is out on the lawn. This time of day, that's her favorite place. Follow me, please.

I followed the nun's rustling gown through the astonishingly beautiful hallways of the Marian Sisters home. Intricately patterned tiles and thick flagstones, flashes of colored light thrown by the stained glass windows, religious paintings in Renaissance tones. How old did you have to be to live here?

The nun led me through an arched doorway and there upon the verdant lawn was Fanny; Aphrodite lay curled in her lap.

No more than thirty minutes, please, Officer, said the nun. You may show yourself out.

The wheelchair sat at the edge of a shadow, Fanny's feet in the sun, her shoulders in shade. Fanny's head was bowed to Aphrodite. She didn't look up as I approached across the lawn.

Fanny, I said, and crouched down beside her. It's the day you've been waiting for, I whispered. We're escaping!

Fanny lifted her head, but her eyes were muddled. Hello? she said. Who are you?

Fanny, it's me. It's Darcy. Don't you remember?

Fanny narrowed her eyes and pursed her lips. I could see her internal struggle and it caused a painful shift in my chest. I swallowed hard.

Take your time, Fanny, I said. There's no rush. You've been waiting a long time for me. Now I'll wait for you. I sat on the grass and reached up to pet Aphrodite. The cat began to purr. We both waited for Fanny to return.

Ten minutes passed, then twenty. Forty minutes, fifty. I wondered how long before the nun would throw me out. I wondered what was happening inside Fanny's head, which neurons struggled to reconnect and how I might help her. I wondered what would happen when I really needed to pee.

I did not let myself think the unfathomable: that I had waited too long.

I reached into myself, deep down into the long-gone memories of home and Murbridge Elementary School, deep down into that envelope of safety and knowledge and certainty. You can never regain that sense, not really, because life only gets more complicated and certainty only more elusive. We try to find it, boy, do we. Taking out mortgages, getting married, planning vacations, reserving a special restaurant for a fortieth birthday party or a fifteenth wedding anniversary. We believe that the future will look more or less like we expect it to. But you can't count on anything, really. You can't even count on yourself. Growth isn't a given, wisdom isn't automatic, but if you travel the same loop again and again you might start to see the patterns. You might begin to find your strength. Perhaps you might dance Neruda's clumsy dance. Perhaps you might find who you truly are.

Slowly I began to recite aloud the names of the presidents.

Washington. Adams. Jefferson. Madison, I said. Monroe. Adams, but a different Adams than the first. Jackson. Van Buren. Harrison, who doesn't really count. Tyler. Polk. Taylor . . .

I was approaching the Nixon years when at last Fanny spoke.

Stop, she said.

I jumped. Fanny?

Don't say Nixon, please, dear.

Do you remember who I am?

Of course I remember you, Darcy. You are the finder of pets who are not lost.

I smiled. That's me. Aphrodite purred steadily. In the grass, fat bumblebees buzzed among the clover.

I'm glad you came back, I said.

Me too, said Fanny. I'd forgotten my presidents. But you, my dear, have an excellent memory for a woman of your advanced age.

Why, thank you, I said. Sometimes I surprise even myself. So Fanny, are you ready to jump this joint?

I began to stand up, but Fanny put out a hand. Not yet, she said softly. I need a moment to regain my strength. Let's just sit.

I settled back into the grass.

Barnaby knew all the presidents backwards and forwards, said Fanny.

You haven't told me much about Barnaby, I said carefully. What was he like?

Oh Barnaby, Fanny replied. He was smart as a whip and the most thoughtful man. He always knew what I needed. Isn't that something? It's good to have someone like that around. He saw through people, through the screens they put up to hide their true selves. We all do it. You do it too, dear. I can tell. Barnaby's aptitude for honesty was uncanny, really. Sometimes he was annoying as hell. Sometimes, hiding is what a person needs. To wall herself away from a hurtful world. To protect her thin skin from cold winter winds. But Barnaby would have none of that. He met everything head-on and thought I should too. He wasn't afraid of a thing. Not one thing.

He sounds like quite a person.

Oh, he was. You'd have loved him. Everyone did. Our one regret, you know, was not having children. We tried of course, but we never got liftoff. And there weren't the kind of options back then that women have today. IVF and all that business. It was my ovaries, you see.

Me too, I said. My doctor never figured out what was wrong with me. But I was the problem, not Skip.

I'm sorry to hear that, dear. Fanny's right hand left the cat and, shaking ever so slightly, came to rest on my shoulder. It weighed so little, as though a bird perched there, but the warmth passed through my hoodie and T-shirt to my skin. I closed my eyes.

You'll be fine, Darcy. Don't worry. Bodies are unpredictable. We are all full of surprises. She lifted her hand and I opened my eyes.

Where did you and Barnaby live? I asked. It was my voice shaking now.

Why, in Murbridge, of course. Thirty-two Lincoln Avenue, corner of Mercer.

I nodded. I know that house very well, I said. My friends Marcus and Dan bought it last year.

We built that house together, Barnaby and I, said Fanny. His father helped with the plans and permits, but we did most of the work. Oh, we had such fun! We couldn't afford any fancy landscaping. We were so young—we didn't know anything about anything. But tulip bulbs—those were easy. And cheap. That first fall, we planted dozens of bulbs in the yard. Red, yellow, purple, pink. I honestly forgot about them over the winter. We had so much snow that year. I didn't think I'd ever see green again. But then spring arrived and the bulbs sprouted and, oh my goodness, Darcy, it was a miracle. Overnight they all bloomed. One morning I looked out the kitchen window and there was an ocean of flowers, all the colors, all those cheerful blossoms. People don't think tulips have much of a scent, but they do. You simply need them in numbers. One doesn't smell like much, but a hundred? They transform into a thing of wonder. Fanny paused. Have you ever smelled one hundred tulips?

I haven't, no.

Put it on your bucket list. You don't want to miss one hundred tulips.

Did Barnaby come here with you to live? I asked.

Oh no. Only women live here. Fanny began petting Aphrodite in long, slow concentrated strokes. The cat briefly opened her eyes and then closed them again.

Fanny, what happened to Barnaby?

Fanny lifted her head. Are you in love, my dear? she asked.

I thought about Skip's recent email. No, I said. But I remain hopeful.

Well then, you will be. Sooner than you think is my prediction. Fanny paused. You want to know what happened to Barnaby?

I nodded.

He died of course. Everyone avoids saying that word. Death is too terrifying to discuss frankly. But Barnaby would have none of that. He was healthy and fit, he weighed the same at seventy-five as he had at twenty-five, and then—Fanny paused. Then out of nowhere he couldn't get out of bed. He was so tired. Finally, after a month of this, I threatened I'd leave him if we didn't get to a hospital. That got him up. A very nice young doctor in Boston did some tests. Pancreatic cancer, he told us, stage four.

Oh Fanny.

Yes. Well, they suggested some treatment but really at that point it was a shot in the dark. Maybe we'd get lucky, but chances were we'd lose his last days to vomiting and hospital visits. He didn't want that. I certainly didn't want that. So we came back.

To Murbridge, to the house on Lincoln Avenue.

Yes. To our home. We had three lovely months together in the end, through the spring and early summer. Just the two of us. We didn't tell any of our friends. Barnaby didn't want anyone making a fuss, he didn't want sadness around him. And for that last season, I wanted him all to myself.

Here Fanny paused and smiled at me, her eyes filled with bright tears. The tulips were magnificent that spring, she continued. And then the blooms began to wilt, as tulips do. First one petal, then another, until only the bare pistils remain. Then it's time to cut the stems. Barnaby was ready to die by then, I had the morphine ready. But the event itself still shocked me. One minute and then—*poof.* Gone. He died on June 10, 1998, and I buried him in the tulip bed. We'd talked about it, of course.

We didn't want to be apart. And he loved those tulips. Fanny paused. I told everyone I buried him in Boston, where he grew up. No one suspected a thing. Darling, said Fanny, I didn't want you to go.

I reached for Fanny's hand and then said gently: I think my friend Marcus may have found Barnaby. He's building a playground for the whole town and, well, there's been a lot of digging.

Fanny angled her head. That's why, she said softly. I suspected something of the sort. So where is Barnaby now?

I grimaced and released Fanny's hand. He's in my friend's sock drawer. At least some of him is.

Ha! Fanny began to laugh. Barnaby would love this story. A dead body, a mystery, a sock drawer, and they send a cat finder to solve the case! It's quite a tale. For years, I've been so worried. I didn't want anyone to know I'd helped Barnaby die. I didn't want to end up in prison. But honestly, Darcy, I don't care anymore. I just want to go home.

Do you remember the officer friend I told you about? I asked her. Fanny nodded.

I know you said no police, but he's going to help us. You don't need to worry, this will all get sorted out. Everything is going to be okay, Fanny. Now let's get you back to Lincoln Avenue.

Fanny put her hands on her chest. That would make me very happy, dear.

I brought my car, I said. It's just a Prius, no convertible, but I can try to peel out.

Wonderful, Fanny said and clapped her hands. I'll go put on my mascara.

I brought the car around to the front entrance. Fanny was standing at the welcome desk, not a nun in sight.

Quick, before someone sees, she said and grabbed my hand. She moved faster than I expected, leaning on my arm only briefly as we descended the steps from the house to the drive. We were almost in the clear, and then:

Fanny Scott, is that you? called a voice from an upstairs window. It's not visiting hours!

Oh good Lord, that's Agnes, said Fanny as I helped her into the car. She's a nutjob. Just ignore her, dear.

But Agnes was not ignoring us. Who are you? she yelled down. Where are you taking Fanny? It's not visiting hours! Kidnapper! Sisters! There's a kidnapping in progress!

She's got some lungs on her, I said as I slid into the driver's seat. Let's hope the sisters are all napping.

The sisters were not napping. An exceptionally large nun rushed out of the building and behind her, several smaller nuns. The large nun jumped in front of the car, a nightmarish vision of swirling black robes and an angry red face.

No visitors allowed outside of visiting hours! yelled the nun, shaking a finger at me through the windshield. And certainly no off-site trips!

Just drive, dear, Fanny said, staring straight ahead. She gripped my forearm. Just ignore her and drive.

And so I did. With a scattering of gravel, I shifted the car into reverse, spun around in the fastest three-point turn ever accomplished by an aging Prius and accelerated away from the finger-shaking nun and the Marian Sisters Home for Elderly Women. As we left the driveway for the road, Fanny let out a cheer.

Oh, you have no idea, she said. You have no idea how long I've wanted to do this. I knew you'd eventually find the nerve, Darcy.

Thanks for having faith in me, I said and smiled. But will you be in trouble? When you get back?

Fanny paused. I may have lost cake, she said. But I can live with that.

I CALLED OFFICER Omar from the car.

We're on our way to the Dash-LaGrand place on Lincoln Ave., I said. I'm with Fanny Scott, the woman I was telling you about. We'll meet you there. And don't forget—be discreet.

When we arrived, the house sat quietly, pristine with its freshly mown lawn and blooming pink rhododendron in front. Burt had moved all his trucks and equipment; the protestors had packed it in weeks ago. We sat for a moment as Fanny gazed out the window.

It certainly does look different, Fanny said quietly. We only had four rooms downstairs, four rooms up. That whole bit there is new. She waved an arm vaguely toward the new kitchen wing. And there—I don't remember that either. She was pointing toward the downstairs side entrance to the boys' bedrooms, interior play area and gym.

The new owners have made improvements, I said.

Improvements? Fanny grunted. Place looks like a sprawling octopus to me. She sighed. But, oh well. In with the new. She turned to me: Can we go inside?

As I helped Fanny out of the car, I heard the distinct sound of approaching police sirens. Oh no, I thought as the sound grew louder. I hope that's not Omar.

It was Omar. A trio of police cars pulled up to the house with a screech and earsplitting *woo-woo*.

Barnaby isn't going anywhere, Fanny said into my ear. There's really no need for them to rush.

Omar jumped out of the first police car.

That's not discreet! I called to him over the noise.

He made a sheepish grimace and ducked back into the car. The sirens cut, but the lights still danced across the house, the street, the sidewalk. Marcus's east-side neighbor opened his front door. Across the street, faces appeared in a window.

As I was helping Fanny out of the car, Marcus rushed outside. Darcy, what the actual fuck, he said. I'm stunned. You completely betrayed my trust.

Marcus, I'm sorry. I didn't think they'd use the squad cars. But bear with me here. I smiled what I hoped was a reassuring smile. This is Fanny Scott, the tulip lady from the Community Board, the previous owner of your house, wife to the bones buried in the backyard. She's the one who put them there!

Darcy dear, said Fanny, I think it's more accurate to describe me as the *widow* of the bones buried in the backyard.

Yes, sorry, Fanny. Widow. I turned back to Marcus. And yes, I called Officer Omar. That's why the police cars are here. He'll take a statement from Fanny, bag up the bones and clear the site so construction can continue. You can still build the playscape, Marcus! There's no smoke! Jake loses!

Darcy, it's too late, said Marcus. We've got a meeting with a Realtor in Greenwich next week. Dan's commute will be easier so he can be home more. The boys can still play lacrosse. We're leaving Murbridge.

My stomach dropped. Greenwich? I said. I thought you were done with Connecticut. And what about the town meeting tomorrow?

Marcus snorted. Are you kidding? What do you think is going to happen? Look at these cop cars. There'll be more protestors here in ten minutes flat, just as soon as news gets out on the Community Board. It's just more fuel for Jake's ridiculous fire. And then tomorrow, Jake and all his gazillions of minions will revoke our building permit, thereby succeeding in his efforts to drive us out of town.

You don't know the permit will be revoked, I said. It's an open meeting. Any town resident can vote. I'm going, Fanny wants to go too. Don't give up on us, Marcus, please.

Marcus looked at me for one beat, two. It's over, he said and turned away. The front door slammed shut behind him.

He sure is grumpy, said Fanny.

He's not usually like that, I replied.

Mrs. Scott? Omar was standing behind us, holding out his hand.

It's a pleasure to meet you. Is now a good time to discuss what happened to your husband?

While Omar interviewed Fanny, I decided to try again with Marcus. I'd never seen him so mad. I decided I'd better knock.

Phin opened the door. Hey Darcy, he said. He was wearing a blue Elsa ball gown and soccer cleats and a feather behind one ear. Daddy says I can't let you in. You are in *big* trouble.

I know. Thanks, Phin.

But Papa wants to talk to you.

Phin stepped aside and Dan, the famed Daniel Dash-LaGrand, broker of deals, earner of millions, flier of platinum frequency, a man in possession of the physique and countenance of a Swedish masseuse, appeared before me.

Hi Darcy, he said. Nice to finally meet you. He stepped outside and closed the door. Sorry, he said, I think it's better if you don't see Marcus right now.

Um, nice to meet you too, I stammered.

I heard you thought I didn't exist?

Not exactly. I laughed nervously. I was just pulling Marcus's leg.

But Dan was serious. The truth is, I don't exist, he said. Not as a responsible partner and co-parent. I'm gone too much. I'm not involved with the boys' lives. I'm stressed out all the time. He paused. I want to thank you for being such a huge support to Marcus this year. Moving to another new town was tough. And after what happened in Darien . . .

Yeah, he told me about the ladies.

You've been a wonderful friend to him. And your carpentry skills are impressive. Marcus is very particular about who touches his table saw.

He's an excellent teacher.

I've promised him we'll make changes, a lot of changes, in our next home.

So you really are leaving?

Marcus thinks it's for the best. I don't want to push him to stay. And listen, I'm sure he'll come around. He won't leave without saying good-bye to you himself.

Okay, I said quietly.

Sorry we couldn't have gotten to know each other better, Dan said. Phin thinks you're the cat's meow, by the way.

The feeling is mutual.

Take care, Darcy.

THAT NIGHT, I opened a dinner from Mr. Kilt Man and picked at the chicken l'orange with toasted Israeli couscous and braised greens. My meal deliveries had been piling up. Mom would have figured out how to freeze them for another, hungrier day but I lacked her refrigeration skills. In fact, I lacked domestic skills entirely. The house needed attention, I realized, gazing around the kitchen with its overflowing sink and full garbage bin. I brought my plate into the living room to improve the view but there too disaster greeted me: discarded clothing, dirty dishes, books, magazines, dust and what looked like a cinnamon roll smashed into the carpet.

When did I drop *that*? I wondered.

I took my dinner out to the backyard and ate it there, balanced on a rickety lawn chair, looking at the back of the Dykstras' house, wondering why in the hell they kept the lights on in every room. Hadn't they heard of energy conservation? Morons. I felt my mood grow prickly, my disappointment in humanity and in myself growing deeper by the minute.

Seven months ago, I'd driven home to an empty house in the dead of winter. I cried every day and wrote weird emails to Skip and never changed my pajamas. Tonight I wore regular clothes—a cute pair of cutoffs Marcus had called twenty-first-century grunge. There was still paint under my fingernails from work on the outdoor mural, my shoulders ached from the electric sander. Last night, I'd dreamt about children swinging on a gigantic swing set, their little legs pumping as they soared higher and higher into the sky. In the dream, I worried that someone might get hurt, one of the kids might go hurtling off into outer space. But they looked so happy that I let them be.

I thought about finding all those pets. *You're an angel, a lifesaver,* those pet owners had said to me. I thought about Murbridge and Marcus and breaking Fanny out of the Marian Sisters home. I hadn't saved anything or anyone. The pets were all just fine. The cats were getting fed; the dogs just wanted a quick wander. The Marian Sisters home was beautiful. There was no saving anyone from that place. And Marcus? The truth was that he had saved me. He had pulled me out of my chickpea stupor with his orange castle and brie paninis, taught me about Lady Marjory and taking risks and independence. He gave me something to do; he showed me what a common destiny looks like.

I began to cry. What had I done with my life? What had I contributed? What had I built? I couldn't even stick it out at the Mushroom Festival ring toss. I had stolen all of Mrs. Pevzner's Tupperware. I'd stopped speaking to my parents. I'd betrayed my best friend. Watching the lights burn in the windows of the Dykstra house, I cried and cried and cried. My self-pity and self-critique grew with every passing minute. Fred, Mr. Kilt Man, Jared the UPS guy, Mr. Castro, Aleeyah, Min, Mrs. Pevzner, Todd, Fanny, Omar, Phin, my fifth-grade teacher Mr. Antizi, who I called Mr. Assy behind his back, my hairdresser in college, whom I never tipped, the driver whose side window I smashed and didn't stop. And Marcus. Especially Marcus. I'd failed everyone I'd ever known.

I stumbled inside to find some tissues. And it was here, sprawled on the couch, tissue box beside me, my nose running, my throat achy from so much wailing, that I heard my name.

Darcy Clipper! A voice yelled through the door. I know you're in there! Open up! A pause. It's your neighbor, Mrs. Dykstra.

I stopped. Mrs. Dykstra? My nemesis, the woman who visited my dreams almost as often as Bianca the skydiving temptress?

What do you want? I yelled back.

Oh Jesus, just open up.

I blew my nose, wiped my eyes, staggered to the door and opened it.

Wow, you are a mess, said Mrs. Dykstra. May I come in?

I coughed. Before me stood a woman I'd never seen before in Murbridge. She was tall, with round tortoise-shell glasses, olive-y skin, straight-across black bangs and a bob à la Uma Thurman circa *Pulp Fiction*. She was wearing a vintage Blondie T-shirt ripped at the neck, a long batik skirt, combat boots and very red lipstick.

Mrs. Dykstra walked past me. Can I smoke in here? she asked. It's just a clove.

I was too shocked to answer. All this time, I'd been expecting a middle-aged, annoyed housewife with manicured fingernails, a huge diamond ring and too much time on her hands. Mrs. Dykstra looked annoyed, possibly middle-aged, but no diamonds and certainly no manicure.

Um, no, my parents would kill me, I said. Let's go outside. I pointed toward the back door.

Mrs. Dykstra sat on a lawn chair and lit up a long, dark cigarette. I've tried vaping, she said, but it's like sucking on a Slurpee. She shuddered. Ugh. She blew smoke from her nostrils like a dragon and held out her hand. Hi, I'm Roxanne. I don't think we've properly met yet.

Hi, I said, taking her hand. Darcy.

Yeah, I know who you are. You're the one who keeps calling the cops on my drone.

That's me.

Listen, I want to put to bed whatever weird psychodrama is playing out between us. Normally these interactions roll off my back, but that Officer Omar said you've had a rough year. So, my apologies if I contributed to your malaise. I know, the drone does sound like killer bees. I've had that reaction before, although never with that much noise. You and Marcus are impressive screamers.

You know Marcus?

I know everyone in this town, said Roxanne. It's my job. She looked at me expectantly. Roxanne *Dykstra*? You haven't heard of me?

I could not have been more confused. No, I answered. I don't think so.

Dykstra Productions? *Bridges to Nowhere*? *Morality's Assassin*?

Excuse me? I said.

You must not be a fan of documentary film.

I did see that one about the tickle guy. He paid people so he could tickle them. Know it?

Hm. Not ringing a bell, said Roxanne. Listen, I'm here to make peace, but also to show you something.

Roxanne took out her phone. I'm making a film about democracy, she explained. New England town meetings, one person one vote. You, Darcy Clipper, are living in one of the last remaining strongholds of pure democracy. Think about that. Everywhere else, it's essentially a figment of our collective naive imagination. But here in Murbridge, with your selectmen and your open meetings, you're living the vision. It's the essence of democracy, the pure unfiltered elixir of the people. Every single goddamn resident gathering together to decide, through peaceful debate, how to manage their community. Honestly, it's beautiful. It knocks my fucking socks off. It's exactly what the founding fathers envisioned. Roxanne paused. Well, not *exactly*. They excluded women, people of color and anyone too poor to own land. But the founding fathers envisioned the *principle*.

Wow, I said. I never knew I was living the vision.

Yeah, most people don't get it. We've all been drinking the fake democracy Kool-Aid for so long—Democrats, Republicans, progres-

sives, independents, neocons, neolibs, Green Party, pool party—
we've forgotten what the real thing tastes like.

Roxanne blew smoke directly into my face. I coughed.

Sorry, I usually smoke alone, she said, waving a hand to clear the
air. So, anyhow, a couple weeks ago I was looking to get some estab-
lishing aerial shots of the town. Nothing fancy, just slow neighborhood pans with nice light. And look at this.

She pressed the play triangle on the phone and Lincoln Avenue
sprang to life. It was dusk, the shadows low and long, cars passing
on the street, a waft of smoke from a nearby barbecue. There was
Marcus and Dan's house, the backhoe, the neighboring red, old colonial, the bus stop and the Little Free Library right out front. Here
the drone lowered and a figure came into view. The figure was male,
middling height, red-haired and red-faced, wearing a backpack and
running shoes. He looked over one shoulder, then the other, pulled
a stack of magazines out of the pack and placed them on the library
shelf.

Wait—I said. That's—

Jake Zdzynzky, presiding chair of the Select Board, said Roxanne.
And look— She reversed the video, slowed it down and zoomed in
on Jake's backpack, his hand reaching in, and clearly legible across
the magazine front cover were the words *Big Bad Babies*.

That stinker, I breathed. Marcus knew it the whole time!

I hate to get involved in petty bullshit like this, said Roxanne. I'm
an observer, not a participant. But I can't let dishonesty win the day.
I tried sending this to the Dash-LaGrands directly, but they've got
one hell of a filter on their service. I kept getting a bounce-back. I
don't seem to have that problem with you. Maybe we use the same
security program?

Maybe? I said and gave her a wide-eyed look of clueless innocence.
Roxanne and I were getting along so nicely; why let on now that I'd
been freeloading off her Wi-Fi for the past seven months?

Anyhow, Roxanne continued, typing into her phone, I just emailed this to you. Do what you want with it.

Thank you, I said. I can't thank you enough.

My pleasure, Roxanne replied and briefly closed her eyes. And listen, don't tell anyone where you got the film. I'm working incognito here and don't want to blow my cover.

So are you, like, famous? I asked.

You could say that, she replied, but no one knows my face. I'm the one behind the camera. I'm the one who tells the story. And I don't want the wrong story told about those magazines.

I'll bring the video to the meeting tomorrow, I said. I'll walk right up there in front of all those people, and I'll look Jake straight in the face and I'll—I'll— I started to choke. My heart was beating faster than seemed healthy.

Roxanne was watching me. Take a deep breath, she said. Most people fear public speaking more than death. She took a long drag of her cigarette. Not me, she said, exhaling smoke. But I get it.

I don't know—I don't know if I can—

Yes, you can. You can do it. It'll be tough, sure, but it's the right thing to do. I understand you and Marcus are pretty good friends.

I nodded.

Would he do this for you?

I nodded again.

My advice is to imagine everyone in the audience flossing their teeth.

Isn't it supposed to be sitting on the toi—

Gross, said Roxanne, shaking her head. Stop right there. Give people their privacy. Let them have their moment. But teeth flossing? It's a bathroom-door-open kind of activity. And it's responsible. I like to give an audience the benefit of the doubt. Give them a chance to be their best selves.

And that works for you? Images of flossing?

Roxanne nodded. Like a charm. And you know why? Because it comforts me to know that deep down, we all have teeth that need attention. Why fixate on our differences? We all need the same things. We all want the same things. A nice meal, a warm bed with a warm body next to you and squeaky-clean teeth. And for the first time, Roxanne smiled at me. We're all just dancing the clumsy dance, she said.

I nodded. And singing the sorrowful song.

Neruda knew what he was talking about, Roxanne replied. She took one long, final drag of her cigarette and then stubbed it out on the patio tiles. I'll be watching from the sidelines at the meeting tomorrow. I'll be cheering you on. Silently, of course, to maintain my low profile, but the cheer will be genuine.

Thanks, I said.

After Roxanne left, I cleared off the couch and opened my laptop. I began an email to Marcus.

Draft email files

Dear Marcus, I'm so sorry but—

_____

Hey Marcus, Remember my crazy neighbor? She—

_____

Marcus, you won't believe what—

And then, finally I wrote:

Dear Marcus, I'm sorry about what happened today, but please don't give up. I have video proof that Jake is a liar and a cheat. I left a thumb drive in your mailbox, and I'll bring the footage to the town meeting and show everyone. I'll stand up and give a speech about how wonderful the playscape will be, how committed you are to the vision. It will be social anxiety training on steroids, but for you and the playscape I'll do it.

Your friend, Darcy

THE SELECT BOARD MEETINGS WERE held in the old Town Hall, down the street from the Store24 gas station, across from the Murbridge town graveyard. The Town Hall building dated back to the mid-1800s and, from the outside, it looked old and imposing: brick with white trim, two massive fluted columns, lots of ivy. Inside, thanks to several decades of cheap and artless renovation, the place resembled a high school gymnasium, minus the basketball hoops. The acoustics echoed and the floor squeaked

Tonight, the place was full. Every folding chair in the joint supported a Murbridge bottom.

Wow, Fanny whispered into my ear after we found two free seats toward the back, I had no idea this many people lived here.

Me either, I whispered back.

All seven members of the Select Board sat at the front of the room, along one side of a long table. On the table was a microphone for board members to share and, in front, a floor microphone for public comments.

And there they were, sitting without any apparent logic or rank. Hildegard Hyman, Pat Pernicky, Lydia Aoki, Allston Highbottom, Rosalia Gonzalez, Pearl Odette, and Jake. I recognized them all from the grocery store, the post office, the library, school field trips to Town Hall, and parties my parents used to throw. I'd rarely spoken to any of them, but I'd watched them age and go gray, send their kids off to college, move to smaller homes. And through all those years, I realized, they had been watching me too.

The crowd shifted and twittered and coughed. Hildegard rapped a gavel on the table and said: Hear ye, hear ye, I call to order this meeting of the town of Murbridge, Massachusetts, on the twenty-second day of August, the year of our Lord two thousand and nineteen.

I feel like I'm in a movie, I whispered to Fanny.

Me too, she whispered back.

Hildegard continued: Today's agenda was tweeted last week and circulated via the Community Board. We have only one item, a proposed revocation of building permit number 7729, for 32 Lincoln Avenue, property owners Mr. and Mr. Dash-LaGrand. A petition has been submitted with—

Jake leaned forward and motioned for the microphone.

Jake, said Hildegard in an indoor kind of voice, there are certain formalities that the secretary must comply with at the beginning of each meeting. That's what I'm doing right now.

Jake shook his head and mouthed something I couldn't hear. Hildegard widened her eyes, but she handed the microphone over.

Hear ye, hear ye, Jake began, my name is Jake Zdzynzky, chairman of this Board of Selectmen. I rule that another item be added to today's agenda. We will consider a new, preemptive building permit application for a future project on the same land. I don't own it yet, but I will soon. My goal as leader here is to make our public meetings more efficient and less wasteful so I'd like to just get the permit approved now while we're all gathered. Capiche?

He handed the microphone back to Hildegard.

But Jake can't do that, I whispered to Fanny. How can you apply for a building permit for land that's not yours!

It's preposterous, Fanny whispered back.

Hildegard cleared her throat. Jake, that's preposterous, she said. You don't even own the land. Let's stick to the official agenda. After the meeting, I can help you understand the correct procedures and protocol. Capiche?

Jake bowed his head. Yielding the floor to Madame Secretary, he said.

Moving right along, Hildegard continued, a "Stop the Build, Save Murbridge" petition has been submitted to the Select Board. There are three hundred seventeen signatories here, she said, flipping pages on a clipboard, although just glancing through I see a few odd names. G.I. Joe? Kylie Jenner? Baby Yoda? Do these individuals reside within Murbridge town limits?

She looked at the crowd as if expecting an answer. There were more than a few giggles, but Hildegard remained solemn. She said: In any event, accepting the full three hundred seventeen as legitimate, this represents approximately nine percent of eligible Murbridge voters. The mic is now open for public comments. Hildegard sat back in her chair.

I looked around the room. After a few moments of busy chair-rattling, throat-clearing silence, a woman in front stood up and made her way to the microphone. I didn't recognize her, but from the back she looked frumpy.

That's one frumpy lady, Fanny whispered to me.

The frumpiest, I whispered back.

The woman began speaking. A verbatim transcript of her comments is unnecessary here, and would likely bore you to tears, but basically she said she was worried that children would make noise while playing.

I'm sorry to interrupt, Hildegard said as she interrupted the woman, but we limit our public comments to five minutes per person. I gather you're concerned about noise?

Yes, ma'am, the woman said.

Thank you. Anyone else worried about noise?

Four hands were raised.

Okay, so we've got five noise worriers. Any other public comments in support of the petition?

The room got quiet. No one moved. No one sneezed or coughed or farted. Could it be? I thought with slow-dawning joy. This silence was the gorgeous sound of Jake Zdzynzky's agenda crashing to the floor. This was the sound of small-town democracy in action.

And then with a squeak of the floor and an alarming crack of his back, Jake himself stood up and took hold of the microphone.

No one? he began. No one else is ready to stand up to save our town? He opened his mouth and stared out at the crowd, his face organized in an exaggerated expression of shock at the utter lack of chutzpah his fellow aggrieved Murbridgeans were summoning tonight.

People, he began. Friends, neighbors, acquaintances. Mi gente of Murbridge. Please, let us not forget the issue that brings us all here tonight, the issue that concerns each and every one of us. I know we don't like to say it out loud, I know we all want to be Peee Seee—here Jake elongated the vowels and used air quotes—but someone must speak the truth.

Good Lord, I hate air quotes, Fanny whispered to me.

Good Lord, me too, I whispered back.

The truth is that where there's smoke, there's fire. And those magazines—those—those dirty, offensive, horrible magazines were sitting right there in a Little Free Library built and stocked by Marcus Dash-LaGrand himself. Little Free Libraries should offer us all a safe place of innocence and learning. A resource for personal growth and enlightenment. *Knowledge* is what a Little Free Library represents. Knowledge and free stuff. And now, this community resource has been sullied, dirtied, defiled by the introduction of deviant sexual material that goes against the family values we hold so dear here in our historic Murbridge. This cannot stand. This *must* not stand. If a man believes it appropriate to circulate pornography within our community, then what else might he deem appropriate? Are the magazines *proof* of evil-doing? No, but do we really want to take a chance with our own *children*?

He's lost me with the logic, whispered Fanny.

Logic schmogic, I whispered back. He doesn't care. But Fanny, hold on to your hat. Things are about to get interesting.

I closed my eyes, inhaled deeply, exhaled slowly. Briefly, I allowed a vision of all these Murbridgeans flossing their teeth, all those bathroom doors standing wide open. These were my friends and neighbors, people I'd known my entire life. Although some, I realized now as I opened my eyes and examined the room, were people I'd never seen before. Most of them, in fact, were complete and total strangers. I felt my pulse escalate, my lungs constrict.

Again, I closed my eyes. Floss. Everyone wants healthy gums. These were people just like me, and they deserved the truth.

I stood up, ready to submit Roxanne's video to the Select Board, to explain what the footage showed and thereby to send Jake Zdzynzky howling from the room. But before I could open my mouth, a voice called out from the back: Jake, you're lying your pants off.

All heads turned. All mouths dropped as Marcus and Dan strode down the central aisle, Marcus carrying a laptop, Dan a portable projection screen. They wore matching blue sports coats and very nice shoes.

Hildegard, I noticed, was smiling.

What hotties, Fanny whispered to me.

The hottest, I whispered back.

After Dan set up the screen and Marcus pressed play on the laptop, after the video aired once, twice and then a third time at the request of two Select Board members, after the crowd's gasps and chatter had died down, Jake pushed himself up from the table and waved his arms.

That video is rigged! It's fake! Jake yelled. That's not me!

It looks exactly like you, said Hildegard.

It does, said Pat Pernicky. I think you're even wearing the same shirt.

Jake looked down. Sure enough, he was wearing the same white collared polo with green and blue argyle stripes seen in the video. This was not a shirt that faded into the background. Shit, Jake said quietly.

The board members all nodded. Hildegard placed a hand on the microphone to allow for confidential discussion. Lydia Aoki leaned in to Allston Highbottom and began speaking intently. Rosalia Gonzalez whispered into Pearl Odette's ear.

There were murmurs from the crowd, head scratching, nods. An unmistakable climate of agreement settled over the room.

That Jake is toast, Fanny whispered to me.

Buttered and burnt, I whispered back.

All color drained from Jake's normally red face. He looked around the room. Well—well—he stuttered. Does anyone else want to speak out about this monstrous construction project? Parking issues? Seasonal employees? High-risk activities? Crime? Drugs? *Gangs*?

Silence.

And what about my idea? Jake continued. An indoor, adults-only pool and first-class spa and movie theater with reclining seats. A nude burlesque show, maybe one of those restaurants where they cook the meat right at the table. We'll pack 'em in, shoulder to shoulder! And eventually, we can bring in a full-service casino. Jake rubbed his hands gleefully. What do you think, Murbridge? Huh? What'll it be?

Silence. And then a woman on the far left raised a slender arm, stood and walked to the microphone. She was wearing a yellow skirt and white cardigan and looked very tired.

Hello, she said. My name is Dierdre Von Dimminger, mother to twin sons Jett and Viggo, forty-six months old. I go by the handle BestBoyMommy22 on the Community Board so hello to all my neighbors. Here she turned and gave a little wave to the crowd. Many of us, myself included, waved back. It's always nice to put a face with a social media name.

She continued: I just wanted to say that I am fully in favor of the playscape project. The public playground here is bad. I mean really really bad. My boys think it's boring. The boringest, they say, and I know that's not a word but it's so cute, I just let it go. This town needs a resource that's not boring. We need a modern, exciting space for our kids and I'm so grateful to the Dash-LaGrand family for using their own private resources to better our community. They're heroes, I think. And thank you for installing trampolines. My boys love to jump and it tires them out like nothing else. Oh, and also, we don't live in Las Vegas, we live in New England. I'm worried that Mr. Zdzynzky is forgetting the history and traditions of our town. That's all I have to say. She gave another little wave and stepped away.

Next, an elderly man shuffled up to the microphone. He forcefully cleared his throat, blew his nose on a handkerchief, folded it carefully and put it in his pocket. *Murbridge*, he began in a deep and crackly voice. I've lived in this town longer than most of you've been breathing. I've seen people come and go, kids pick up and leave, friends die, my wife, Delores, too, God rest her soul. Lots of change and most of it not the good kind. Crime. Gangs. All these teenagers running around with their pants dragging down, tattoos, crazy hairdos. Whatever happened to good old-fashioned fun? Playing cards, racing derby cars, listening to the radio? Sock hop. What the hell ever happened to sock hops? Well, I'd like to see Murbridge kids do something other than stealing packages, ringing doorbells and smoking crack. I think this whole playground development is a good idea. Positive change for once. I don't even mind that these two men are homosexuals. Their intentions seem honorable to me. He snorted. I don't care about some dirty magazines. Hell, we've all seen a few of those. So, yes, I'm in favor of the new playground. He nodded toward Hildegard, gave a little bow and shuffled back to his seat.

And so it went. Person after person, Murbridgean after Murbridgean, taking the stage, voicing their support for the playscape, publicly and loudly. Georgina talked about how useless her husband was at watching their four children and would Marcus and Dan consider adopting a few more? The crowd laughed nervously at that one. Mrs. Pevzner talked about visits from her grandchildren and wouldn't it be nice for them to have someplace special to go, all together. The blond owner of Hamish the golden retriever took the mic. Several other pet owners I recognized from my previous occupation: Puneet with the pet boa, Lillian with the Labrador, Consuelo with the schnauzer. A trio of Marian Sister nuns wondered if some of the elderly residents might volunteer at the playscape. Or maybe use the trampolines themselves? One woman even offered to make lunches for the kids on weekends. All the soup they can eat, she said shyly.

Toward the end of the session, I felt a draft of fresh air as the door opened, a rustling of footsteps as more people entered the hall. I turned and it was the Birdwatcher and his posse, a smaller group than the one I'd encountered on my mushroom trip but a dozen people at least. They all wore pocket vests, binoculars strung around their necks.

The Birdwatcher strode to the microphone, his boots clomping, and as he walked, people in the crowd looked at him with trepidation and—could it be?—fear. Chatter broke out, one man pointed and leaned into his wife: *Gangs,* he whispered loud enough for the whole room to hear. More heads turned. There were nods, whispers, narrowed eyes. The word *gang* moved across the room.

Unperturbed, the Birdwatcher began to speak in his calm, measured voice. I'm not a Murbridge town resident, none of us are—he gestured toward the others in his group—but we highly value the avian wildlife that populates this part of the state. We're members of Flock, a Boston-based amateur ornithologist club for people of color. Many of us frequently travel out to these small towns to see what we can find. As an avid birdwatcher since childhood, I'm particularly thankful that the Murbridge town government has pre-served and maintained the wetlands area here as a refuge for so many threatened and endangered species. He gave a head tilt to-ward Hildegard, who tilted hers back in thanks.

The crowd, I noticed, was now completely silent. Everyone watched the Birdwatcher as he spoke.

My comments today are twofold, he continued. First, I'd like to express my support for the playscape and my opposition to this new casino development proposal. I'm sure the latter would offer eco-nomic benefits to the town and to *some* of its residents, but I ask you all to consider the larger costs. The nature of Murbridge would change fundamentally. I urge you to preserve the natural space you're lucky enough to enjoy here. It's a rare and special place.

He paused and, in the silence, I thought I heard some muffled weeping coming from the front. Several people, I noted, were now slumped down into their chairs as though trying in vain to disap-pear. *Sheepish* was the word that sprang to mind. Sheepish and em-barrassed.

The Birdwatcher resumed speaking: And second, if the playscape project continues to fruition, I'd like to offer birdwatching instruction and short guided treks to the children of Murbridge and their parents. The natural world offers so many wonders, but we need to learn to listen and observe from a young age. We invite you to join us in ap-preciation and celebration of the miracles that surround us every day.

Now I definitely heard weeping. The man who had whispered *gangs* wiped his eyes. His wife laid a hand on his shoulder and nod-ded as if to encourage him. And then, the man stood up.

I'm sorry! he cried, turning to face the Birdwatcher. I'm so sorry! I'm such an asshole! I thought you were a gang! He gestured toward the group. All of you. I just—I'm so worried about crime and nega-tive home equity. And I'd never seen vests like those before. But I get it now, I see that I was wrong. Please forgive me.

The man, still weeping, sat back down. His wife handed him a tissue.

Well, said the Birdwatcher. He cleared his throat. If anyone has questions about our group or the local birdlife, please feel free to stop us while we're out and about. You can also get in touch via our Facebook page. And that's all I have to say. Thank you for listening and we'll see you around town. He stepped away from the microphone to the sound of applause, scattered sniffles and nose blowing.

I want to go birdwatching, Fanny whispered to me.

Me too, I whispered back.

After the Birdwatcher and his posse left the hall, there was a moment of silence. No one else raised a hand, no one else took the floor. Hildegard looked to each of the Select Board members in turn; each nodded with finality. Hildegard pounded her gavel.

All righty, then, she said. Let's open item five hundred eighty-nine for a vote. All in favor of rescinding the Dash-LaGrand building permit, say aye.

One lonely voice called out a thin *aye!*

Those in opposition to rescinding the building permit?

The *aye*'s started quietly, like that tickle in the back of your throat before a cough or those first drops of rain before a downpour, and then the *aye*'s rose up, louder and louder, all those voices, high and low, young and old. The *aye*'s shook the floor, they shook the roof and the sound went on and on. Marcus and Dan stood at the front of the room, holding hands and wiping away tears. I hugged Fanny. Hildegard was poised with her gavel lifted, waiting for the sound to crescendo and begin to fade. As she waited, I believe I saw the glint of a glisten in her eyes too. Then at last she pounded the hell out of that thing.

The motion is rejected, Hildegard called. The building permit stands.

I cheered, Fanny cheered, we all cheered for kids and old-fashioned peace, love and understanding.

Quiet! Quiet, please! Hildegard was again pounding her gavel. What now? I wondered. Cookies for everyone? A public flogging for Jake? A salary increase for the school crossing guard?

The cheers died down. Hildegard surveyed the crowd.

Thank you, she said, for coming tonight. This is the highest attendance we've ever had at a Select Board meeting. Generally it's us— she gestured toward the selectmen—Joyce there in the front, Bob Cokes, who generally forgets his hearing aid—*HI BOB*—and occasionally three or four others. But that's it. If we see a dozen people in this room, it's something. So. While you are all here, I want to urge each and every one of you to participate. Pat, Lydia, Pearl, Rosie, Allston and myself have served every post on the Select Board for the past twenty years. We rotate positions because the bylaws state that only two consecutive terms are allowed for any one member. This year, it was Lydia's turn to be chair, but her sciatica was acting up and then Jake decided to run. And, well, we all know how that ended up. Hildegard raised her eyebrows.

We're all so lucky to live here in Murbridge, she continued. Of course it's not perfect, there are problems, people don't always say or do the right thing, people don't always agree. But this place is special because *we* get to build it. Everyone here gets a say. This is your town, your home. This place is what *you* make it. There's only one catch— you must show up. You must participate. It's that simple.

A yelp came from the side of the room: Yes! We got it! That's the shot!

I looked over. Roxanne, wearing a blond wig and gray sweatpants, was perched on a stool at the side of the room, filming the meeting with a very small, very expensive-looking camera. Next to her, discreetly holding a microphone on a long slender arm, stood a tall thin man in horn-rims and seersucker.

Sorry, folks! Roxanne called. Proceed, please! We're not here, just ignore us! She motioned to Hildegard and mouthed *sorry*.

Okay then, Hildegard resumed, this Select Board meeting is officially adjourned. She pounded her gavel. Have a good night, everybody! We'll see you next month to discuss the purchase of new soccer goals for Murbridge High. And don't forget to grab a cookie on your way out.

Snickerdoodles? Fanny whispered to me.

Fingers crossed, I whispered back.

Slowly, all Murbridgeans filed out of the meeting, each clutching a cookie and, I like to imagine, considering Hildegard's words. Did they wonder about the lunatic with the camera? Did they think Hildegard had overstepped? Did they agree that we all need to show up? Did they vow to do better?

I hope so.

THE NEXT MORNING, I slept late and woke slowly. In my half-asleep head, I replayed the town meeting and then the after-party at Marcus and Dan's house. Margaritas, scheming with Burt and Marcus about the next steps in construction, Omar popping in to just say hello and then staying for hours as we googled the hell out of Dykstra Productions. Marcus gave Fanny a tour of the house, Fanny gave Marcus a tour of the old tulip bed. That had been hard and beautiful in unexpected ways.

It was only me, Marcus and Phin who walked with Fanny away from the patio and the party, toward the dark rift in the earth where the pool excavation had stopped midway. Phin led Fanny to the spot where he thought he'd found the skull, but she cocked her head, narrowed her eyes.

No, she said, *there*, and pointed to the western edge of the hole, farther from the house. We walked to the spot and stopped. The night was clear, the stars bright. Yes, she repeated, looking up at the sky, I put Barnaby right *here*. She didn't cry or even look sad. Her body straightened up a bit, her face relaxed. Darling, she said.

I'm sorry, Fanny, said Phin. I got confused about where I found it. At first the skull scared me, but only a little.

Oh, dear, I'm the one who's sorry, said Fanny, leaning down to look Phin in the eye. You know, Barnaby loved scavenger hunts. We used to hide little gifts around the house and yard for each other to find. It was so much fun. He'd have been so happy you found him, Phin. Truly.

Phin smiled. And then he yawned extravagantly, his eyes watery, his little body sagging with all the excitement of the day. Thanks, Fanny, he said. You're an awesome old lady.

Marcus picked Phin up and hugged him. I think someone needs to go to bed, he said.

Noooo! Phin objected, but weakly, and then laid his head on Marcus's shoulder. I'll be back in ten, said Marcus. Don't talk about anything good while I'm gone.

Fanny and I sat on lawn chairs near the lip of the pool. We held hands and did not talk about anything. I thought about Mom and Daddy. And Skip. Skip would never, ever, ever hide gifts around the house for me to find. We didn't have that kind of fun. We didn't have any kind of real fun, I realized. Was fun the essence of love? Was holding and helping another person the common destiny? Had I finally learned to dance the clumsy dance?

And then I registered that I was drunk and overly sentimental and very sleepy and so I closed my eyes and woke up only when Marcus was shaking my arm gently and saying: Darcy, let me drive you home.

Darcy.

Darcy.

Darcy.

Now I was fully awake in my black bedroom at home and somewhere someone was saying my name. Not someone—some ones. The voices were muffled but distinct. The voices were coming from downstairs.

What the hell? I leapt out of bed and grabbed a pencil, then a ruler, then a bowling pin. Where did I get a bowling pin? I wondered, but the heft seemed right, the weight just enough to knock out a potential intruder. I took the pin in hand, opened my bedroom door and crept slowly, carefully down the hall.

Mumble, mumble. Darcy. Mumble, coffee, mumble mumble, blocked. Mumble, crap.

Were they robbers? Squatters? Jake's minions? I tried to proceed quietly and confidently, but my heart beat hard in my chest and I thought I might throw up.

I tiptoed down the stairs, avoiding squeaky stairs four and seven, and paused in the downstairs hall, steps away from the kitchen. The voices started up again.

Stan! Get away from that toilet! You're not good with a wrench!

The voice was my mother's.

Not squatters, then; just my parents.

I threw open the door. What the hell are you doing here? I said.

My mother jumped. Why are you holding a bowling pin? she asked. Have you taken up bowling?

No, of course I haven't taken up bowling. Mom, why aren't you in Arizona?

Oh Bunny, she replied and ran to hug me. I let the bowling pin drop to the floor and leaned into her hug, smelling the overly sweet gardenia perfume she always wore, the weird mustiness of the hair she never brushed. Sigh. I'd missed my mom.

I missed you, Mom, I said into her shoulder. And then I heard another, deeper voice coming from the bathroom.

Stan, I think you need a Phillips, said the voice. I know where the tool kit is, just hang tight.

Skip Larson, my hypothetical husband, erstwhile love of my life, breaker of hearts, diver of skies, emerged from the downstairs powder room with a wrench in one hand, a roll of toilet paper in the other.

Oh wow, Darcy, he said as our eyes met. You're not dead.

Mom and I stepped out of the hug. Nope, I said. Still kicking.

And then my dad yelled from the bathroom, Darcy! Darcy, is that you? Hallelujah, saints be praised! You're not bludgeoned! There was the sound of heavy breathing, thumps, a very loud *oh shit* and then my father emerged, his jeans slung low, an unidentifiable stain on his shirt, his hands very very dirty.

Darcy, we were so worried. We didn't know where you were! He too enveloped me in a hug, this one reeking of plumbing and toilet water, and released me almost immediately when I began to retch.

Sorry, he said. Skip and I thought we'd kill time by fixing that leaky john.

What—why—how—I thought you were in Arizona, I said. And you—I said, turning to Skip—I thought you were in Bianca.

Darcy, Mom began, we got this bizarre phone message from someone named Matteo? Matthew? Marbles? Anyhow, he said you were lost, and you were last seen volunteering at the Mushroom Festival. Ha! Of course I assumed the call was a prank, but then you didn't answer your cell phone and I got so worried about you and so I talked your father into coming home. She paused. And, to be honest, I missed Murbridge.

Arizona heat, not as dry as advertised, said Daddy, shaking his head.

Don't get me wrong, said Mom. Arizona is an interesting place. I love what they do with turquoise down there. And the sweetest little geckos lived in our rock garden. They ran every which way when I was out there doing my morning Pilates. But—

We belong here, said Daddy. We're not going back to Little Valley.

And I'm not going back to Bianca, said Skip. I want to come home to you, Darcy.

I had momentarily forgotten Skip was there, but now I turned to face him. Same Skip eyebrows, same Skip mouth, but our separation, I noted, had not been kind to Skip's waistline.

Bianca must be one hell of a cook, I said.

Skip shook his head. No, she's really, really bad. We ate out most of the time.

Hmmm. That makes sense, I replied. Well, I don't know what to say to all of this. I just woke up. And also there's been a lot of activity around here. A *lot*.

So you forgot to charge your phone, said Mom.

Yes, okay? Yes. I forgot to charge it! I've been super-bonkers busy, so it slipped my mind. And then I also got lost in the Murbridge swamp and ate a shroom, um, accidentally and went missing for twelve hours.

Mom rolled her eyes. Really, Bunny? Even I can remember to plug in my phone.

Skip stepped forward and took hold of my hand. He gazed into my face. My eyes, I was guessing, were bloodshot. My face, still caked with yesterday's makeup. My odor, not so great. And yet Skip looked at me as though I was the most beautiful person he'd ever seen.

Darcy, he said. I made a horrible mistake. I'm so sorry. Please forgive me. Please can we be married again and live in our condo? I miss bingo. I miss us.

Skip, I said. Can I ask you just one question?

Of course.

Does Bianca have a third nipple?

What? No.

Was it all that body hair?

Darcy, for crying out loud.

So?

Skip shook his head and then answered. She spoke really loudly all the time. Like THIS. ALL THE TIME. Skip raised his voice and we all took a step back.

Wow, I said.

I think maybe her hearing is damaged by skydiving. The airplane, all that wind. He shrugged. It's loud up there.

Thank you for the explanation, I said. And now, Skip, I think that—I began to cough and then caught my breath and then coughed again. I couldn't stop. Tickle—I said, waving a hand. Tickle in my—water—wait—

I stumbled into the bathroom and ran the faucet into my mouth. The water splashed over my chin and cheeks and I began to finally and truly wake up. My senses surged to life, the water ran coolly down my throat. I patted my face dry with the only clean hand towel and noticed with interest a new wrinkle at the corner of my left eye. I smiled, the wrinkle deepened. I smiled again, broader this time, and a wrinkle popped on the right side too. Awesome, I said to myself in the mirror. You are a woman wise enough to have smile lines.

I left the bathroom.

Mom and Daddy, I said, I'm so glad you're moving back to Murbridge. I really love this town. It's my home and I think I'll stay awhile. Skip, I'd like us to put the condo on the market or you can buy me out. I'll give you a decent deal, no worries there. I'm just not super into the idea of continuing our marriage. In fact, I definitely want a divorce. Like, definitely absolutely. So why don't we just go with that, okay?

But—but I said I'm sorry.

Yeah, I heard you. I'm not mad about Bianca anymore, I wish you all the best. You're not a bad person, Skip, just uninspiring. A little boring. Clueless. I just want something different. You know?

Skip blinked slowly. He opened his mouth and closed it again. Then he turned toward my dad. Good luck with that john, Stan, he said. Use the Phillips number four. And Jeanine, it's always a pleasure. You roast a fantastic chicken. He did not say good-bye to me. Skip Larson walked out my front door.

Well, that was certainly awkward, Mom said. But honestly, I agree. Don't you agree, Stan? Skip was one big yawn.

My dad shrugged. I don't get involved in matters of the heart, he said. Whatever you want, Bunny, that's what I want too.

Thanks, Daddy, I said and hugged him, stink and all. Then I jumped back. Oh no! I said. I forgot to do something.

Darcy, just leave a sticky note on the bathroom window: *charge your phone,* Mom said. It works wonders for me.

No, I answered. This is much more important.

I opened the side broom closet and out tumbled a mountain of Tupperware containers and lids, different shapes, sizes and shades of pastel.

My mother yelped. Please tell me that's not what I think it is, she said.

It's Mrs. Pevzner's Tupperware.

My mother screamed. Stan, can we still go back to Arizona? I don't think I can show my face in Murbridge anymore.

I'm staying out of this one, my dad said, and returned to the bathroom.

It's okay, I told my mom. I'm going to organize the Tupperware and return it all in one neat package to Mrs. Pevzner. And before I do that, I'm going to bake some snickerdoodles and bring those over as a peace offering.

My mother was watching me with suspicion. Have you been watching baking shows? she asked.

Of course not, I said. But my friend Marcus makes the best snickerdoodles ever and he promised to share the recipe.

And so, later that day, I appeared on Mrs. Pevzner's doorstep, Tupperware in a large paper bag, four dozen snickerdoodles in a large ziplock. I left them both on the Pevzners' porch with a note:

Dear Mrs. Pevzner,

   I'm sorry it's taken me so long to return your Tupperware. For some reason, your containers provided me with comfort during my time of emotional upheaval. Thank you too for all the blondies. I couldn't have gotten through the winter without them. Please tell Todd I say hi and I forgive him for what happened when we were in high school. I know the unfortunate events of our disastrous prom night have plagued him for a long time. I hope he finally feels at peace. I sure do.

Best wishes, Darcy

Autumn

I'VE ALWAYS LOVED AUTUMN IN Murbridge. Piles of golden crunchy leaves ripe for jumping, clear sunny skies undercut with chill, pumpkins and apples and maple trees tapped for syrup. Autumn, I think, is the true season of new beginnings. No matter your age, there's that fresh pencil smell of going back to school, the excitement of seeing your friends, of new routines and new meaning. New Englanders can't really handle summer. There's too much activity, all those heady water sports and long buggy nights. By the end of it, we're ready to placate our sunburns with a heavy coat of aloe and retreat inside to read by the woodstove. Good luck to you, Los Angelenos. Fare thee well, Floridians. In Murbridge, we turn the calendar to September, warm up a mug of apple cider and breathe a deep sigh of relief.

Marcus and I sat on the patio, blankets on our laps, drinking tea. It was 4:30 p.m., school was out and kids swarmed the playscape in the waning afternoon light. Up and down slides, bouncing on the trampolines, hanging from the monkey bars, climbing the magical tire tower. Jake Zdzynzky sprinted across the lawn, paintball shooter in hand, pursued by a handful of second graders.

You know, I said to Marcus, Jake has really surprised me.

Me too! I had no idea he was such an ace shot with that thing.

No, I mean the turnaround. The public apology, the genuine contrition, his willingness to volunteer with the kids. He's learning how not to be an asshole. Mom was right: everyone has the capacity to change. It warms my heart.

Well, I'm not entirely convinced of Jake's moral transformation, said Marcus. I'm still keeping an eye on that one. He's investing with Dan now, did I tell you? Normally it's a three mill minimum. Zeus Capital had, ahem, a tad less than that, but Dan's the boss. Jake is poised to make a killing. Dan is never wrong.

Never?

Never. According to Dan, 2020 will be the year of staying in. Crafting, streaming video content, bread making. It'll be the Etsy-Netflix-sourdough year.

Seriously? I laughed. Where does he get his intel? That can't be right.

I know. Who wants to stay home all day? Marcus shrugged. But Dan's track record is pretty good. He flagged Uber back when they had only twelve drivers and were called Guber. It was Dan who told them to drop the *G*.

Marcus, Darcy, I made some shortbread! It was Fanny. She was carrying a full plate out from the kitchen, carefully stepping across the lawn to avoid discarded soccer balls, lacrosse gear and a full croquet set. She placed the plate on the patio table.

Oh my God, Fanny, your shortbread is ridiculous, said Marcus. Seriously, what's in this?

Well, Fanny began, first you take six sticks of—

Stop right there, Marcus said, holding up a hand. I don't want to know. He handed me a shortbread and took three for himself.

Fanny, I said. Come sit with us.

Fanny pulled up a chair. She'd been living with Marcus and Dan for the past few weeks, helping with the kids, baking up a storm, teaching Phin how to play bridge. The Marian Sisters Home for Elderly Women was closing next month. Residents would be transferred to in-state nursing homes or back to their families. Without children or any surviving relatives, Fanny had found herself unsure where she would end up. Unsure, that is, until Marcus invited Fanny to live in their guest cottage.

On the day of the invitation, we gathered on the patio, where Marcus poured tea and sliced some cake. I couldn't help but notice that his hands were shaking.

Marcus, are you okay? I asked. You look like you're about to throw up.

Across the lawn, Burt and his crew were engaged once again in pool excavation. Noise rose and fell as they worked.

I'm fine, Marcus said. But there's something important I need to discuss with Fanny.

At this unfortunate juncture, Brendan started up the backhoe with a loud mechanical growl.

Fanny, Marcus said solemnly, would you like to move into our guest cottage?

Move? she replied. Yes, it's too loud out here. Let's go inside.

No, Marcus yelled. I mean *permanently*.

What, dear?

Permanently! Marcus yelled. Forever!

Fanny cupped a hand around her ear and squinted. *What?*

Forever! Until you die!

Just as Marcus said the last words, Brendan cut the backhoe's engine and the word *die* traveled across the now quiet yard.

Ouch, I said.

Fanny blinked. Marcus dear, she began, if you want to talk about death, that's fine. It's healthy, I support you wholeheartedly, but please find a trained counselor. Just because I'm old doesn't make me an expert on the subject.

Marcus resumed speaking in a normal voice. Fanny, I was wondering if you wanted to move into our guest cottage, permanently, with me, Dan and the kids. We would love to have you.

They had already invited Harriet the nanny to live with them full-time, one of the many changes Dan and Marcus were making to improve their work-life balance. And Harriet, it turned out, was also trained in eldercare.

Not that you need much care, Marcus said quickly. You're fit as a fiddle, Fanny Scott, but better safe than sorry, and Harriet is just wonderful. Her older sister passed away a few years ago. Harriet has been lonely without her. I think you two will get along famously.

Marcus beamed with satisfaction. Sometimes plans come together in the most marvelous ways.

But Fanny didn't answer. She turned her head out toward the pool, where her tulips used to grow.

Marcus glanced at me nervously, but I only shrugged. There was nothing I could say. This was Fanny's decision to make.

Fanny, Marcus said, taking hold of her hand, the boys adore you, Dan and I adore you. This invitation is coming from all of us.

Fanny cleared her throat. She did not smile and for one brief torturous moment, I thought she might turn Marcus down. But then her face broke into a grin, the laugh lines and smile lines and life lines spreading wide.

Oh, what a delightful idea, she said. I accept. Wholeheartedly. I have only one condition.

Anything, Marcus and I said in unison.

It involves Barnaby.

And so two weeks after Fanny accepted Marcus's proposal, Barnaby's bones were interred in the Murbridge town cemetery. The ceremony was simple, the crowd sparse. There weren't many people left who remembered Barnaby Scott, the local pharmacist, the guy who still spoke with a Boston twang after fifty years in Murbridge, the guy who would play tag with kids along his block and hand out extra candy on Halloween. The man who married the love of his life, who built his own home, who planted one hundred tulips. I cried my eyes out during the service, but Fanny remained calm, stoic. Beside Barnaby's plot was an empty one for Fanny when the time came.

And beside Fanny, in the car ride back to Marcus and Dan's, sat Barnaby's skull.

I told Marcus that was my one condition, she said as the limo pulled away from the church. We found a plastic one at the dollar store—they're already stocking Halloween decorations, can you believe it, dear? We gave the fake to the funeral home and I kept the real one. No one asks questions when you're a grieving widow. She winked. Marcus made sure there's a special place for him in the tulip bed, somewhere the landscapers won't touch. She patted Barnaby's head. At least part of him will still be with me at home, our real home.

And now it was three weeks later, more than a month after the triumphant Select Board meeting. I chewed Fanny's ridiculous shortbread. The magic tire tower began to play John Lennon.

Dear, Fanny said to me, what do you think about planning a New Year's Eve party? Don't you think that would be nice?

I swallowed my shortbread and said, You're a genius, Fanny Scott! That's the best idea ever. We could invite everyone in town. What if we put a dance floor over the pool! I saw a picture of that once in a magazine. I'm sure Marcus and I could figure it out. It's a new decade, we should usher in 2020 with a real celebration.

From the driveway came the sound of car doors closing, the side gate opening, and across the lawn walked Dan and Omar, both of them just off work.

How was your day? I asked Omar.

Boring, he answered. The good kind. He stood behind me and squeezed my shoulder. I reached up to take hold of his hand.

Dan leaned over and kissed Marcus. They'd been seeing a couples' counselor recently, working on the division of household labor, carving out more family time, letting Harriet take on more responsibilities. Marcus was going back to architecture school to finish his degree. UMass Amherst was a trek, but Dan had agreed to cut back on his travel. He wanted to spend more time with the boys. They were growing up so quickly, after all. And Dan had already missed so much. Marcus said their marriage was still a work in progress, but he also looked calmer and happier than I'd ever seen him. And Dan never missed Friday falafel night.

Omar and Dan pulled up chairs and we all sat, eating shortbread, watching the kids play, catching up on our days. The sky began to darken, parents to pop in and collect a forgotten backpack or lunch box. Kids called, Good-bye! See you tomorrow! Car doors closed, bikes whizzed down the block, lights flickered inside warm houses.

I gazed at the children playing, at the gleaming finished playscape, at Fanny and Harriet, Dan and Marcus, Omar. Was this all too good to be true? Could something so sweet and lucky as this life endure? I knew the answer. The turn of a doorknob, the beat of a heart. But this moment, now, trembling starlight and Omar's palm and my strong heart and laughter. *Stay.*

How about dinner? Dan asked. It's my night to cook. Tacos sound good to everyone?

Tacos sound fantastic, said Omar.

Dan's been working on his guac technique, Marcus told us. He's made remarkable progress.

Laughing, Dan gave Marcus the finger and headed inside.

I sipped the last of my tea and was folding my blanket when Phin appeared suddenly, breathless, his cheeks flushed with excitement and happiness and cool, fresh air. He wore red swim trunks pulled over Winnie the Pooh pajamas and ballet slippers with purple socks.

Come! he cried. Come here, quick! Phin was pointing at us.

I need to run interference in the kitchen, said Marcus. Your papa's still new at food.

But Phin was shaking his head no. Not *you,* he said to Marcus.

Fanny smiled sweetly. Dear, I need to pee. It'll take me a while to make a round-trip. She began rocking forward and back in her chair, and then Harriet was beside her, helping Fanny to stand.

But Phin was still shaking his head. Not you, Fanny! Not you, Harriet! he said with a cheeky grin. He shook his finger. I need Darcy!

Me?

Yes, come here, quick! Come see!

But I—

Darcy, Phin repeated, come on! I need you!

Go, said Marcus gently. We'll clean up here. Phin needs you. Marcus waved his fingers to shoo me away, and in that gesture I saw all my fears—of children and touching, germs and isolation, abandonment and risk—fly away, out into the darkening night.

Okay, I said and turned to Phin. He was dancing up and down, rolling his eyes at the utter ridiculousness of grown-ups and the glacial speed with which we walked across an expanse of lawn. I took Phin's warm hand in mine.

You won't believe what we made, he said, looking up at me. We worked so hard, all of us together. And now it's the most beautiful thing in the world.

Show me, I replied.

Acknowledgments

First off, thank you, dear reader, for making it through quarantine and COVID, through all that was lost and all that was gained, and here you are, on the other side, holding a book in your hands. You made it. I wrote most of this novel during the first eighteen months of the pandemic: quarantine, remote schooling, political chaos, social isolation, confusion, fear. I wrote it to make myself feel better and to make myself giggle. I wrote it because I missed my friends and extended family, my hairdresser and the barista at my favorite coffee place, my kids' teachers and coaches and so many more. I wrote it with a profound belief in the fact that all human beings want the same things and that those things—laughter, safety, love—are most easily found in community, despite our individual and collective foolishness, ignorance, anxiety and fear. Believing in community, working against the foolishness and toward the safety and the love, are noble goals upon which to build a life. To the election workers, school board officers, select board members, crossing guards, newsletter editors, community board moderators, librarians, brownie bakers, fundraisers and organizers—all the Pat Pernickys and Hildegard Hymans of the world—thank you most of all.

As always, I am enterally grateful to my agent Michelle Brower and editor Kate Nintzel for their wisdom and guidance. To say I owe these two my undying gratitude and respect is a vast understatement. They are smart, funny, strong women who I am honored to now call friends as well as colleagues. My thanks to the entire team at William Morrow / Mariner Books who designed, perfected and promoted this weird, tricky book: Dan Funderburgh and Ploy Siripont for the gorgeous cover; Rachel Berquist, Tavia Kowalchuk (again and again!), Jennifer Hart, Molly Gendell, Karen Richardson, Eliza Rosenberry, Kelly Rudolph and, of course, Liate Stehlik for her continued support and fierce leadership at HarperCollins.

I benefited greatly from the encouragement of my thoughtful and wise early readers and dear friends Mari Hinojosa, Cynthia Fierstein and Elissa Steglich. To Christopher Roberts, thank you for your insight and enthusiasm during a particularly low moment. To Ron Rossi, thank you for introducing me to Barnum and so much more. To Allison Augustyn, Margot Case, Elisabeth Eaves, Elise Hooper and Carrie LaSeur, thank you for your writerly advice, inspiration and friendship. To my interstate, indispensable community of women: Carrie Barnes, Ellen Barry, Jennifer Beatty, Laura Conklin, Riisa Conklin, Cheryl Contee, Naomi Donnelley, Kim Dozier, Sarah Jacobson, Jody Lindwall, Susannah Lipsyte, Amy Mushlin, Amy Predmore, Paige Smith and Ruth Whippman my enduring love, admiration and gratitude for your badassery and strength. And thank you to all the friends (too many to name!) from Menlo Park to Miami Beach, who, upon learning I was writing a book based on a certain neighborhood messaging app, sent me their favorite posts, silliest stories and the best and worst community scandals and controversies.

To my children, as always, you three are my light and life, and every word I write is striving, somehow, to make your world a better place. And to my parents, Christina and Jay, who decided to move from a tropical, hippie paradise on Saint Croix, USVI, to western Massachusetts in the middle of winter: I forgive you. And I also thank you. It has been thirty years since I lived in small-town New England, but I still can't seem to leave it behind.

About the Author

Tara Conklin is a writer and former lawyer who lives in Seattle, Washington. She graduated from Yale University, New York University School of Law, and the Fletcher School of Law and Diplomacy. After seven years working in New York and London as a corporate lawyer, she began writing a short story that became her first novel. *The House Girl* was published in 2013 and was a *New York Times* bestseller, #1 IndieNext pick, Target book club pick, and Goodreads Choice finalist, and was translated into seven languages. Her second novel, *The Last Romantics,* was an instant *New York Times* bestseller and was chosen by Jenna Bush Hager as the first-ever pick for the *Today* show book club. Her third novel, *Community Board*, was written during COVID quarantine and was inspired equally by her neighborhood message board and the push-pull of isolation and community. She loves to hike, swim, practice yoga, drive over the speed limit, embarrass her children, and laugh with her friends and family. You can find her at www.taraconklin.com.